Encounter at River's Edge

T.A. Galloway

Gazelle
PRESS

Mobile, Alabama

Encounter at River's Edge
by T.A. Galloway
Copyright ©2019 T.A. Galloway

ISBN 978-1-58169-7087
For Worldwide Distribution
Printed in the U.S.A.

Gazelle Press
P.O. Box 191540 • Mobile, AL 36619
800-367-8203

Table of Contents

Acknowledgments

Master artisans never view an empty canvas, block of marble, or unhewn wood. Their eyes and spirits already know and are intimately acquainted with the completed work. The painter knows it will take hundreds of brush strokes to bring to life on canvas what is living within his soul. The sculptor knows it will take hundreds of hours and countless hammer blows to bring life out of the lifeless block of stone. The Master does not count the brush strokes or the hammer blows. He rejoices as the lifeless material takes on form and beauty.

The Master Creator of the universe employs life to fashion his workman. I am so thankful for the many family members and hundreds of friends that have been the brush strokes used by God to fashion me into the Christ-follower that I am today.

Without the love and support of my wife, Donna; my children, Marily, Hilary, and Ana; and my grandchildren, Allie, Ayden, Avery, and ? this story would continue to be locked within my heart.

1

Horror Steals Al's Soul

The chrome I.V. pole disappeared into the drab gray paint. Al was one of dozens of broken bodies and scarred minds on the military medical flight. His moaning brought the flight nurse to his side. The morphine injection she gave him afforded him some relief from the pain but not from the images and sounds so fresh in his mind.

Four hours earlier, Al and a young soldier, Pfc. Williams, were witnessing what no human eyes should see. The city was under attack, and Al was trying to find safety in a bunker. As shells were getting closer, the young marine glanced at Al saying, "Sir, you better get inside the bunker. These shells don't care who you are." Within seconds the rounds were landing within 10-20 yards of the bunker.

Al said, "I want to get a couple more shots."

Just after those words were out of his mouth, he stuck his head around the corner of the sandbags. Turning to Williams, absolute horror disfigured his face. Stuttered words tried to escape his mouth, "A little girl…"

Quickly the private peered around the corner. Both men watched in perfect clarity. Al could see the dirt streaked on the front of her white, buttoned shirt. Strangely, Al suddenly remembered his own white shirt from first grade.

Running as fast as her little legs could move, she had tears streaming down her cheeks that told of the terror that filled her heart. Another explosion was closer still, and the two men watched as a woman tried to catch the child. She had come from the shops and was just seconds behind the little girl.

Williams scrambled around behind Al, screaming in his ear, "I'm gonna go grab her. Stay here."

Glued to the corner of the bunker, Al had his camera ready. He wanted pictures of the marine. Al heard Williams say, "Dear God, protect us."

Almost in slow motion, while Williams was moving behind Al, a deadly metallic projectile headed towards the bunker. In the millisecond before the concussion of the blast threw Al and Williams backward, the small girl, in her dirty white shirt and tear streaks on her cheeks, vanished in a red mist.

Trying to move forward, Al could sense something warm in his ears and on the back of his neck. He began yelling at Williams, "Where's the girl? Where's the little girl? Where in the hell did she go?"

Williams, lying next to Al, shouted back, "She's gone! She's gone! Dear mother of God, she's gone."

Four hours later, Al again was trying to focus his eyes. Gray blended with drab green as Al's blurred vision tried to focus on the green cots that surrounded him. The only clear sense to Al, the war reporter, was the deafening roar of the massive turbo-prop engines. Al's disquieting movements brought the nurse, morphine, and sleep.

The turbo-propped ambulance was heading to Japan with her cargo of coffins and cots. The blast had ruptured both of Al's eardrums and propelled him backwards into a steel post. A file, with his name on it, rested in between one of a soldier who lost his right leg and another who could never read again. His file read, "Severe head trauma and possible brain injury."

After a month in the hospital filled with tests, x-rays, and bed rest, his doctor stood at the foot of his bed. He said, "Al, you are one lucky guy. The injury to your skull is healing. Your hearing may continue to suffer for a while, and some hearing loss may be permanent. That, my friend, is the good news."

Al responded, "I didn't ask about the bad news."

"Well," the doctor said, "you may not have asked for it, but I have to give it to you straight. A small portion of your brain suffered significant damage. It might heal itself, or it might not. I have sent a report to your main office. I think you need to take it easy for three months. That's what I told your office."

Two days after the doctor's prognosis, Al found himself knocking on the front door of a stately old Victorian home. As the front door opened, Al thought for a second he had gone back in time twenty or thirty years. The woman standing in the entryway had her hair up in a bun, wearing a dress that nearly touched the floor.

She said, "Why, you must be Al. It's so nice to meet you. I have your room ready for you. I'm Harriet and welcome to my home."

Smiling, Al replied, "Thank you for having a room for me. I was afraid I wouldn't find one. I just have this one box and my old suitcase. Traveling pretty light these days." With his box tucked under his left arm, he reached down to grasp the old leather handle of the suitcase.

Harriet interrupted his movement and said, "Please let me help you with the suitcase."

With his suitcase in hand, she climbed the front staircase,

holding on to the sturdy oak banister. Just down the hall, she opened the door to Al's room.

"Now," Harriet said, "If you need something, just ask. At the end of the hall is the staircase that leads down to the kitchen and back door. I'll tidy the room twice a week and change the bedding. Dinner will be at six in the main dining room."

Glancing around, Al thought, *I must have stepped back into the days of Mayberry. Harriet reminds me of Aunt Bee, and this place looks like a Life Magazine story from twenty or thirty years ago.* It took him just a few minutes to put his clothes away and from the bottom of the box, take out his bottle of Kentucky Bourbon.

At five minutes before six, Al headed down the back stairs and pushed the kitchen door open. The heavenly aroma from the kitchen quickly assaulted his sense of smell. As he entered, the absolutely intoxicating smell of the peach pie on the cooling rack was an attack of the most pleasant kind.

With her back to him, he asked, "Can I help? Figure if I help, I might get some favoritism here."

Looking back over her shoulder with her hands still stirring a pot on the stove, she chuckled and said, "Enjoying your dinner and my home is all I ask. That will get you plenty of favoritism. But right now you can help by taking the vegetables into the dining room."

Once everything was on the table, Harriet introduced Al to the other boarders. She had six others sharing in her hospitality. Except for one, all appeared to be Al's age. The oldest at the table was a small man with wire glasses and a thinning hairline. Al thought, *He could have been one of my journalism professors.*

Harriet said softly, "Let's silently ask God's blessing on our food."

A minute later, the only sound coming from the dining

room was the tinging of silverware on the serving platter and the scraping sounds from the large bowls filled with mashed potatoes and candied carrots.

Al placed the food in a methodical manner on his plate—the chicken breast on the front side, baked carrots on the left, and mashed potatoes on the right. He had heaped the mound of potatoes together and made a crater with his spoon, filling it with chicken gravy. The potatoes were heavily peppered, but the chicken and carrots had more subtle seasoning.

With the chicken platter empty and one small carrot and a spoonful of potatoes left in the bowls out of politeness, Harriet announced dessert as she backed her way through the swinging door. When she turned around, Al's eyes took in the full magnificence of her peach pie. The crust of the pie was the color of light oak. Small cuts in the top had allowed the sweet juice to erupt and cover parts of the golden brown treasure.

Small dessert plates were stacked on the buffet, and within moments, they were bearing their riches to each diner. Voices were quiet as taste buds weighed, judged, and measured each sterling silver forkful. Even the forks seemed subdued when they came into contact with the plate as if the noise might lessen the excellence of both peach and crust.

Al sat and looked at his piece of pie for a few seconds as if he had to decide when and where his fork engaged the treasure. Placing it against the crust, only a moderate amount of pressure was needed to get the golden brown treasure to yield. Once in his mouth, the crust seemed to melt.

Almost in a stupor, Al asked her, "What on earth makes this pie crust so delicious?"

Harriet, with a slight smile, replied, "Lard."

After dinner Al found himself in the kitchen helping Harriet clean up, much to her discomfort and protest.

"Harriet," he said, "you remind me of a favorite character from my childhood. She went by the name of Aunt Bee. Would you mind if I called you Aunt Bee?"

With a smile and covering her mouth out of embarrassment she replied, "Oh Al, I don't mind if you want to call me Aunt Bee."

2

Nightmares Invade

On the mend, Al covered his first stories with enthusiasm. Soon, the stress-free assignments got boring, and he was champing at the bit for more. He went to his chief's office and asked, "So, how do you think I'm doing? I'm ready for more; you know I'm a good reporter. Put me on something that gets my juices flowing."

His bureau chief asked, "So tell me how you're doing physically. Your doctor says you took a bad blow to your head."

Al responded, "I'm fine, had one or two minor headaches, used some aspirin. That took care of them." He was not going to admit to the ever-present bottle of liquid medicine in his nightstand.

His persistence paid off. The following week he was called into the chief's office. He said, "There's a big rally in D.C. this weekend. I'm sending you and two other guys north for the weekend. After the march, I want you to get inside the heads of these protesters. Find out why they hate the war, or why they're marching. You might be surprised to find out it's also a good way to meet a girl." Both men chuckled.

Back at the boarding house, Al got his things in order. Meeting Bee in the main living room, he said to her, "I'll be gone over the weekend and should be back Sunday evening. I don't care what desserts you serve, just save me some."

Her nervous habit showed up again as she covered her mouth, trying to disguise a very slight chuckle. She reached across and placed her small hand on his arm. Bee promised, "I'll save you some dessert and cold fried chicken and meatloaf. You just be careful, young man. God bless you."

Al and the other two reporters drove one of the company cars north to Washington and checked in at the motel. Al was glad that he didn't share a room. He didn't know what his peers might think of the bottle in his suitcase.

The first part of the rally was supposed to be a massive march down Pennsylvania Avenue and then a gathering at the mall. The staff reporters were to cover the march as the Capitol police expected around a hundred thousand protesters. Afterward, they would report on their individual assignments.

The march began without much fanfare. Al was surprised by the size of it, yet even more by the marchers themselves. The longhairs and beards were mixed with average looking kids that could have come from any midwestern neighborhood. The marchers were an equal mix of women with prairie skirts and bare feet and men with blue jeans and baggy shirts. For some crazy reason, the girls with headbands and flowers in their hair brought a smile to Al's face.

As usual, Al found a person who knew what was going on and asked a few questions. A moment later he eyed a spot near the end of the mall, closest to the Lincoln Memorial. He was wearing his press pass around his neck, even though he didn't want to. He thought the pass made him a target. But if there was trouble, that little ID tag might keep him out of it. A few of the protesters started heading to the memorial.

Many of the first to arrive at the mall looked like normal, everyday college kids. When a couple saw him standing with his press pass, they began talking with him. One kid, looking like he was straight from the Midwest and wearing blue jeans and a paisley shirt, approached him.

The kid asked, "So tell me, what are you looking for today? Are you looking for some kids hating their country? That's not me. I'm here because I have a brother over there."

Al replied, "I'm open-minded about the whole thing."

The crowd started to grow as more young people gathered, and Al found himself as the center of attention of a group of around twenty protesters. He was talking with a few of them about the march and the war when a young couple maneuvered their way up to him.

The young woman was dressed in a long prairie skirt and billowy peasant blouse, the young man in jeans and a flannel shirt. To Al, the clenched jaw of the young man spelled attitude. He was standing only a foot or so from Al, looking at his press tag, and asked, "Why aren't you carrying a sign and protesting a government that's killing thousands of children?"

The protestors' words of ignorance brought instant images of horror. Right in front of him, the protestors evaporated into ghostly images. An innocent girl took perfect form in his sight. His gaze focused on her dirt-streaked white shirt, tears running down her smudged cheeks, absolute terror on her face. Racing death, she seemed to be reaching out for the safety of strong arms, only to disappear in that God-forsaken red mist. As Al stood there, his stomach started to tighten, and he could feel sweat beginning to form on his neck. He had to jar himself back to the mall and the words of the ignorant young hippie.

Al said, "Bombs and bullets don't care who they kill. They are tossed at opposing sides with equal stupidity."

The young man said in a challenging voice, "What gives you the right to blame both sides when America is the Superpower?"

Al's answer was short. "I've seen enough to know you're a stupid ass."

His words ended the conversation. He did notice the young woman with the California Dreamin' clothes on. Her light brown, wind-blown hair hung down past her shoulders, and there was a sort of country attractiveness to her. When the young man confronted Al, she stepped back as if she were a part of things but not a part of what was taking place between Al and the guy.

With the protest over, he wanted to get a good cup of coffee and relax. It was an absolutely beautiful day in the city. The sun was warm, and the breeze was gentle as he made his way to a coffee shop. He ordered his coffee and sat out on a bench near the park. He stared into his coffee, and his mind went back to the bunker and a tear-streaked little girl. *Damn war,* he thought, *damn the politics; she was just a little girl.*

He was suddenly startled out of his reverie as he looked down at bare feet and a prairie skirt. The girl with the light brown hair and peasant blouse was standing in front of him, her smile as bright as the sunshine.

Looking up at her, he asked, "Care for a cup of coffee?"

She answered, "Is that an offer—are you buying?"

Al nodded and they walked inside together.

She said, "I'll take mine black, please."

"Now," Al said, "I was positive that you were a cream and sugar person. Most people that I know who drink their Joe black are either late night workers or military."

After he paid for the coffee, they went back to the bench. Sitting together, they both tried to ask the same question, "What's your name?" Chuckling, maybe from the awkwardness, Al said, "I'm sorry. You go first."

She responded, "I'm Sarah, and I know you're Al."

He was surprised, and the look on his face told her so. She said, "It's right on your press card, in pretty big letters I must say."

The two sat on the bench chitchatting until Sarah asked him a straightforward question, "When were you over there?"

He hesitated a moment and then asked, "How did you know?"

She said, "I could just tell by the way you talked."

His reply was brief and brusque, "Just a couple of months ago."

With a tear forming in her eye, she said, "I lost my brother a year ago. He was killed in the delta."

Not knowing what to say, he repositioned himself on the bench. To him the war meant a little girl vanishing. In an instant of perfect clarity for him, the entire war was captured in the image of the innocent little girl trying to outrace death.

He pulled up the words, "I'm sorry about your brother."

After a sip of her coffee, she said, "That's why I protest the war, for my brother and the hundreds of other brothers."

He nursed his coffee, and they made small talk about the weather and the mall gathering. He looked at her, sometimes just out of the corner of his eye, sometimes straight on. She seemed so free, so full of life and beauty. He was struck at how the wind blew her hair. Her scent was like some type of flower. He thought for a moment, his brain landing on a lilac. When she smiled, he felt alive. With their coffee gone, Al felt awkward. He wanted to ask her if she lived in the D.C. area.

Knocking him for a loop, she said, "I want to see you again. Just give me your phone number, and I'll call." Fumbling with his pocket notepad, he dropped it on his shoe, and when he reached for it, his hand shook. Embarrassed, he quickly picked it up, jotted down two numbers, and handed her the paper.

"The first number is my office, and the other is Aunt Bee's. I'm usually done at the office by six and back to Bee's by six thirty."

"Aunt Bee, who is Aunt Bee?" she asked. "Oh, sorry if I'm too nosy."

Al said, "She's the old lady that runs the boarding house. She's a fantastic cook and a nice lady."

"She sounds like my grandmother. And I bet she wears dresses to the floor and her hair up."

Al burst out laughing. "You must have met her."

Heading back south with the other staffers, in his mind he replayed the coffee time with his free-spirited friend. Sarah had asked for his number, and he never even thought of asking for hers. *Man oh man, what is happening to me?* he thought.

Getting back to Aunt Bee's around six on Sunday evening, he found a note on his door. It read, "Cold chicken and pie in the fridge, gone to church for a couple of hours."

He devoured the chicken, wondering how she could know his love for cold fried chicken. The peach pie, well, that treasure was not just devoured—each crumb of crust, every tiny speck of peach, and each droplet of juice had to be examined by each taste bud before it was unwillingly swallowed. And each swallow took its proper place in his memory bank.

Feeling satisfied in mind and stomach, he decided to turn in. The excitement of the last two days, along with some stress, had drained him. He reviewed the weekend, his mind cataloging the important from the inconsequential. Before dozing off, he smelled lilacs, watched long brown hair blowing in the breeze, and felt intoxicated by a smile.

A few short hours later, captured by his own words, "Where in the hell is she?" and Williams's voice echoing back, "Dear mother of God, she's gone," the haunting red mist shook Al out of his nocturnal torture. Swinging his legs over the side of the bed, he pulled the sweat soaked t-shirt away from his chest. Aunt Bee's hand-embroidered pillow cover with red and yellow roses was discolored where his head fought the losing battle with his mind.

Holding on to the bedpost to steady himself, he lurched for the bathroom door frame. Gaining support from the solid oak, he staggered the next few steps into the bathroom. Drops of sweat burned his eyes as he tried to focus on the toilet. The twisting and grinding in his stomach put him on his knees in front of the stool. Half-sitting and half-lying on the cold tile, his head rested on his right arm. The cool ceramic bowl touching his skin was in sharp contrast to his burning face.

Sometime later, when he was sure his stomach was empty, he tried to get off the floor. With his left hand on the sink and right hand on the stool, he pushed himself upright. Gripping the sink, he began splashing the cold water into his face. The old mirror revealed dark and sunken eyes. His always combed and neat hair looked as if it had been greased and slicked down.

Muttering out loud, "Don't you look like hell! If this is gonna be what my head feels like, well…" Turning away from the mirror, he reached for the door frame. Steadying himself, he made his way over to the bed, and with one hand on the night-stand, he flopped down.

The voice in his head asked, *What kind of headache is this? The others were nowhere near this bad. God, I'm not sure I can take too many of these.* His trembling hand reached over and opened the bottom drawer of his nightstand. Pulling out his glass friend, he placed it between his knees and unscrewed the cap. Using both hands, he raised his friend to his lips and took a long gulp.

Looking at the old windup alarm clock, he decided the red

mist would leave him alone as long as he didn't sleep. He stared at the clock, but the hands moved slowly until it was finally near dawn. Back in the bathroom, he stepped into the hot shower. While the water ran down from his head and shoulders, the warmth eased the tension in his neck and back. Buttoning his shirt in front of the mirror on the medicine cabinet, he muttered, "You still look terrible."

He soon found Bee in the kitchen. With her back turned she said, "Good morning, young man. I have scrambled eggs and ham for breakfast, or you can have French toast."

A little off guard, Al responded, "Now how did you know it was me? And, I'll have both, if it is alright."

She chuckled. "First, I know how you walk—with determination. Second, of course you can have both. Just sit yourself down with a cup of coffee, and I'll bring them to you."

With his back to the kitchen, he sipped on his first cup of coffee. Bee came through the swinging door and around Al's right side. She came close to spilling the plate when she set it down and looked at his face.

Gasping, she asked, "What on earth is wrong? My, Al, you look dreadful. Are you feeling alright? Can I get you something to help?"

Al's response was short but not reassuring. "I'm alright, just had a bit of a headache last night."

3

Sarah Fights a Pizza

The paper ran a couple of stories about the protest. They put in a small piece that Al submitted highlighting the different kinds of people at the protest. It didn't take long for him to forget about the march and rally at the mall but not about the prairie-skirted beauty. During the day he found himself back at the park bench, sipping on coffee and watching the beautiful free spirit with the light brown hair, intoxicating smile, and the smell of lilacs.

On Wednesday his office phone rang. When he answered, it took him a moment to gather himself together. Sarah's voice surprised him. After he recovered, he said, "I'm really glad you called. I feel like a real fool for not getting your phone number." Her laughter at the other end was a vitamin for his heart.

Their chit-chat lasted for ten or fifteen minutes. He hated the thought of hanging up, so he promised her, "I'll call you tomorrow. It's so nice to hear your voice. And really, you must think I'm some kind of idiot for not getting your number." She laughed again, and his phone receiver transmitted more than her voice. After hanging up and a little taken aback, he thought, *Why would she call me, why? It doesn't make much sense.*

The next day he made the promised phone call during lunch. There was so much he didn't know about the smiling mystery. He didn't know where she was from or where she lived.

Oh, he had her area code, but that didn't help much. As they talked, he made some mental notes telling himself not to be so stupid.

When he hung up, he knew a few more things. First, he knew he would be calling her again. Next, he knew she was from a small town not too far from the coast. She had told him, "Down off Lynnhaven Road. It's part of the coast that invites beach walkers and coffee sippers."

Feeling some stirrings deep in his soul, he felt the days drag by. His preoccupation didn't go unnoticed by his boss. He called Al into his office and asked, "How are the headaches these days? Anything else I need to understand?"

Al said, "I'm doing alright; the headaches come and go."

The reply from his boss was blunt, "Then I expect you to get your head together and do some great work and not just good work."

He and Sarah had decided that it was time to spend some time together, not just on the phone. She had told him that she was living at her dad's cabin not far from the coast. Her dad, a naval commander, was on maneuvers and wouldn't be back for a couple of months. He figured the drive from Aunt Bee's to the cabin on Lynnhaven Road might take him about three hours.

He made sure he had the weekend off and that another staff reporter would be on call. From Fredericksburg, he'd sail down the freeway to 64 and then over to 225 and to Lynnhaven. He wanted to be in Lynnhaven by six Friday evening, find a motel close by, and meet Sarah for their first real date.

Glancing at his watch, he saw it was two o'clock and time to get going. Twenty minutes later he pulled into Aunt Bee's place. He met her in the kitchen and with his hand on the doorknob, ready to sprint up the stairs she stopped him.

"Why Al, it's just past two. Aren't you home early?"

With his hand still on the knob and turning to face her, he said, "Yes, I guess I'm early. Sorry, but I should have told you yesterday that I would be gone for the weekend. I should be back Sunday afternoon."

With her back to Al, she was smiling when she asked, "Do you have to work this weekend?"

Opening the door and taking the first step up, he said, "No, I'm just going away for the weekend. Probably head over to the coast." Aunt Bee's smile was evidence of her perceptive heart.

The drive downstate was a mixture of relaxation and anxiety. It was relaxing because he liked the rural countryside. The fields, farms, and last of the mountains brought a calmness that he hadn't enjoyed for a while. The anxiety started as he got closer to Lynnhaven and Sarah. The closer he got, the more confused he felt. He had been around the world and had witnessed the worst and best of mankind, yet he couldn't get a handle on what was going on in his head and heart.

He saw the sign and pulled in the drive. The Lynnhaven Road Inn had been around for at least a hundred and fifty years. Rumor had it that General Lee spent time there and used it as a command post for the better part of six months. Al checked in at what looked like an old bar. The luster of the dark wood displayed character and generations of experiences.

An elderly man was sitting at an old roll-top desk with his back to him. The man turned and welcomed him. "You must be Al," he said. "Got your phone call and the room is ready. Pretty sure you will like it and this place. We kinda think this is one of the best places around."

It was just past six when he tossed his small bag in his room. He picked up the phone and dialed Sarah's number. Within one or two rings he heard music and a voice saying, "Hi there, this is Sarah, can I help you?"

Almost dropping the phone, he recovered. "Yeah, this is Al," he said, "I'm at the motel and—"

Before he could finish the sentence, she said, "Great. I can't wait to see you. Just down the street is the best pizza place around. I'll meet you there in a few minutes. Bye." The phone went dead.

When Al asked the old gentleman at the desk where the place was, he responded, "It's just a piece down the road, might be a quarter mile or so, right next to the post office and the drug store. Sign hanging right in front of the place." Al smiled at the old man's demeanor and evident southern charm. He enjoyed the way the old guy put his words together.

His pace walking down the side of the road was as determined as ever, but the rumbling in his stomach was set in a queasy dance. As he got close, he could see Sarah sitting on what looked like an old church pew on the porch of the pizza place. Lynnhaven Pizza, lettered on a battered metal sign, hung out from the eave of the pizza joint. The closer he got to her, the more vivid his memory of their first encounter. This evening she was wearing another long skirt, sky blue with some type of lace.

When he was three or four steps away, she jumped up from the pew, her smile as big as ever. "Al, Al," she said, "I'm so glad to see you." To say the least, he was surprised at her excitement and smile. She ran the few feet and kissed him on the cheek. The smell of lilacs invaded his senses, and every cell in his body was under her control. "This place has the best pizza in the world," she told him.

Inside they took a booth near the front window. Al, looking around like a reporter, took in the setting. A single row of booths lined both walls, and a row of tables went down the center. The counter at the end served as the place to order and pickup, and an old chrome soda fountain stood to the right of it. He thought, *Man, I haven't seen an old soda fountain in a long time.*

Sarah, as excited as a child at Christmas said, "I'll order the pizza; it's my favorite, and I know you'll love it."

After she said that he thought, *I'd love it if it was only cardboard and ketchup.*

She seemed to spring from the booth, and in a flash, was at the counter ordering the pizza and then two glass mugs of root beer from the soda fountain. She carried the root beer to the table and set them down. A moment later her upper lip escaped the icy mug covered in foam. Al snickered a bit as she said, "What, never seen a root beer mustache?"

When the pizza arrived, it was smothered with fresh wild mushrooms, sun-dried tomatoes, fresh shrimp, and three kinds of cheese. He watched Sarah in between taking tasty bites. She ate her pizza like she lived—unfettered and loving every moment. When he laughed, she asked, "What's so funny?"

He chuckled as he said, "I swear it looks like the shrimp and mushrooms are trying to escape their trap."

They talked long after the pizza was gone. Al learned a lot about this long-haired, free spirit. She was the only daughter of a naval commander. In a quiet moment, she said, "My mom died three years ago from cancer. Jerry, my brother, wanted to walk in my dad's shoes. He graduated from the naval academy and was second in command of a patrol boat. The only thing I know about his death is what my daddy told me. He and two other sailors were killed on their boat."

He was beginning to understand where the war-hating, peace-loving Sarah was living. Little did she know, they shared a few things in common? Al hated conflict. His nightmare of a vanishing tear-streaked girl was the cement that held his convictions together, convictions of the utter stupidity and futility of solving political issues by killing people by the thousands. He also knew enough of human nature to realize that men would always kill each other.

At eleven a voice from the back said, "Sorry, Sarah, I have to close up."

She responded back, "Okay, Mr. Robb. We'll be out in a minute. We're just going to sit on the porch for a while."

Out on the porch, Sarah asked, "Now will you tell me about your family? You know all about me, now tell me about you, the reporter."

Shifting his position on the bench, he glanced at Sarah. "Do you really want to know about my family?" Sarah seemed hurt at his question, and he could sense it. "Okay," he relented, "I'll tell you all about them. My dad was a reporter during World War II and earned a lot of awards for stories and pictures. He told people he was the best, second only to Ernie. And then Ernie got himself killed, which made him the best. My dad and I haven't gotten along for a while."

"And," Sarah said, "what about your mom and brothers and sisters? Tell me about them."

He answered back smiling, "My mother was, is, a very kind and quiet lady. She always supported my dad. She always smiled when people talked about how great my dad was, and how she was so lucky to be married to such an important person. They didn't see the torture that my mom lived with. They didn't know about the drinking and how my dad had to be the best, no matter what."

Sarah, looking right into his eyes, said, "I'm sorry for asking about your family. Your dad seems pretty messed up. We can talk later. I better get back to the house, and you better get back to the motel. That old guy likes to tell stories." With that de-

20

cided, Sarah jumped up and headed down the street, and Al headed back to the motel.

Early the next morning Al was sitting in the Inn, enjoying a cup of coffee in the quietness. The old man dusted the bar and polished the dark brown wood.

At one point Al spoke up, "This place seems pretty special to you, how come?"

The old guy answered back, "My great, great-grandfather worked here. Near a hundred years ago, he was able to buy the place. Been in our blood that long."

After finishing his coffee, Al left and headed to Sarah's place. Her directions were perfect, and within two minutes he pulled in front of the cabin and pressed down on the chrome car horn. Right away, Sarah sprung out the door like a butterfly from its cocoon. Remembering his manners, he got out to open her door, and she beat him to it.

When he reached for the handle, she grabbed his hand and kissed him on the cheek. With a smile as bright as the sun, she asked, "And, my sweet Al, how are you this beautiful morning?"

She didn't wait for an answer. She helped him open the door and glided onto the seat. Pulling the door shut, she said, "Come on, I have some great places to show you. Hurry up." As they drove east, she talked nonstop of the coast and days spent as a child hunting seashells. An hour later she guided him to a spot on the side of the road. As soon as he parked, she was out of the car, running down to the beach, and hollering back, "Hurry up, slowpoke."

For the next few hours, they walked the beach. Al couldn't remember the last time he walked barefoot with soft sand squishing up between his toes.

"Sarah," he said, "slow down. I don't have shorts on or a dress."

Laughing at his comment, she said, "Aw, come on, just roll your pant legs up and enjoy yourself."

He watched as Sarah ran around the beach like a child. Picking up a large shell, she held it to her ear and then ran to Al. "Here, listen, you can hear the ocean." Holding the shell to his ear, she giggled. "You can hear the ocean, can't you?"

Glancing into her eyes, he said, "I hear the ocean and much more." His heart was racing as he bent down, the scent of lilacs filling his senses as he kissed her.

As they sat on the beach, Al was flexing his toes in the sand. Turning his head, he asked, "Where's a good seafood place?"

"There's a place up the coast called the Sea Mistress, and their food is really good. You want to go there for dinner?" Without even waiting for an answer, she was on her feet.

They headed back, and Al dropped Sarah off at the cabin and went back to the motel. Standing next to the bed, he chuckled to himself about his selection of clothes and asked himself, "Do I wear the blue oxford shirt or the yellow? Sure not gonna wear a tie. Blue oxford it is, with my camel hair jacket and jeans. Casual, yet pretty good look if I say so myself."

Sarah came into the Inn and greeted the old gentleman at the antique desk. "Hello, Mr. Johansen," she said.

He replied, "Well, hello there, Sarah. How is the commander doing?"

"Fine, I guess. I haven't heard from Daddy in a couple of weeks. Next time I talk to him, I'll tell him you asked."

Glancing at Sarah with a bit of a smirk he said, "Nice-looking young man you seeing. Is it serious?"

Leaning over the counter she replied with a twinkle in her eye, "Now, Mr. Johansen, that's not a polite thing to ask a young lady." Just then Sarah heard the horn on Al's car and with a smile and a wave vanished through the front door.

They arrived at the Sea Mistress a few minutes before seven. The evening was wonderfully comfortable with a breeze coming off the ocean. Out on the veranda, they enjoyed a glass of white wine at a table for two. Al was mesmerized as the breeze blew Sarah's hair back, and the sparkle off the bay made her hair look alive.

As he was looking at her, she turned and smiled. "What?"

"Nothing really," Al said.

"Oh, come on. I saw you looking at me."

Trying to recover he said, "If you must know, I was thinking about the mystery of the ocean. We can only see what's on top. What's below the surface is the real mystery."

Sarah's response was slow in coming, quite unlike her. "Most people are like the ocean. It's really hard to see what's underneath."

As if she turned on the excitement switch, Sarah got up from her chair and said, "Let's eat out here. I'm going in to get our waiter." She was back within seconds in her seat smiling at Al.

Their waiter came to the side of the table, and Sarah said, "I'll have the Mistress Platter."

Al responded next, "I'll have the Flash in the Pan, and please be sure the flounder is pan-fried."

Raising the wine glass to his mouth was a good disguise in covering his smile. Taking a slow drink, he kept his eyes on Sarah. He thought, *There will never be a more perfect picture. No camera in the world could do her justice.*

The service was excellent, and the warm food arrived a few minutes later with lots of visual appeal. Sarah's plate was overrunning with shrimp, oysters, flounder, napa slaw, and hush puppies. He looked at it and laughed.

She said, "Really, don't laugh; I'll eat every last bite." His plate was not as big but still filled. His fare was flounder smothered in scallops, all on a bed of wild rice. Dinner lasted for almost three hours. As the staff was preparing to close, he was holding the hand of his free-spirited wonder.

They drove the few miles back to Lynnhaven, listening to the radio and enjoying the breeze. He dropped her off at her dad's place and headed to the Inn. The entire day with her was now replaying in his mind. Her smile was enchanting; her laughter was music to his soul. That night the bottom nightstand drawer stayed closed. He slept like a baby and woke to the sun just beginning to rise. His morning coffee was the best he could remember. The fresh cool morning air, hot coffee, smell of lilacs, and her smile all pointed to a magical day.

Al picked Sarah up before ten in the morning. She jumped into the car and said, "I want to take you to one of my favorite spots on the coast. It has a wonderful view of Chesapeake Bay."

Al responded, "I'll drive anywhere you want to go." They drove the thirty or so miles, talking about how much fun they had walking along the beach and how great dinner was. He snickered when he remembered her eating pizza and talking.

"What's so funny?"

With a smile, he answered her, "I was just remembering the pizza, and the mushrooms and shrimp trying to escape while you laughed."

Within the hour, she had pointed the way to a drive off along the two-lane highway. From their vantage point, the Atlantic was right in front of them, and the Chesapeake Bay was to their left. With her standing in front of him and the sun shining through her hair, he said, "I'll always remember this view. And I'm not talking about the ocean." She laughed at his comment, grabbed him by the hand, and spun around like a ballerina.

Heading back to Lynnhaven he said, "I have a story I need to cover first thing in the morning. I'll need to head back before dark." Silence filled the car, and even the noise of Al's shoe on the floor of the car echoed. He glanced over at her and said, "This is one of the best times I can remember in a very long time. I want to come back soon." She smiled at his words, yet her smile was not quite the same. He detected sadness.

He pulled his car into the commander's drive. Turning off the ignition, he turned to her. He tried to say something but had to clear his throat first. He spoke quietly, yet trying to be firm, saying, "Sarah, I think I'm falling in love with you."

She moved a little in her seat and softly kissed him. With that she opened her door and seemed to spring out of the car.

"Have a safe trip back and call me," she said. Her words coming back through the open window made his heart race even more.

4

Meeting Rose

The car sat motionless for a few seconds before Al put it in gear. The three-hour drive back to Bee's seemed to last forever. He finally parked behind Aunt Bee's. When he got out of the car, he wasn't the same guy who had left close to forty-eight hours earlier.

Coming in the back door, he carried his bag and headed up the back stairs. Before he was two steps up, Bee was behind him. She said in her ever-pleasant voice, "I've got pot roast, potatoes, and carrots still warm in the oven."

He turned, smiling at her and said, "I'll be right back down."

He put his few things away and headed back down the stairs. Bee's pot roast was delicious, and he cleaned his plate with a slice of her homemade bread. He said, "Bee, you'd be rich if you had a place that served this food."

She replied as she moved around the room, "I'm happy taking care of folks and seeing them smile and enjoy my cooking. I don't think I would like that many people."

As Bee fussed around him, he said, "I have an early assignment. Thanks for keeping dinner nice and hot. I'm gonna turn in."

She asked, "Well, what was your weekend like?"

Her effort didn't pay off as he replied, "Someday I might tell you." Just after saying that he smiled and thought, *What am I doing, she is not my mother, and I'm not a teenager.*

His early morning assignment lasted into the evening. He got back to the boarding house after seven and had leftovers from the dinner hour. Bee had set out homemade biscuits and creamed chicken. After Al had cleaned his plate, he went upstairs and reached for the telephone. Sarah must have been sitting right next to her phone because she answered before the second ring. Al smiled as he heard her voice.

They talked on and on. Well, she did most of the talking. Al thought that the excitement in her voice was as if a field of wildflowers were singing. Near the end of the conversation, he said, "I want to come down, as soon as I can get away."

She answered back, "I had such a wonderful time. I can't wait to see you again."

He explained, "It's gonna have to wait for the following weekend. This coming one, I'm on an assignment. I wish I didn't have to wait."

A few minutes later the phone line was silent but not the hearts of the two in love.

They talked on the phone every night that week. His weekend assignment was at the naval base in Norfolk. The navy was making some big news about new ships and war strategy. He did a great job covering the story. His chief remarked at how detailed his information was and that he did a great job.

Getting back from the assignment, he called Sarah. It was good to hear her voice, and they reminded each other of the coming weekend. He laughed over the phone when she said, "I will remind you every night until you pull into the drive."

He would have a hard time describing how he felt when she called. His wildflower could transform a bad day into a great one.

Near the end of the week, Al got a phone call from Ray, his former chief in DaNang. They hadn't talked in months, and Al couldn't remember exactly when it was. His old boss was telling him that he was retiring from the paper, and he and his wife were buying a small weekly paper up near the Canadian border.

He told Al that when he wasn't fishing a famous trout river, he might be working. Al said, "You mean it the other way around, you old newshound. You might find time to go fishing."

Al congratulated him, and before he could hang up, Ray said, "If you ever find your way up north, you'll always have a job, although you might only get paid in coffee and Kentucky's finest." Al scribbled down the phone number and put the scrap of paper in his wallet.

Al left town on Friday afternoon and headed down the freeway, thinking about Sarah the entire time. His radio was playing his favorite rock-and-roll, he was in love, and life couldn't get much better. Lynnhaven Road increased his pulse. As soon as he pulled into the commander's driveway and pressed down on the chrome ring for the horn, Sarah flew out the door. He was hardly out of the car, and she was jumping into his arms. Her smile, laughter, and the smell of lilacs melted his heart.

They decided that pizza with wild mushrooms and shrimp was the dinner for tonight. Al was famished; he hadn't eaten since leaving Bee's that morning. Smiling, talking, laughing, and Sarah fighting mushrooms and slippery shrimp filled his heart with joy. Every smile, every quirky look from his spring flower cast him deeper into the well of love.

After the pizza, they sat on the old church pew and talked. There was so much he wanted to tell her, so many things she didn't know about him. He wanted to tell her of the headaches and dreams. He wanted to talk to somebody who cared.

Close to midnight, he pulled back into the drive to let Sarah out. Their embrace on the porch lasted until the morning light came over the marsh on the coast. Morning coffee was beyond description. Sarah asked him if he wanted to spend the early part of the day along the beach.

He replied with a smile, "You name the spot, and we're there."

The minutes along the beach added to his love as more smiles and laughter only dug the well deeper. He thought, *What kind of life did I have before I met Sarah?* The morning soon turned to afternoon, and the laughter and smiles along the beach continued.

Within a couple of hours before sundown, Al looked at his lilac-infused love and said, "Let's go find an out-of-the-way place for dinner. I'll point this old wreck south, and let's see what we find."

Sarah replied, "Getting adventurous, are you? I'm game. Never know what we might find along any old road."

Sixty miles down the coastal roadway, they spotted a road sign that captured their attention. Sarah said, "I've been down this road dozens of times, and I have never seen that sign before."

"Well, it looks as if it has been there for years and years. Let's go and see what the place is like."

The sign was easy to read, "Food—Best on Road." Al pulled the car onto the parking lot of gravel filled with potholes. The place was rundown and in need of paint and a few repairs. He held Sarah's hand, leading her up the front steps that creaked and sagged under them. When he opened the flimsy front screen door, it creaked, and the spring twanged as it pulled the door shut behind them.

Glancing around, Al shrugged his shoulders as if he was

asking Sarah if she wanted to stay. Just seconds after the door slammed, they heard, "Just have a seat you two, and I'll be right with ya." With a grin, Sarah took a couple of steps and sat at a window table.

A puzzled look crossed their faces. He whispered, "How did she know it was just the two of us?"

A rotund black woman came out of the back room. Her smile filled her face as she said, "Well, hello. How are you two love birds doing this glorious evening? You can't hide love from Rose. I've seen it a million times, maybe more." Al thought she was being far too forward and inconsiderate. Rose's next sentence made his jaw drop. With a hand on her hip, she said with attitude, "Yeah, I know you think I'm rude and forward. Well, I guess I am forward. Now, this is the best place to eat along this road for miles."

Recovered, Al asked, "So how's the gumbo?" Rose's reply was short, "It'll be the best gumbo you ever had, or it's free."

Al looked over at Sarah and asked her, "Are you up to trying the free gumbo?"

Sarah smiled, getting the jab, "Sure I'll try the free gumbo."

Rose turned with a chuckle, "Free gumbo. When they get done, they'll be willing to pay twice. Free gumbo, I'll give 'em free gumbo."

As they sat waiting, Al said, "Look around this place. It's an absolute mess. These tables and chairs must be forty or fifty years old." As he finished, Rose came out with two large bowls and set them on the table.

Standing next to Al she said, "So, my place looks dumpy. Yeah, the tables and chairs are close to fifty years old. But you know what? Folks don't come in here to eat my tables and chairs."

Reaching over and putting her hand on Sarah's shoulder, she

smiled and said, "If it's too spicy put a tad of sour cream on your bread and take a bite as you eat the gumbo."

Sarah took her first spoonful, and the look on her face was priceless. Gasping, she said, "I think I'll try the sour cream."

With those whispered words, Al and Rose took to laughing. Al laughed for a few seconds, his eyes never leaving Sarah. Rose was laughing to the point of tears.

After trying the sour cream, Sarah said, "It works. Thanks."

Rose responded, "Can't have you not liking my gumbo, now can I?" With that said, she let out another laugh and returned to the kitchen.

Their entrée was blue crab with fresh sweet corn, roasted potatoes, and hush puppies. They ate until they were stuffed; it was as if the more they ate, the more was on their plate. At long last, Al wiped his mouth on a paper towel.

Rose walked to the table and smiled. She asked, "So, you two, how was it?"

Al said, "Of all the places I've been and the different food I've eaten, this is the best."

Rose smiled as big as possible and said, "I just love making people happy and knowing that I satisfied their hunger. You know, I can tell when people are in love, and you two are perfect examples." Her next words were as much of a puzzle as was Rose. She said, "Remember, love is like a rose bush—such beauty and fragrance fills the senses, but the thorns on every bush bring pain. Both of you lovely kids are gonna experience both the fragrance and the pain."

As Al and Sarah reached the door, Rose said, "Now don't go and tell lots of folks about my place. I don't want to get overrun."

The two lovers smiled at each other as the rickety screen door slammed behind them.

Getting back after dark, he parked in the drive at Sarah's. That night he never made it to the Lynnhaven Inn. Al sat with his left side against the massive side of the bench. Sarah sat close and snuggled under his arm. After a few minutes of listening to the night chorus of bugs and frogs, she shifted her position. Looking at him she said, "Please tell me what happened when you were there. I know that something is eating at you, like I knew there was more to the death of my brother."

Shifting on the bench, he looked straight at her. "Okay," he said, "We had been hearing that there was going to be some kind of attack. The signs were there. The shopkeepers were telling us that there was going to be trouble. The military knew the enemy was moving large weapons and stockpiling supplies."

As Al talked, Sarah watched his hands clench and relax over and over. With his voice quivering, he said, "An explosion knocked me out of bed that morning, and the artillery barrage started working its way down the road towards the shops and a bunker we were in."

She was looking into Al's eyes, and his tears were moving her heart.

Just above a whisper, he said, "I watched a little girl running towards me. I could see her tears and her dirty white shirt. She looked like she was trying to reach out to me. The young marine next to me, a Pfc. Williams, he was going to move behind me and try to reach the little girl. And. . .and. . .in an instant, right in front of me, she vanished, in a damned red mist. I just kept yelling at Williams, 'Where is she, where is she, damn it, where is she?' And. . .and. . .he hollered in my ears, 'Dear Mother of God, she's gone. She's gone! She's gone!'" At the end of the words, Sarah was holding on to her love, wet with tears and sweat.

Al headed back to the city Sunday afternoon. He felt that

he had experienced an inner cleansing when he had spewed out the poison that had been eating his mind and soul for the past months. He held nothing back as he talked with Sarah. Now she knew of his headaches and the nightmares. He shared the deepest pain and secret of his soul with the wildflower of his life. Just closing his eyes brought her smile, laughter and the smell of lilacs to his soul.

On Monday, Al walked into his space and found a note waiting for him that said, "See me right away" and was signed by his chief. Al went to the office and found two other staff people already there—one was a reporter and the other a photographer.

"Al," his boss said, "This afternoon you'll be part of our staff heading to Southeast Asia. There are talks of negotiations beginning, and I want you to be there. You're the only one with any experience, and I want your opinion as one who has been there."

Before Al could object, agree, or utter a word, the three were told they had the rest of the afternoon to prepare, and the plane left at seven.

Back at his desk, he dialed Sarah's number. The knot in his stomach began to tighten as the phone rang.

"Hello, this is Sarah," she said.

Before she could say more, Al said, "Hi Sarah, this is Al. I've got bad news. I have to leave this afternoon and head overseas on an assignment. Looks like I will be gone for a while." Al heard her crying on the other end.

He asked, "Why are you crying? I'll be just fine." He didn't know if she was upset about his leaving or what he had experienced. A second later he found out.

"I love you," she said. "And this scares me."

He said, "I'll be alright as long as I have you waiting for

me." The knot in his stomach did little to reassure his heart. With a strangling lump in his throat, he said, "I love you. I'll call you the first chance I get."

On the other end, he heard Sarah choke back tears. She said, "I love you too. Please be careful. I'd die if I lost you."

His flight landed twenty hours later. He was tired, needed sleep, and wanted a drink. About an hour after landing, he felt the beginning of a headache coming on. His stomach was grinding, and he knew the flashing lights would begin soon. He knew too well how this was going to play out. When the pain in his stomach was nonstop, and the flashing lights were strobes, the migraine hammer would begin crushing his skull.

After checking into the hotel, he went straight to his room, turned on the air conditioner, minus the front panel. He downed three fingers of bourbon, stretched out on the bed, and covered his head with a pillow.

The pillow was always a failed attempt to mitigate the pain and shelter him from the hell to come. As the little girl with her arms outstretched ran towards him again, his pleas were the same. "Why, O God, does it have to continue? God forgive me for being a jerk. I just wanted one more picture. Please let it stop." His often repeated confession never brought relief.

The news conference the following morning didn't amount to much. Al thought, *Just a few men who think they're important talking about peace coming after forty years of war.*

Within an hour Al was back at the hotel. He went to his room and pulled out Sarah's phone number. The International Operator put him through, and after a few seconds of waiting, her phone rang.

The instant she picked up he said, "Sarah, O God, it's good

to get through. I've been dying to hear your voice. You don't know how much I miss you."

She answered, "I'm so glad you arrived safely. I was worried about you. I wish you didn't have to stay."

He could hear her holding back tears. He couldn't bear to listen to her crying. "Sarah," he said, "I love you, and I'll be back as soon as I can get out of here. I have to go to a meeting. I'll call again tomorrow. I love you."

After he hung up, a lone tear trickled down his cheek and dropped onto his trousers. A few seconds turned into a few minutes of stillness. In the quiet his mind replayed what his heart was feeling. He watched her attack her pizza, walk along the beach, and turn red eating gumbo. He remembered how he smelled her hair when he nestled his face close to hers.

During the news conference the following day, a few questions were asked and answered. The talks would take place in Paris. All sides in the conflict would be represented. Al and the staffers with him were told that they were to go to Paris and cover the set-up of the talks. *That could take a week or a month,* he thought. His heart ached for Sarah, her smile and lilacs. As he was leaving the hotel for the flight to Paris, his phone rang in at the front desk. The receptionist listened to Sarah's voice asking, "Is this Al's room? Can I please talk with him?"

She answered, "I'm sorry ma'am, the entire team of journalists just left for Paris."

After settling in at the hotel in Paris, Al called Sarah. She sensed the tension in his voice and asked, "What's bothering you? Is it Paris? Are you having those headaches?"

"No," he replied, "It's none of that. I, I love you, and being away from you is driving me nuts."

His heart melted under his shirt as he heard, "I love you too, and I can't wait to hold you."

A few minutes later, the phones went dead.

The talks in Paris dragged on, and little progress was being made. The main office decided to call the team back to Washington. But as luck would have it, Al heard a rumor about a snag in the set-up of the talks. He phoned a contact in the State Department, and they met for coffee. The connection told Al that the set-up ran into a snag over something stupid—the shape of the negotiations table. After coffee, Al knew what he had to do. He called his chief and told him what was going on. Instantly he regretted the call. The other members of the team were to leave. He was told to stay behind to see what was going on.

Back in his room, he picked up the phone and dialed the memorized number. On the second ring, his wildflower answered. "Sarah," he said, "It's me. I don't know how to tell you this. I'm not coming back for a while, maybe up to a week. I love you so much. This is driving me crazy. I miss you so badly."

Both of them talked through tears. Al was dying inside, he missed her so much. A moment of silence was interrupted by Sarah.

She said, "When you get back, there's something we need to discuss."

"I know'" he said. "We have a lot to talk about, and I don't want to do it over the phone." The connection went bad, and both of them were holding onto receivers that failed to carry a loving goodbye over the miles.

When he hung up the phone, the grinding in his stomach began. He tried to soothe it with three fingers of Kentucky. It didn't work. An hour later, the strobe lights started flashing, and he began fighting the headache. Soon he was covered in sweat with his head under the pillow. Almost in a stupor, he prayed, "Dear God, keep her away from me, please." His prayer went unanswered. It was a night of flashing lights and a vanishing girl.

It took a full week for the negotiators to decide on the shape of the table. He wondered if he should write about the hundreds who died while idiots tried to agree on the shape of a table. At the end of the week, Al phoned Sarah to tell her he was leaving.

He couldn't move fast enough as he gathered up his things and headed to the airport. His editor decided, against the common sense of any good editor, to give Al a first-class seat. Within minutes of takeoff, he had reclined and was enjoying his beloved Kentucky. The flight was uneventful, and as the plane was on approach, the image of Sarah was filling his mind and soul. He knew her smile and lilacs were waiting for him.

When he had cleared customs and immigration, he rounded the corner to find Sarah. She was wearing his favorite—the prairie skirt he first saw her in and the peasant blouse. Her smile was bright and beautiful and warmed his heart. Their embrace lasted as her soft lips met his, and the beauty of lilacs filled his senses. He grabbed his bag from the carousel, and they headed out the door, knowing he had two days to relax.

The drive to the coast and the commander's home was pleasant. The sun was warm, and the windows were down in the car. He had planned only a brief stop for gas and then to the coast, good food, a walk along the beach, and Sarah's arms. As he got closer to Lynnhaven Road, he sensed that Sarah was pre-occupied.

"So," he asked, "so tell me, what's going on in that beautiful head of yours."

She smiled and said, "After dinner, we'll have time to talk."

For whatever crazy reason, Al wanted to go south along the coast to the shabby place they went to weeks back. He remembered the sign, as dilapidated as the eatery, it said, Food—Best on The Road. He found the place and parked on the dirt and gravel drive.

When they went in, the voice of Rose greeted them, "Well, I'll be. Are you two coming back for more of Rose's food?"

Al had two bowls of the gumbo and then Sea Bass with mushroom stuffing. Sarah had a shrimp salad and scallops for her main dish. She was picking at her food, and Al was sure that something was bothering his wildflower. Sensing her uneasiness, he declined desert and went to the counter to take care of the bill.

As Sarah headed out the door, Rose came to the counter. She said, "I could tell that the two of you needed some quiet. That's why I didn't stick my nose in earlier. Remember what I said about the rose and the thorns, I'll be seeing you later." Her statement went right past him.

Back on the front porch of the house, they sat on the large bench. For some time, the two were seemingly molded into one. Not a word passed for what must have been an hour. Al just sat and felt the texture of her light brown hair. With each breath, the smell of lilacs filled his mind and his heart.

He finally broke the silence and said, "What's been bothering you? You seemed distant all the way down."

She started to fidget and sat on the edge of the pine bench. Staring at her sandals, she said, "I'm pretty sure I'm pregnant."

The lump in his throat didn't help his loss for words. Pausing, he asked, "Are you sure?"

Quietly she said, "I'm pretty sure, I'll know more in a few days. I first suspected when I tried to call, and you had left the hotel." Her next words left Al stunned. She said, "I don't want to be pregnant. I'm not ready to have a child."

She continued, "Al, I love you so much, I'm just not ready for a baby. There's so much more I want to do before I have to settle down." His wildflower wanted to continue to be just that, a beauty that moved with the breeze of freedom.

He held her hands and looked into her eyes and professed, "I love you, I will be with you, and together we can face this."

They spent the next day walking the now familiar beach. Their conversation was missing something; a sense of heaviness seemed to fill the very air around them. That night on the porch, Al sat against the armrest built into the bench, and Sarah curled her feet and sat tight against him, wrapped in a soft fleece blanket.

Near sunrise, with Sarah asleep, Al moved to the old mountain chair and gently lowered Sarah onto the bench. His attempt at sleep was pitiful, and the thoughts of a child kept him restless. Gusts of cool air and the sun splitting between two trees stirred him back to life. Getting up from the old chair, he went into the cabin, showered and changed.

The aroma of coffee reached Al as he pulled on his shoes. He heard the familiar sound of ceramic cups and saucers being moved. Coming from the bathroom, Al stepped behind Sarah, put his hands on her shoulders, and whispered, "I love you."

"I love you too," she replied softly.

"I have to be back early this evening, Sarah," he said taking his seat. "I have a story to submit first thing in the morning. The boss has been chewing my rear lately, so I better give him some good stuff."

The coffee and toast tasted bland, and Al and Sarah's conversation was devoid of their usual enthusiasm. The rattle of the coffee cups against the saucers echoed in the silence.

Clearing her throat, Sarah spoke up, "If I'm not pregnant, that will be great. If I am pregnant, then I guess I know what to do. There's a clinic in New Jersey that I know of. If I have to, I can go there."

Shifting on the kitchen chair, Al said, "I'll help in any way that I can." Sarah's comment about the clinic seemed confusing to Al. *Why,* he thought, *would she have to find a doctor that far away?*

On the drive back Al replayed the conversation with Sarah over and over. He kept telling himself that he didn't want to be a father. Memories of his childhood and his father's failure to be more than a tyrant brought vivid images of his father yelling and cursing at his mother or anyone else guilty of disagreeing with him.

Pulling into the back at the boarding house, Al sat for a moment. He hoped to avoid Bee by going in the back door. She was standing at the sink and turned to Al. The look on his face told Bee that something was bothering him. He headed up the back stairs.

Standing in the doorway, Bee said, "Al, Al, there are leftovers in the refrigerator. I set aside cold chicken and potato salad for you." She was convinced something was wrong when he didn't acknowledge her.

In the late night hours, Al looked at the glowing hands of his alarm. He tried to focus on the green glow from the clock although his head was throbbing, and his stomach was churning. Curled in a ball, with his pillow over his head, he pleaded with the God he didn't believe in, to stop the headaches and dreams. When the sun came up, he found himself half asleep on the bathroom floor.

5

Sarah's Decision

Al's office phone rang. It was Sarah. After a second of silence and an awkward hello she said, "I found out I was pregnant. Yesterday I drove to Jersey and went to the clinic. I have to take it easy for the next few days, but the doctor assured me that I would be alright. It was a decision I had to make for myself."

As the haunting words penetrated Al's heart, his mind shouted, "No way in hell is this my wildflower." If he could snatch the next words out of the air and stuff them back in his mouth he would, but they were out. He spewed, "What gave you the right to kill our child without even talking about it more with me?" With the words out, the phone went dead.

Al sat at his desk for the longest time, just staring at his old typewriter. His boss must have noticed because he hollered his name and told him to come into his office. Al walked into his office and said, "I have to leave, I might not be in tomorrow. I have some personal business that I need to take care of." With the words out, he turned and left his boss' office.

Late that night, Al stumbled in through Bee's back door. Making it to his room, he opened the bottom drawer and wrapped his hand around his bottle. At that moment, he heard a knock on his door. He set the bottle between his feet. There was another quiet tapping on his door and then Bee's voice. "Is everything alright Al?" Her voice was as pleasant as ever.

Trying to disguise his distress, he said, "I'm alright, just tired." Bee wasn't convinced and asked if she could come in. She took his silence as approval. Opening his door, she found him sitting on the side of the bed, holding his head in his hands.

She stood near the end of the bed, and Al could see her worn-out black leather shoes. She asked, "Dear, sweet Al. What's wrong? I've known something was bothering you ever since you came. I've heard you late at night when the house is quiet. I've heard you crying. I wasn't going to say anything, but tonight I knew I just had to."

Al began sobbing. Bee moved a chair to the side of the bed, sat down, and put her arm around his shoulder. The long sleeves of her cotton housedress rested on his neck. Her touch moved his heart, and he began to tell her about the past months. Bee wept as Al told her about his nightmares and the vanishing girl in the red mist.

Al's words were filled with pain and anguish as he said, "Sarah was going to have a baby." As he tried to start the next sentence, he began to choke as the words tried to come out. "She ended the pregnancy; she decided to end the life of our child." Now he could hear her praying, praying for Sarah, praying for him, and praying for the little life in the arms of Jesus.

Bee tried for some time to comfort him and said that God was holding his baby and there was forgiveness. Still choking back tears, he looked up at Bee and said, "I don't think God cares. With all the killing going on and the little children dying, what kind of God is that?"

She sat by his side for the longest time. He could still hear her praying, just above a whisper. After what seemed like an hour, Al gained his composure. He said, "Thanks, Bee, for just sitting by me."

Getting up slowly, Bee went over to the bedroom door. Turning she said, "I promise to keep praying for you and Sarah. Al, my dear, you are like the son I never had."

Al stirred as the sun was coming up. Sitting on the side of the bed, he was sure that the sounds of a crying infant had come from the hallway. Wondering if Bee had gotten a new boarder with a baby, he listened for another cry, but the old house was quiet.

Later that morning, with most of the other boarders gone, Bee fixed Al breakfast. She moved about quietly, and even her long housedress seemed silent. As he sat sipping his first cup of coffee, Bee came and put her hand on his shoulder. Her touch didn't bother him; he found it comforting.

She said, "Your eggs, ham, and biscuits will be ready in a minute."

The eggs and ham were tasteless, and he had to swallow hard to get the buttermilk biscuit down. He left one egg untouched, and the remaining ham was cut and arranged in two rows on his plate. As Bee came into the room, he said, "I'm sorry Bee, I'm just not very hungry this morning. I think I'll go up to my room for a little while."

Sitting on the edge of the bed, he regretted the words he had spoken to Sarah. Thinking that a phone call and trip to the coast would help, he dialed her number. The phone rang for more than a minute with no answer. He called five minutes later and let it ring, still no answer. In his heart, he watched her walking outside the cabin. He watched her bend down to smell a flower, and laugh, dancing with the butterflies.

He decided that if Sarah wasn't answering her phone, he would drive down. He left Bee's before noon, confident that they could work things out. As he drove, he relived in vivid detail the first time he drove to see Sarah. The sun seemed brighter then and the breeze was cooler. Sarah eating her pizza had stolen his heart and captured his soul.

It seemed like his car was on autopilot as he turned the corner onto Lynnhaven Road. A moment later he was parking in the Commander's drive. Getting out, he looked around the yard expecting to see Sarah. Going up the front stairs, he rested his hand on the porch bench and smiled as he remembered her sleeping on it.

Al opened the screen and rapped hard on the heavy inner door. Waiting just a few moments, he knocked harder and waited. The door opened slightly, only inches. He could see Sarah through the screen, and she opened the door and stepped out onto the porch.

Al said, "I had to come down so we could talk. I tried to call, but you didn't answer. I'm sorry for the way I sounded."

In a hushed tone, Sarah said, "I said some things that I regret too." She took a deep breath and put her head down as the front door reopened. Al pivoted and stood in the presence of the young man from the protest.

Al asked, "What's going on here? We talked only a few days ago. You never mentioned anybody else."

Sarah seemed at a loss for a moment and then said, "I called Jerry yesterday, and he came right down. He understands the way I feel, and he agrees with my decision."

Not acknowledging Jerry's presence, Al looked directly at Sarah and said, "I love you, and you said you loved me. I want to work things out."

Her response was as deadly as a bullet or knife. She said, "It's over for us. It was nice, but now I know how you feel about some things. Jerry and I are going out west. If you had gotten here just a little later, I would have been gone."

Unable to speak and sure that the blood from his broken

heart was running down his shirt, he turned on his heels and stepped off the porch. Tears were forming in the corner of his eyes as he reached his car. Pulling out of the driveway, he turned onto Lynnhaven Road. He headed north to the city, to Bee's house, the only security he had. For the next three hours, his hands never left the steering wheel.

The countryside that had captured his mind was now drab and nondescript. Farmland and pastures, perfect in their tranquility, were simply miles of dirt and vegetation now; two hundred-year-old estates were just collections of stone, brick, and board put in some order. Al knew that his life as it had been was over.

He pulled into town but not to Bee's place. He stopped at the bank and took out the little amount of savings he had. He told himself, "At Bee's place, her eyes and voice would be much too painful. It's just better to head off, anywhere, everywhere, off the face of the earth." The car headed north with Al, just a mindless, heartbroken passenger, going nowhere and anywhere.

Just north of Washington, his car took the freeway northwest hoping to reach oblivion before dark. It was headed towards the small town of Frederick. As the car and Al pulled into town, he spotted a small motel and a party store just across the street. He entered the motel and paid cash for one night and walked across the street.

Inside the party store, he bought two bottles of Kentucky. Walking back across the street, he reminded himself that Kentucky had never taken advantage of him; the opposite was true. His Kentucky always gave him exactly what he was asking for. He trusted his glass friend. It never lied to him, never kept a secret, never betrayed his trust, and always did what was needed.

His room smelled musty, and the bedding was threadbare and cheap looking. The stand next to the bed was empty, not even a phone on top. As he reached to open the drawer, he stopped. He set the bottles on the top of cigarette burns and white rings stained into the wood. Out of habit he opened the drawer and noticed the Gideon Bible. *What in the world is that doing in this dive of a place?* he asked himself.

His Kentucky was beckoning, and soon he was obliging his old friend. That night their friendship increased until exhaustion sent Al into a form of sleep and his empty friend onto the floor. Sometime in the darkness, the cries of a baby woke him. Sitting upright in bed, he strained his ears to hear where the noise was coming from. And, like at Bee's place, the night was empty of sound.

During the night when sleep restores the body and soul, the cries of an infant returned and haunted Al. Past midnight the infant cries were joined with the innocent little girl he knew so well, running with her arms outstretched, vanishing just a few steps in front of him. Near daybreak, soaked in sweat, he woke again and felt that his mind, sanity, and life were vanishing, just like the child in the red mist.

He checked out of the motel around eleven and continued his mindless journey. He needed the protection of a blank mind and a cold heart. He couldn't allow himself even one thought of Sarah and his lost child. Just outside of Harrisburg, he found an old four-story hotel stuck between the freeway and an industrial park.

Pushing open the dirty, salt eaten door, Al faced an old man at the front desk. The hotel rate sheet hung behind the old man. Al reached into his front pocket, pulling out some bills and said, "I'll pay for a week." The old man grabbed the cash. As he did, Al noticed his fingers stained a raunchy yellow and brown from unfiltered cigarettes.

"Suppose you really don't need a receipt, do ya?" the words coming out of the old man like a belch.

"Can you tell me where the nearest party store is?" Al asked.

"Yeah," the old man answered, "You can get your booze at a place a couple of blocks away, near an empty warehouse. Yeah, empty, just like everything around this godforsaken place."

"Thanks," Al said, and turned on the grimy floor and left.

Al found the party store just as the old man said. The shelves were bare except for booze and wine. As Al cradled three bottles of his faithful friend, one slipped, and the bottles bounced against each other. The man behind the counter could have been the twin of the old man at the hotel. His stubble was peppered with gray. His sky blue shirt was missing a button at the top, and his t-shirt was stretched down and frayed.

"Ya need anything else?" asked the old man.

Al answered, "No, this is it. Thanks, just tell me how much."

The answer back was unexpected, "Nope, this isn't all you need, but expect that'll come later. Give me twenty bucks for the three bottles, and we're even."

With the old man's comment swimming in his head, Al reached into his shirt pocket. Pulling out a tangle of bills, he stripped a twenty out of the mess, put it on the counter, and headed out the door.

With the door open, Al heard the old man say, "Expect I'll be seeing you again."

Al spent the next two days in self-induced mindlessness. During those two days, Aunt Bee and Al's boss had been talking on the phone. Bee told him she had no idea where Al had headed off to. Almost in tears, Bee told him she still had Al's room ready for him to come back. Al's boss in response told Bee that he would keep Al's job for him for another week. He said that he tried the cabin on Lynnhaven Road, and the phone went unanswered.

The next few days were a hazy mixture of bourbon and

nightmares. Three of the nights found Al on the edge of the filthy bed, shivering and rocking back and forth. The cries of the baby and the red mist were now transformed into a devilish trio with headaches that brought on hours of vomiting.

Without a dollar in his pocket and empty bourbon bottles in the room, it was time to check out of the hotel. Standing at the hotel counter, burned by hundreds of butt-end cigarettes, Al put the room key on it. As the old man reached for the key, Al asked, "Do you know anybody that might need a car? I bet I can get a few hundred bucks out of it."

The old man answered, "There's a bar down the way a few blocks. You might find some guy in there who needs one. I doubt it, though. Most of the guys in there are only a bit better off than you are."

Al said, "Thanks, if I find a buyer I might be back for a few more days. This place is kinda growing on me."

It took Al just a couple of minutes to find the bar. Going in the front door, he was greeted by the snarl of the bartender asking Al, "What do ya want? If ya don't have any money get out of here."

Al's senses were attacked by the smell of beer and spirits. He offered, "I've got an old car out here, and I'm looking to sell. The old man at the hotel told me you might be interested or know somebody that might be."

The look of disgust on the bartender carried over to his voice, "Well, it won't hurt to look."

As he came out of the dark bar, the sunlight temporarily blinded Al. He stood in front of the car, his shoes grinding in the small bits of gravel and cigarette butts. The bartender walked around his car and asked Al, "How much ya trying to get out of it?"

Al said, "I think it's worth at least a couple of hundred."

Looking right at Al, the man said, "Listen, guy, I guess you need some cash, and I'm sure you've got some sob story about how life stinks. It's pretty easy to see you need more than a few bucks. I'll give ya a hundred dollars cash, right now. Take it or leave it. No negotiating, no bull."

The gravel grinding under Al's feet sent the bartender a message. Al said, "I was really hoping for more."

Almost with a snarl, the bartender shot back, "Take the hundred bucks or go find somebody else."

"I'll take the hundred. The papers are in the glove box." As the bartender handed over the cash, he said, "I don't really care about the papers."

Tucking the cash into his front pocket, Al walked back towards the hotel. Before turning the corner, he stopped at the party store and left with four friends that didn't complain or ask questions. As he entered the front door of the hotel, the four bottles clanged in the bag.

The old man turned when he heard the bottles. Al said, "Looks like I'm gonna enjoy this fine establishment for a few more days." Pulling some bills from his pocket, he tossed them on the burnt counter.

The old man said, "I'm glad you're back; the maid wasn't gonna get to your room for a while." Trying to laugh, the old man went into a coughing jag. Al thought, *Old guy, probably smoked a few hundred packs of those unfiltereds.*

After he downed three-fourths of a bottle, the all too familiar ritual started—lights flashed across his eyes, and soon he was doubled over in pain. He tried to bury his head through the mattress, but the pounding in his head reached his stomach. Soon his bedding reeked of sweat and bourbon.

During his torture of flashing lights, sweat, and pain, the relentless little girl kept running and running, her small outstretched arms trying to reach Al. Like so many times before, he watched himself try to reach out to her, only to have her vanish in that godforsaken red mist.

In the early light that found its way through the filthy windows, Al moved slowly on the floor. His shirt, soaking wet, clung to his chest and arms. His hair appeared as if it were streaked with grease. In the light he reached for the nightstand; pulling himself up, he turned and sat on the edge of the bed.

As if grabbed by an unseen force, he started shaking. Soon the shaking was uncontrollable. With his head in his hands, he was unable to stop. Tears were flowing down his cheeks. Amidst the shudders, his mind was invaded by the suicide army. It was as if they were chanting, "Why don't you just give up and die? This is never gonna end. That little girl will cry and reach for you till your last breath."

Later that morning, Al pushed the dirty aluminum door open and left the hotel. Walking around the warehouse district, he saw that the town was like so many others. Areas that once were alive were now corpses of steel, glass, and concrete.

After walking for a while, he was feeling better. He thought the walk and fresh air must have done him good. Coming in the front door of the hotel, he heard, "Hey Al, want a cup of coffee?"

Looking at the old man, he said, "Sure would. Ya know all the time I've been in this fine establishment, I've never learned your first name."

"I'm Stan," he said. "Now let's have that cup of coffee." Al watched him reach underneath the counter and pull out a creamy white mug. Stan muttered, "Best check it for dirt." He swiped his yellow and brown fingers in the cup and set it down. The steam and aroma from the old electric percolator filled Al's sense of smell and his memory of Bee.

The coffee was strong, and Al savored the aroma. Stan asked, "How are ya doing? I heard some disturbing sounds coming from your room."

Al responded, "Just bad memories and headaches, nothing much."

"Well, you better get rid of the demons in your head."

Al replied, "It's just stuff I've seen, not demons."

Stan instantly shot back, "Stuff stuck in your head is the same as demons. I know that's a fact, I know."

"Ya know Stan," Al said, "that coffee has done me good. I'm feeling the need to eat something. Is there a café anywhere around?"

Laughing and choking, Stan got out, "The word café doesn't really fit the place. Just past the highway is an old diner. It used to be busy when the trucks were using the warehouses."

Al answered back, "Think I'll head that way."

Al had to go through an overpass to reach the road. The area was filled with booze bottles of every color; the lingering smell of urine was nauseating. A block past the highway, a sign hung on an old building. "Food" was all the sign proclaimed. As he got closer, he could hear the sign swinging in the breeze. A rusted chain announced its creaking age.

Al went in and sat on a stool at the counter. The black covering on the seat was split, exposing the old and dirty cotton underneath. The chrome was a mixture of shine and dirt; the floor looked to be covered with years of dirt and floor wax. A voice from the back told Al that his presence was known, and he would be attended to right away.

The swinging door soon opened, and a middle aged woman came out. She greeted Al and told him her name was Rosie.

Rosie, he thought, *I've heard that name before. Must have been a popular name years ago.*

Rosie said, "I make the best chili around, and my ham and cheese on rye is known all over these parts."

A bit sarcastic, Al said, "Looks like you could use a little more business."

She ignored his comment and said, "I use aged sharp cheddar, salted country smoked ham, and my rye is the best, not that store bought stuff you can blow through."

She set down coffee in front of him and said, "Could tell you needed some and liked it strong and black."

A bit surprised by her demeanor, it took him a second to reply. "Okay," he said, "You sold me. I'll have the ham and cheese on rye and a bowl of chili with extra onions and cheese on top."

After putting in the order, Rosie walked to the counter, returning with the coffee pot. "So," she said, "When I get back with your food, are you gonna tell me about Al?"

With the coffee cup almost slipping out of his hand, he said, "I didn't tell you my name. I just came in and sat down."

She responded confidently, "I'm sure you did, just after I told you I was Rosie."

The coffee, chili, and ham and cheese on rye were delicious. While he enjoyed his third cup of coffee, Rosie came around the counter and sat on a stool, leaving an empty one in between them. Again she prodded him asking, "So what trouble brings a young man down here?"

Al shot right back, "What makes you think I have troubles?"

Looking right at him, Rosie said, "Nobody who's trouble-free comes to these parts, let alone comes in here. I can see it in your eyes. You've been hurt, and the hurting wants you dead."

Getting up to leave, he tossed a five on the counter. Coldly he said, "My troubles are my own, and they don't concern a short-order cook who thinks she's a shrink."

Rosie shot back, "Say whatever you want about me, but I'll be seeing you again, someday, not too long from now."

Al walked for hours among the abandoned buildings. He thought, *I'm just like this ugly place. I'm a broken, empty shell, like broken glass, or dirt and garbage littering the sidewalks and alleys.*" Sarah's voice and the scent of lilacs filled his head and overpowered the smell of trash and exhaust. His heart and mind joined voices, "She was the best thing that ever happened to you. Her smile made you happy. She gave you something to live for."

Near dusk, he made it back to the hotel. Passing by Stan, he said, "Found the place, and the food was good. Don't care much for the nosey lady. Thinks she must be some kind of shrink."

With a monotone voice Stan said, "Well, if ever a man could use one, it would be you." Al ignored the words and went up the stairs.

Getting to his room, he noticed that Stan had left some sheets on the floor. Picking them up, he tossed them on the bed. On his nightstand stood his last solitary friend and comforter— a lonely sentinel, pledged to keep him company. It took him only a minute to put the clean sheets on the bed, and soon he was sleeping but not alone.

Close to midnight, Al felt like he had been soaked in gasoline and set on fire. Sweat had already drenched him. The inferno was joined again by flashing lights streaking across his eyes like lightning. The headache came crashing and crushing his skull and had him on his side. The pillow over his head offered no escape, and within minutes he was retching, his stomach emptying itself of Rosie's food.

The headache's conjoined twin was always the dream that played over and over, like some malfunctioning movie screen. The little girl, with her tears and dirty shirt, reaching out her hands and begging Al to leave his fortress and save her. Just before any arms could snatch her away from death, she vanished in the haunting red mist. In the midst of drowning in the ghastly images, Al screamed, "Why does she try to reach me? Why does she always reach out with her tiny hands? Dear God, doesn't she know she's dead?"

Around one in the morning, Stan was beating on Al's door. He knocked so hard that a few of the others down the hall stuck their heads out to see what was going on. After close to a minute of beating on the flimsy hollow door, Al opened it.

At the sight of Al, Stan uttered, "You look like hell. What's going on?"

Al asked Stan in and said, "It's these dreams and headaches I have. My head feels like it's ready to explode."

Pointing his discolored yellowish finger right in Al's face, Stan said, "The demons will kill you unless you kill them first." Before he left the room, Stan pushed his cynicism up a level saying, "I don't think you have the guts to face the truth. So, the advice from this sick old man is: give in and let the demons win; let them dance a jig over your sorry carcass."

6

Agape Station

Al didn't really know how close to the truth the cigarette-stained old man was. By the end of the week, his liquid friend had dried up, his rent was up, and he had nothing in his pockets. Stan had little choice and said to Al, "You have to be out by noon. The rules are the rules; I don't make 'em."

Al said in his most sarcastic tone, "I'll be glad to be out of this roach infested dive. You can have this hole."

He left the room carrying just a small bag with his only clean clothes, a shirt, and a pair of underwear. The biggest piece of luggage was on his back. As he left the run-down hotel, he was carrying Sarah, his child, the vanishing girl, and more.

Al found himself walking past the warehouse district and the little eatery. His aimless wandering took him past more old and broken-down steel and concrete edifices. In his heart Al felt he was no different than the steel and concrete skeletons he passed, except he was a lot younger. His mind attacked him again, *Have they outlived their usefulness, just like you? Or had some man in a suit decided their fate? Aren't you useless? You're a drunk, spent and done.* He wandered that night and made it to the other side of downtown.

Just past the high-rise office buildings, Al found himself in an alley behind a strip of businesses. The back doors told him where he landed. To his left was "Harry's Clothier" and to his right, "Java Café." The space between their garbage bins cut the wind and provided a hiding place.

Night brought little sleep as the smell of cardboard under his head blended with coffee grounds. When night brings the blessing of peace and sleep to the world, it doesn't visit Al. His nighttime demons are as regular as the morning sun arriving on time. The cries, the red mist, and the ebbing preservative nature of his bourbon had transformed the once top-notch reporter into an empty casing. His was a body with a broken soul, a heart devoid of life, a shell fitting the garbage cans where he hid.

Sometime after sunrise, Al was sitting with his back against a fence. With the sound of metal scraping, the back door of the coffee joint opened. A young man came out carrying a large plastic garbage can. He stopped with the garbage, took the lid off the large container and dumped his load of cups, coffee grounds, filters, and paper napkins.

Looking at Al, he said, "Looks like you could use a cup of coffee." A moment later he was back. Reaching down to Al, he handed him the cup with Java Café printed on the side.

Al offered up a weak, "Hey, thanks for the coffee." The young man went back in, escaping the smell of garbage.

With his back against the fence, he sipped at his coffee. Images of his wildflower filled his mind, and small tears coursed their way down his dirty cheek. Soon, the broken man began sobbing so intensely that his shoulders shuddered. Great tears ran down his cheeks and off the end of his nose. With his head between his knees, the tears flowed for minutes. Words that could break the hardest heart could be heard escaping the broken soul, "O Sarah, my wildflower. O how I love you, our baby, we were gonna....you're gone."

With his head still down between his knees, he didn't hear the back door open. He had no idea how long he had been sitting on the dirty asphalt in agony. The coffee-bearing young man asked, "What are you gonna do? You better not sit back here all day. The police don't take kindly to the homeless."

The word "homeless" hit hard. Even as the young man stood in front of him, his thoughts centered on the word. In his mind the message was playing, *Homeless, me a war reporter, now homeless. Whatever happened?* His mind came back as the young man was talking to him.

"Hey, mister," he said, "down the street is a place called Agape Station. The reverend and his wife help people. You can get a meal and a place to sleep. They are real nice folks. People start lining up around five, but it wouldn't hurt to be there a little early."

Al sat in the alley for another hour or so. The sun was warm and enticed him into something close to sleep. When he tried to get up, it took all of his strength just to prop himself up against the fence. Almost a full minute later he was stable. His feet were numb from sitting so long, and his lower body felt like it was dead weight, as if his legs were bags of cement. Once steady, he walked out of the alley and turned left in the direction where the kid said Agape Station was.

After walking a few minutes, he stood looking at a sign hung at a right angle to the storefront that said, "Agape Station, Love in Action." Al remembered enough Greek to know the word for love. The entire front of the building was filled with windows. From about three feet from the sidewalk to over eight feet high, the windows stretched for fifty feet or more. Within seconds, the messages covering the front windows captured Al.

All the messages appeared to be done in white shoe polish. Some were done well while others looked like they had been put there by children. One seemed to flash at him, "My end was my beginning." He gazed at the length of the window and thought that there must have been close to a hundred messages. Some were: "Jesus saved me," "Jesus loves me and you," "Repent or die," and "God used this place to save my life." A few were done in a straight line while others trailed off towards the bottom of the window.

After the messages, he realized that the sidewalk was deserted. He thought, *I must be real early. You'd think a few people would be standing around. Man, what I must look like, a bum standing outside a mission hoping for some food and a bed.*

Instead of just standing around, Al decided to take a walk. As he headed away from the message-filled storefront mission, an elderly couple walked towards him. As they got closer, he stepped aside to let the elderly lady have room.

"God bless you," she said.

The old man looked at Al and gave his head a bit of a tilt as if to acknowledge his act of respect. Al continued on and walked for an hour or so.

Heading back, Al could see a crowd gathering around the front doors. The sign read that the doors would be unlocked at five. Al had wondered why they needed to keep doors locked to a mission that was there to help people and give them a meal and a place to sleep. When he got closer, he could understand why.

It appeared to Al that every type of person was waiting at Agape Station. Quite a few of the people were using various kinds of wheeled gizmos to move and carry their stuff. Such a mixture of humanity was gathered in front of him. There were elderly men and women—some had on heavy coats and others wore two or three shirts. He was disturbed to see a few children standing with a woman.

A young man inside appeared at the front doors, and Al heard a key turn the lock. As if some signal had been given, the poor and beaten souls quieted down, and two very orderly lines formed. Standing back at first, Al watched the folks enter the mission and then joined them.

Going inside Al sat down near the back on an old metal folding chair. It was hard to tell what color it had been in its younger years. Most of the paint was scratched off so it could have been dark brown or beige. As he looked around, it was easy to see that the mission was in sharp contrast to the world just outside. The walls were clean and painted soft beige. The floor was tiled dark brown, and the air smelled clean.

Al watched as more folks came in. Inside he had a better chance to look at the carts and trolleys filled with coats, bottles, newspaper, cardboard, plastic sheets, and unrecognizable stuff. Every person who came in with a cart or trolley kept it close to them. Al smiled, thinking of the ingenuity behind some of them. After they waited for what seemed like half an hour, a little old lady came to the front of the room. It was the same lady that Al had stepped out of the way for.

When the elderly lady raised her hand, the large gathering became quiet. Welcoming everyone, she asked the group to bow their heads and pray with her for the blessing of the food that was before them. Hesitantly, Al bowed his head as did every person around him. Her prayer was simple: "Lord, bless this food to the nourishment of our bodies and bless the hands that have brought this food to us. Amen."

Table by table the gathering moved to the front of the room where the food was set out on two large tables. Taking a plastic spoon and fork, Al tucked them into his front pocket. The meal was creamed chicken on a biscuit with peas. Walking back to the table, Al set his plate next to a man who was rocking back and forth in rhythm with his bouncing feet. Soon they were joined by a man wearing a stocking cap.

The table was quiet as they ate. When Al was just about

done, the man in the stocking cap asked Al, "Hey, you gonna take a dive when the preacher gets up there?"

"Take a dive," Al said, "What does that mean?"

"It means the preacher and his wife try to get people to come to the front and pray at the chairs. Some tell me you get better treatment if you take a dive. Now me, I've never done it, so I get no special attention. I eat my food, listen to the preacher, and leave. Not sure Jesus is gonna help too many of us. Just don't seem like it to me."

Al watched as the gathering of struggling souls finished eating. The lady who had prayed brought out a small music stand. She set it near the front next to a portable speaker and microphone. A young man came through a doorway carrying sheets of paper stapled together. A young woman took some of them and started at the front of the gathering and passed them out.

Al's pages were pretty worn out. They had been folded back and forth so much that the papers had been re-stapled. The first words to jump off the paper to Al were, "Amazing grace how sweet the sound that saved a wretch like me." Looking at the pages and thumbing through the stained and tag eared sheets of sacred songs, Al began to feel uncomfortable.

Watching the young man pass out the song sheets, Al recognized him from Java Joint. He was the youngster who brought him the coffee. While this was going on, another person pushed out an old piano on wheels. It was set at an angle to the simple set-up in the front. To the left and right of the piano and music stand, a row of folding chairs was set side to side, with the back of the chair away from the gathering.

After a moment of shuffling through papers, the kindly lady sat at the piano and began playing a few notes. Soon a few of the folks started singing. Sitting there, Al didn't recognize the music or the hymn. The guy next to him said, "It's Amazing Grace, she always plays that one first."

As she played, the elderly man whom Al had met outside approached the simple music stand/pulpit. Clearing his throat, he said, "Welcome, everybody, I greet you all in the name of Jesus Christ. I am Reverend Daniel Williams, and that tiny wisp of a lady at the piano is my wonderful wife, Elizabeth. Welcome to Agape Station, a place of caring and love."

The reverend stood at the microphone, and his deep voice bellowed out the words to the hymn they were singing. Al thought, *That giant of a man can't carry a tune in a wheelbarrow. But his wife, well that is one talented lady. She plays like a concert pianist.* They sang two more hymns led by the reverend, and then he announced his Bible reading.

The Bible story was about a woman at a well giving Jesus a drink. Al was listening as Reverend Williams told the gathering the woman was from the other side of the tracks, a place the Jews hated. She wondered why Jesus being a Jew would even talk to her.

As Reverend Williams preached, his voice began to boom. With Al's full attention, Reverend William's said, "Jesus doesn't care where you are from. He wants you to know where you are going. You can't be any worse off than the poor woman he met at the well. You see, she couldn't hide anything from Jesus and you can't either. Jesus knew she had five men in her life, and the guy she was with wasn't her husband."

As the reverend was talking about hiding anything from Jesus, Al began to get a strange feeling in the pit of his stomach. His chair was getting harder, and he was getting tired. The old reverend ended with a prayer and asked anyone in the gathering that had a need of Jesus in their life to come forward to the prayer chairs. When the words left the preacher's lips, the guy in the stocking cap elbowed Al. As the Mrs. Reverend played and sang, "Just as I Am Without One Plea," a couple of folks walked to the front of the old transformed grocery store. Al was not one of them.

After the service, anybody wanting to sit around for another cup of coffee was welcome. And seeing that Al never refused a cup of black coffee, he stayed. As he was drinking the coffee, Mrs. Reverend walked up to him and said, "I remember you, young man, you were respectful to me outside."

He said, "Yes, ma'am, that was me." He was thinking, *She seems like a very pleasant lady with a very relaxed kind of way about her.*

As he worked on his coffee, she asked, "What has brought you, an intelligent sounding young man to Agape Station?"

Sensing her sincerity, he answered back, "It's a long story, and I don't know that you want to hear my troubles."

She responded, "Any man's troubles are mine to pray about and the Lord's to deal with."

Al was getting uneasy and decided he needed to escape. As he was getting ready to excuse himself, the reverend walked over and introduced himself. His handshake was firm, and the look in his eyes told Al that he was a man of experience. Before Al knew it, he was sitting down again drinking another cup of coffee.

Al said in a matter-of-fact tone, "I don't know who makes the Joe around here, but it's good." At the words, Joe, the reverend and his wife looked right at him.

"Joe, you said," responded the reverend, "Haven't heard that word for coffee in a while. Spend time in the military did ya?"

Al answered, "No, I wasn't in, but spent time with some grunt marines."

There was something about the reverend and his wife that

Al liked. He was trying to decide if it was their friendliness or their sincerity. Al sensed they were trying to make a difference in the world. He wasn't too sure the mission was a place for an elderly lady. He chatted with them for a few more minutes, and then the reverend announced they needed to leave.

Standing to leave, Reverend Williams said to Al, "I will be here in the morning before nine. We ask everybody who spends the night to leave around nine. That way our folks can look for jobs and keep appointments to see the local clinic doctors or other issues. But I'd like to see you in the morning if you plan on staying around."

Al said, "Well, my life is kinda up in the air right now. I'll be here, I guess."

A few minutes after Reverend Williams and his wife left, one of the volunteers at Agape Station explained the process for getting a cot and spending the night. It seemed pretty simple to Al: sign your name on a sheet of paper and agree to keep to yourself. The men stayed on one side of a hallway, and the women stayed on the other. The men lined up down the hall, and as they entered the room, they were each given clean sheets, a pillow and pillowcase, and a blanket.

Walking carefully between the narrow rows of cots, Al found one over in a corner. Under his cot was a plastic tub for personal items. Al was surprised to find a few men stretched out already since the setting sun was still coming in the western windows. Al put his bag in the tub, arranged the cot, and stretched out too.

Lying on his back and staring at the ceiling, the ceiling tiles seemed to be a mosaic of lines and holes. Al was imagining designs and figures in the ceiling. He wondered what kind of stories the room could to tell and imagined the ceiling telling of good men who had good jobs and families, losing everything through booze and drugs. He knew stories firsthand of soldiers suffering emotional and mental problems from stress. Living on the street, they were casualties that walked around, dead in their soul, just waiting for their body to catch up.

Al spent most of the long night thinking and reliving the hours and days he had spent with Sarah and the smell of lilacs. The sounds in the night were a mixture of men rolling over on small cots, coughing, snoring, and other body noises. The smell of dirty feet and unwashed bodies hung in the air. As daylight began to brighten up the eastern windows, Al could smell coffee, the lifeblood of the street people.

Sitting in the large meeting room, Al was on his second cup and feeling like he might survive. As he spotted the reverend and his wife approaching, he got up and opened the door for them. There was something about Mrs. Williams that grabbed ahold of Al. He couldn't put his finger on it, it was just something about her—her smile, her soft voice, and something more.

When they came through the door, Mrs. Williams was smiling and took Al's hand. "Good morning, son," she said. "I trust the Lord gave you a good night."

Al responded, "Let's just say I've had two cups of coffee, and I'm ready for the third."

Standing in the doorway, Reverend Williams was an impressive figure, especially standing next to his wisp of a wife. He laughed and said, "I can well imagine what a long night might be like with such a mixture of people." Reverend Williams extended his hand, greeting Al. With their hands clasped, Al saw the unmistakable Marine Corps insignia on his ring. It didn't take but a second for the wheels in his coffee-filled brain to begin moving. *Last name Williams, Marine Corps insignia on his ring. No, it couldn't be possible. Better just to keep it quiet,* he thought.

The Mrs. broke the awkwardness of the moment when she said, "I never had the chance to tell you my first name, and it's Elizabeth. I'm so glad you came yesterday. I sense God has a special reason you're here."

Over the next hour or so, Al and Mrs. Williams' talked. He disclosed very little about his life and problems. He did tell her that he was a reporter and enjoyed it.

Mrs. Williams asked, "Do you have a special lady in your life? You're such a nice young man, surely. . ." She stopped and seemed embarrassed. "I'm so sorry for asking. It's none of my business, please forgive me for being so forward."

"That's okay," he said. "Yes, there was a very special person; her name is Sarah."

Mrs. Williams asked, "Would you mind telling me about her?"

Al said, "On our first date we went to a pizza joint, and she ordered a marvelous pizza, covered with wild mushrooms, sundried tomatoes, and shrimp. I laughed as she tried to talk while a shrimp was trying to escape from her mouth." As soon as he said that, it became quiet.

Mrs. Williams spoke softly, "I sense that you loved her deeply. I could see it in your eyes and sensed your spirit." With those words from Mrs. Williams, Al got choked up. Trying to compose himself he looked down. Mrs. Williams put her hand on his shoulder and asked, "Is there anything else you would like to talk about?"

He said, just above a whisper, "Thank you, maybe later." After regaining his composure, Al asked, "Is there anything a reporter can do to help you folks?"

Without hesitating, Mrs. Williams said, "Let me get my husband. We've been talking about some projects we would like to see done." With that said, she went to the office area, returning with Reverend Williams.

"Honey," Mrs. Williams said, "Al wants to help out. We have been thinking and praying about a newsletter and some type of poster. What do you think?"

Reverend Williams half grinned, saying, "Well, praise the Lord. There are so many folks that support us here, and I would like to have a way of telling them what we're doing. I'd like to tell them about some of the marvelous transformations we've seen here. I'd like to put out some flyers so folks know what we're doing and what help is available."

Al agreed, saying, "That'd be great. I'll get started since I have so much time on my hands."

Al got busy taking notes on the activities of Agape Station. As he started digging into the various programs, he was surprised to learn how much was going on. Along with the meals and a place to sleep, he learned of a program that touched his heart. The mission arranged medical visits and provided transportation to clinics, hospitals, and veterans' centers. The mission also worked with the local college to help with remedial and tutoring services. And three nights a week, the mission was the meeting place for alcohol and drug support groups.

After a long day of gathering information, the evening meal time was approaching. Al decided he was going to sit with a few different people. Noticing a table with a couple of older men and three women, he approached them. Al asked, "Mind if I sit here with you folks?"

An older guy, with long white hair, nodded his head. Not wanting to interrupt their meal Al was thinking it was best to wait before he asked a few questions. When everyone was done eating, Al asked, "Is it alright for me to ask you folks a question? I'm just trying to figure out if folks like what's going on here. You know what I mean." The other folks at the table looked at the white-haired man.

Shifting in his chair, he said, "I'm Joe, and guess I've been coming here most every day. I think most of us are grateful for this place. The street is a mean place. Some of us like the way we live; most of us just got used to it. Now, the Mrs. Reverend, she's as sweet as they come. We think of her as our Godmother. The Reverend, now he's a straight shooter, an honest man; he's trying to do good round here."

7

A Blind Soldier with Vision

During the middle of the week, the mission conducts a worship service followed by the usual coffee and talking. It differs in that the local folks and regulars at the mission get to participate by singing, giving their testimony, or reading something important to them. Al had heard from Reverend Williams that he might be surprised at how good the local talent was.

With the meal over, the front of Agape Station was transformed from dining hall to sacred setting, complete with music stand/pulpit and prayer rail made from chairs. As Al was listening to the singing, he was amazed. An elderly lady was the first to sing. She was known to the folks as Sweet Pea. She shuffled her feet as she stood at the microphone. Al noticed she was dressed in blue jeans that were way too big and under her coat was a dark green sweatshirt.

Sweet Pea's voice sent Al into shock. He didn't know the song, but he thought her voice was almost angelic—gentle and sweet, almost airy. He sat up and concentrated on the words, "For His eye is on the sparrow, and I know He watches me." The softness and purity of her voice were in shocking contrast to her appearance. As she ended the song, Al's heart hoped for more.

As Sweet Pea finished, Reverend Williams was on his feet, approaching the music stand. In his booming voice, he announced that he was going to be reading from the twenty-fifth chapter of the book of Matthew. Al was listening to Reverend Williams read about people receiving talents and how God was expecting people to use them.

Reverend Williams said, "Those who use their talents are recognized and given more. The fool, who takes what he was given and hides it, is rebuked and punished. We just witnessed Sweet Pea use her gift for the Lord. She is doing what the Good Lord intended." Al thought, *Sweet Pea might be blessed with a talent, but I kinda doubt that many in this crowd of drowning souls have much to offer.*

At the end of his sermon and prayer, Reverend Williams said, "We have a real special guest this evening that is gonna come up and sing a couple of songs for us. This young man has a powerful testimony, and I know he's gonna share some of that with us tonight. His name is Joshua, and he was blinded while serving in the Army. Now, let's listen as this young man blesses us."

In the front and to Al's left, a young man with a cane was guided to the front and sat down by the music stand. The microphone was lowered, and the young man held it as he moved his chair closer.

"Hello," he said, "my name is Joshua White, but friends call me Josh. Only my mother calls me Joshua." The young man smiled as a few folks chuckled. "And," he continued, "I'm glad to be here and glad to know that Jesus Christ died for me and now I belong to Him and my heavenly Father."

As soon as the young soldier gave his testimony, Reverend Williams shouted out, "Amen, son, amen."

Josh continued, "Before I sing, I want to say a few things to you folks. First thing is, don't feel sorry for this guy up here. I'm the luckiest guy around; well, I shouldn't say lucky. I'm the most blessed man in the world. You see while I was in combat I lost my eyesight. But the best thing is, today I can see clearer than ever. Now don't misunderstand me. For a while, I was mad and depressed. I hated the world. And then a nurse told me to quit crying and look to God.

"The first song I want to sing is a real old hymn, 'The Old Rugged Cross.'" At the name of the hymn, Al remembered hearing it when he was just a young kid. His mother used to play old gospel albums during Easter season. As the young man sang, Al began to feel strange. He thought, *How could this young man, his eyes stolen from him due to the insanity of man, thank God? This just doesn't make sense. A man is supposed to be angry when his eyes are stolen.*

Joshua sang two songs, and after the second one, he said, "I'm gonna sing one more song. I wrote this one when I was trying to deal with my blindness. The words have to do with suffering, Jesus' suffering, to be exact. You see, Jesus suffered for the entire world and every person that will ever live or has lived. I hope you'll listen to the words."

On the first note from Josh, Al's mind was in the presence of the tear-streaked innocent little girl who vanished right in front of him. Lost in pain, he only heard Joshua sing that Jesus took our sin and suffering so we could be free of pain. As Joshua ended his song, everybody was on their feet clapping for the wounded warrior. As he stood with the rest, Al's vision was blurred with tears as was the vision of many in that sacred, renovated storefront.

During coffee time, Reverend Williams approached Al. "Al," he said, "I want you to meet Joshua. I think I'd like to write a piece about this young man and how he brought such a blessing to Agape Station."

The two men walked over to the table where Joshua was sitting and talking to a younger man. Not wanting to be rude, they waited a moment.

Al introduced himself, and the singer responded, "Call me Josh."

Al said, "Okay, Josh it is. I was with the news service up in the north."

Josh said, "So you were with a bunch of grunts. Man, I used to feel sorry for those guys, having to tramp through the jungle and bush. I was lucky. I was with a bunch of bad boys that got to ride around on Huey's."

Al asked, "Would you mind telling me what happened?"

"Sure I'll tell ya," Josh said. "I was blinded by tiny shell fragments. We were under small arms fire, mostly AKs. I turned my head to holler up front when a couple of fragments got me across the front of my face. I got pieces through the eyes and a bigger one across the bridge of my nose. The Doc said if I had my head out another inch, well, I wouldn't be singing."

Al asked, "How can you have such a good attitude about the whole thing? Aren't you mad?"

To Al's surprise, Josh said, "It's about Jesus. What I couldn't see with these eyes, I learned to understand with my spiritual eyes. I was blind, really blind before I met Jesus Christ. Now don't think I'm some kinda nut. Oh, I could see the world, but I was blind to the real world God has. I'm so glad that God gave me spiritual sight. I'm so much better off than I was."

Al asked, "How long are you going to be in the area? I'd like to get together again before you leave."

Josh said, "I should be around for a couple of days, then I'm heading to Washington."

"Washington," Al said, "I've spent time there, in my other life. I covered a few big rallies." His words triggered an instant image of Sarah, smiling, running along the beach, mushrooms dangling from her mouth.

A minute later Reverend Williams came up behind Al, placing his huge hands on his shoulders. He said, "Excuse me, but I have to get Josh. He'll be back tomorrow, right Josh? He agreed to let us tell his story in our newsletter. Remember Al, our newsletter, that you're gonna start for us. We might as well begin with Josh's testimony."

Josh was back the following afternoon, and Al was waiting for him in a small lounge area near the front. When Al saw the front door open and the massive figure of Reverend Williams fill the doorway, he was on his feet. Al extended his hand, and his fingers complained under the older man's grip.

Walking over to the lounge area, Reverend Williams said, "You boys sit right there and talk. I have business to take care of. I'll join ya later."

Josh was first to speak, "So, I told you a bit about me, tell me about being a correspondent."

Al said, "I was at the desk in DaNang. I went with the marines on a few patrols. Man, I had a lot of respect for those guys, going out at night, never knowing what might be waiting."

Almost interrupting Al, Josh said, "Did you know that Reverend and Mrs. Williams' son was with the marine detachment where you were? He was there when there was a major attack. A month later he was killed as he tried to help a local woman escape a firefight. The marine had written his parents about the attack and how bad it was. He even mentioned a guy who was working for a newspaper. He told his parents he was sure this guy saved his life."

8

Poison Surfaces

Frozen in sudden realization, Al was unable to move. Josh heard him attempting to breathe, and soon Al was choking back tears. Clearing his throat, Al tried to regain his composure. The blind soldier looked right into Al. He reached across, fumbling for a moment until he found Al's hand.

Al said, "I was the guy with Williams." Al was now trembling and choking back tears and continued, "When the shelling began, I found myself in a bunker with Williams. The shells started walking down the street right at us."

Al's words were now mixed with faint sounds coming from deep within. His body was shuddering, and the hand held by Josh was quivering.

He continued, "We saw a little girl running down the street towards us...and Williams, he, he was going to get her. And then there was a blast, and that poor little girl vanished right before my eyes. Dear God why? Why did that poor little girl have to die? She never hurt anyone. I can still see her little buttoned white shirt, streaked with dirt, and her tears. Dear God, why, why, why?"

Unknown to Al and Josh, Mrs. Williams had come in and sat behind them. She was sitting quietly with her head down like she was praying. Al was having trouble getting his composure when he felt another hand on his shoulder. He turned on the old metal chair and looked into the glowing face of Mrs. Williams.

Moving her chair around so she could see both men, she said, "It was days after that attack that my Joey was able to write to us. In his letter he told us a little about what happened. Joey told us that you saved his life. The medic that attended my Joey told him that if he had gotten around you, he would have been killed. The medic said that the blast shattered your big camera, and the front of the bunker was shredded. You see, son, you saved my Joey's life."

The saintly Mrs. Williams continued, "It was the Lord that saved your life and my Joey's. The Lord knew you were going to be in that bunker. You see, you saved my son so he could go on. My Joey knew he was in the hands of God from the very beginning. Please understand, he wanted to serve God and his country. He was gonna be a preacher, just like his daddy, that is before the war. He was the youngest of the children the Lord blessed us with. You know, he wasn't even ten when he told us God wanted him to be a preacher, just like his daddy."

The Mrs. Reverend continued, "Even Agape Station was my son's idea. He told us that when he was discharged, he would attend Bible College and then find a place to preach where the gospel reaches into the life of everyone. He even knew what he would call the place, "Agape Station," he said. You see, Al, we've only been here just a couple of months. When the news of our dear Joey's death came, we knew what we had to do. My dear husband had been preaching for years in a small town close to a hundred miles south of here."

As Mrs. Williams continued, Al broke in, almost oblivious to what she had been saying. He stood up from his chair, shouting, "You don't understand; you don't understand! If I hadn't been so crazy about getting a great photo, your son would have been able to get to her, or I could've dropped the damn camera and gotten to her myself. She could still be alive."

As those last words were expelled, Al collapsed back on his chair. Now his head was bowed low, and Josh and Mrs. Williams listened to his sobs. In his tears they could hear him mumbling, "She vanished right in front of me. She simply vanished. One second she was running and crying, and I could see her dirty shirt and her tears, and then she was gone. Dear God, she just vanished."

Joshua and Mrs. Williams continued to hold onto Al. The Mrs. whispered to Al and got up. A moment later, she came back with her husband. Reverend Williams moved one of the old folding chairs, the rubber-capped bottom squeaking on the tile floor. He sat right in front of Al, within inches of his face. With his head bowed for a moment, he took Al's hands in his. His large hands, calloused and slightly bent, swallowed Al's.

Reverend Williams looked into Al's eyes and said, "Now you listen real good to what I'm going say to you. God is the ultimate authority. We might never understand why or how things happen. We're human, and we will never have all the answers. But He, He knows and understands. All things are in His hands. You can't know for sure the little girl might have been saved by my son or you. Just like you didn't know you saved my son's life. Some things are left unknown."

Joshua, the warrior, was engaged in a different battle as he wept and prayed for Al. Just above a whisper, he prayed, "Lord Jesus, help my friend find peace and security in your great love. Heal his soul of the pain he has carried."

Mrs. Williams was also praying. She held her handkerchief in one hand while her other was still on Al's shoulder.

Three saints of God held onto Al, a suffering and nearly destroyed man. They prayed for his healing and peace. They prayed that God would take away the images of horror in his mind. They prayed that he would reach out to Jesus for forgiveness and purpose for his life. Even when the praying stopped, the tears kept flowing. Mrs. Williams reminded them that tears wash the soul. The four, a wounded and blind soldier, an old man of God, his saintly wife, and a man dirty, smelly, and broken, sat in quietness for a few moments.

Minutes later, in the back of the meeting room, Mrs. Williams said to her husband, "There's still something hurting his soul. There's still some great pain deep in his heart. He tries to pretend it isn't there, but it is. I can sense it."

Her husband said, "I trust your spiritual insight. We need to pray more that the Lord will help him understand how loved he is. He's a troubled soul and has witnessed more evil and death than any man should have to."

Al spent the rest of the day in silence. He moved around the center slowly, every move deliberate and planned. He drank coffee and on two occasions talked with his new heart-bonded friend, Josh. Deep inside, Al admired the young soldier more than any other person in his memory. He was amazed at how a warrior could find peace by losing his eyes. He kept telling himself over and over that it didn't make sense. Josh was supposed to leave the next day, so Al wanted to have more time with him. They decided that after the meal and the gospel service, they would take time to talk.

During meal time, Al was quiet. He never realized it was time for the service until Mrs. Williams tapped on the microphone. They sang two or three hymns, and then Reverend Williams got up to bring his Bible message. He read the miracle of the blind man and how Jesus touched the eyes of the blind man with some dirt and spit and then told him to wash his face in the pool that was nearby.

Reverend Williams said, "You see, real vision has nothing to do with our eyes, our physical eyes. Real vision is being able to recognize the hand of God. It is recognizing his hand in the world, yes, in the mountains, flowers, the sky, and the birds. Real vision understands through the eyes of the spirit that without Jesus we are lost. We are sinners in need of a Savior. When we understand that, we can really see. That, my friends, is what real vision is."

Even before Reverend Williams asked the gathering of folks to pray, Al stood up. He didn't know what he was supposed to do, yet he knew what he had to do. Walking ever so slowly up through the aisle of old folding chairs, he dropped to his knees at the prayer rail.

Unseen by the others, Reverend Williams motioned to his wife to come up to the music stand. When she did, he pointed to the hymn he wanted her to sing, "It Is Well with My Soul." As she sang, "When peace like a river attendeth my ways, when sorrows like sea billows roll," the preacher went around the chairs, bent his old and tired knees, and put his arm around his friend, Al.

Al, kneeling in front of a chair, with his arms resting on it, spoke words that were direct and simple. "God," he said, "I need you. I'm not sure how to even believe in you, but I know I need you. I need what my friend Josh has. I need peace in my life; my memories keep haunting me. I need a new purpose in my life; I've turned into a drunk, a drunk because love almost killed me. Jesus, if you are as real as they say you are, come into my life. Forgive me of my sins and help me."

Al's blind warrior friend was at his side. As Al was praying, Josh was in two-fold action. He was pleading with God to hear the prayers of his friend and demanding Satan to be judged by the blood of Jesus and cast away from Al's life.

The Mrs. Reverend had finished singing, and she was sitting in the row of chairs just behind Al, Joshua, and her husband. Her hand was still holding her bleached and laced handkerchief. Her face was glowing. Her pure white hair was but a symbol of her grace and purity of soul. The reverend placed his hand on Al's head and prayed, just above a whisper at first. And then as he prayed further, his voice raised in volume and intensity. "Dear God of heaven," he prayed, "bend down your faithful ear. Hear the prayers of your dear child, kneeling here in the holiest of places, in your presence, O God."

Not one person inside that heavenly cathedral stirred. After some lingering moments, the service ended. The folks at Agape Station went back to the streets until lodging time. Al, Josh, and Mr. and Mrs. Williams sat at a table for a couple of hours talking and praying. At times there was laughter, at times just silence. At one point Mrs. Williams said, "Let's just listen to the Spirit. Holy silence is so good for the soul."

Reverend Williams broke the silence. He said, "I have to get Josh back. He's heading to Washington first thing in the morning. I'll stop here in the morning for a minute so everybody can have their goodbyes."

Al got up from his chair and took Josh by the hand and helped him up. With Josh on his feet, Al was hugging his new friend. Al said, "I'll see you in the morning."

Still embracing, Josh said, "You sure will. Sleep well and remember what God has done in your heart."

Turning to Reverend and Mrs. Williams, Al said, "I'm feeling pretty drained, guess the emotions of the past few days have kind of worn me out. I think I'll go find my cot." Mrs. Williams stepped over to Al, coming just to his chin. Wrapping her arms around him, she whispered, "God loves you, and so do we. Good night."

Just as the sun was beginning to transform trees and buildings into recognized shapes and forms, Al began to sweat and vomit. As he tossed on the cot, he tried to talk. The guy next to him heard him and asked, "Hey Al, are you okay? What's going on?"

Al looked over at him, started gagging, and vomited again. A moment later the night manager was at Al's side. "Hey Al, he said, "This is George, are you alright? Can you talk to me?"

The look on Al's face was one of fright and confusion. He was unable to respond to George. Seconds later George was on the phone to the ambulance station. The next phone call was to Reverend Williams. The ambulance arrived within minutes. The medics had been to the building many times, usually to assist someone suffering drug or alcohol problems.

As the medics tried to assess Al's condition, Reverend and Mrs. Williams came through the front doors. The emergency personnel told the reverend and his wife that they had no idea what was wrong, and they were taking him to Saint Joseph's after they got him stable and on the gurney. As the medics were getting ready to move Al, the elderly saints placed their hands on him, their misty eyes visible to everyone around them.

A couple of hours later, the doctor who met them when the ambulance arrived, came back down the clean and shining hall. While they had been waiting, Reverend Williams found a payphone and called Josh. The family that was putting Josh up brought him straight to the hospital. As he approached, the elderly couple were on their feet. Their blind friend stood still as he heard their shuffling and the movement of the chairs. The three children of God embraced. The door opened, and a doctor entered the waiting room.

The doctor suggested they go to a room where they would have privacy. At the privacy suggestion, Mrs. Williams gripped her husband's hand all the tighter. The four of them went into a consultation room, and the door closed with a very distinct metal against metal sound.

"Please have a seat," the doctor said. Reverend Williams spoke up, "Thank you, sir, but we're fine. Please just tell us of our dear friend."

"We're at a great disadvantage with your friend," the doctor began. "We do not know any of his medical history."

Reverend Williams said, "I know he was in DaNang and had suffered some type of traumatic brain injury, but he seemed fine these past days."

"That explains a lot," the doctor said. "There is clear evidence of trauma from some time ago, but that is not the most severe problem. His X-rays indicate some type of cyst or tumor within his brain. We just can't handle that here. I'm sorry."

The words, professional, cold, and textbook perfect sucked the breath out of the three people of God. As the doctor walked out the door, Josh was grasping for hands. He found Mrs. Williams' frail and tiny hand, and then the massive hand of the reverend's found his. With their heads bowed in the presence of their Creator, silence engulfed them.

The warrior then began to pray and pleaded with his Healer to touch the life of his friend. In the midst of Josh's praying, Mrs. Williams began to pray and then she fell silent. Her last words were choked off by the pain in her heart for the young man lying in the emergency room.

It took a few minutes for the three to get their composure and leave the privacy of the consultation room. Standing in the hall, Josh said, "I've made some friends during my time in the hospital and rehab. I'm gonna make some phone calls and see what can be done. I'll find somebody to get Al's records, and we'll go from there. I have to leave for Washington, but before the day is over, I'll call you. Our Lord is not going to leave us hoping and praying for answers."

Joshua called Reverend and Mrs. Williams later that afternoon. He informed them his doctor made a phone call to a hospital and cleared the way for Al to be admitted. The fact that Al had been a war correspondent afforded him some special treatment. The problem of money and transportation had to be dealt with. Al would need to be taken by ambulance to the hospital, a hundred miles away. Reverend Williams told Joshua that the ambulance would be taken care of and thanked his friend for his devotion.

The ambulance made the hundred mile trip to the City of Brotherly Love in less than two hours. A neurosurgeon met Al, and he was quickly admitted. More X-rays and tests were performed, and the results were phoned to Josh's friend, who in turn called Josh.

Joshua called Agape Station, and Reverend Williams answered. "Reverend, this is Josh. The doctor told me that Al is going to have to undergo serious brain surgery. They're going to begin right away, and it's going to take them six or seven hours."

"Thank you, son. Mrs. Williams and I will be leaving the moment we hang up. I want to get there to pray with him before the surgery."

Reverend and Mrs. Williams didn't make it to the hospital to pray with Al. It had been a long time since they had been to Philadelphia, and the traffic proved to be a roadblock to their heartfelt wishes. Arriving while Al was in surgery, they asked at the front desk where the waiting room for surgery patients was located and made their way there.

Reverend Williams was holding his wife's hand as they walked in, his grip as tight as the knot in his stomach. While they were sitting in the waiting room, an administrator asked them if they were family or friends. The young woman told them that they were trying to find family members. Reverend Williams informed her that as far as he knew, Al had no other family members.

Almost a full eight hours after the Williams arrived at the hospital, the attending surgeon came out and led them to a private room. He said, "I removed as much of the growth as possible. There were finger-like parts that penetrated deeper into the brain that couldn't be removed." In a monotone manner, he continued, "He'll be in recovery for the remainder of the evening and overnight. You're welcome to stay, but he won't be awake for some time."

For the next ten hours, two of God's servants sat by Al's bedside, a man they had known for just a short time. They knew little about him, his life, his past, his family. What they knew came from talking, praying, and listening to a broken heart leaking out of a man's soul. On and off for those hours, God bent down listening to the prayers from the hearts of an old preacher man and his gentle wife. Numerous offers from the nurses for places to rest or food were politely declined. Mrs. Williams said to one nurse, "We will be by his side when he wakes up."

During the night the alarm in Al's room started going off. Reverend and Mrs. Williams, asleep in two armchairs, jumped at the noise. The attending nurse calmed them and said, "The alarm was set to get our attention should he start to move around on the bed. With his type of surgery, we really don't want him trying to get out of bed."

Her smile and slight laugh brought a welcome sense of relief to the startled prayer warriors. As she left the room, she said, "Your friend is in the best of hands, he's in God's hands and your prayers."

As Mrs. Williams was looking through the window, the sun was just beginning to break through the brick and steel forest. With her back to Al, his stirring caught her off-guard. By the time he opened his eyes the gentle saint was smiling at him. Holding his hand, with IV needles and bandages, she bent over the bed and kissed him on the forehead. She said, "My husband will be right back, he has to have his morning coffee."

Clearing his throat, Al asked, "Do you suppose he'll bring me back a cup?"

Still holding his hand, she chuckled just a bit. A small tear appeared in the corner of her eye, and after a few seconds it ran down her cheek. "Dear Al," she said, "God has answered our prayers."

A moment after she finished her words, Reverend Williams came back into the room. Standing at the foot of Al's bed, he was a pretty imposing figure. He stood over six feet tall and had the frame of an athlete. Al looked at him and asked, "Where's my coffee?"

Reverend Williams was quick with his reply, "I already drank yours." Al smiled at his friend

"So," Al said, "What's the verdict? When am I getting out of here?"

Reverend Williams chuckled and said, "Well it's gonna take a couple of days. We'll be taking you to our house. I think you're going to need some tender loving care." He glanced over at his wife, and they both smiled.

It was a week before Al was able to leave the hospital. The surgeon explained to Al the extent of the growth and what he had been able to remove. In professional bluntness, the doctor told Al what he might expect later. He said, "I have no idea if

the growth will regenerate or stay dormant. You will probably continue to have serious headaches. I did all I could."

When they pulled into the drive at the Williams' home, it struck Al as to how the house fit his image of the couple. The home was modest in size, and the outside was red brick. There were two trees in the front yard, a large white pine and a red maple. Around each tree was a circle of white stones with edging. The approach to the front steps was a mixture of low-lying bushes, daisies, and roses. Part of the porch was covered, and hanging in the shade were two baskets overflowing with flowering plants. On the front door, for all to see, was a banner with a single star in the center. It was their declaration of sacrifice and love of their country.

Al found the inside of their home just as fitting as the outside. The entrance was bright with cut flowers on a small table just before the archway into the living room. The walls of the living room were filled with pictures and casual photographs of family. Al was amazed at the number of family pictures on the walls. Along the top of the main wall were graduation pictures of all the children, complete in cap and gown. All the children carried the same smile and sense of pride.

Underneath one picture hung another one of a young marine's graduation from boot camp. Al recognized Joe, a distinguished and handsome marine in his perfectly prepared dress blues. Mrs. Williams asked Al to follow her to the room he would be staying in. It seemed to be perfect to Al. The colors were neutral with beige walls, and the bureau was next to a window. The blinds were up, and sunlight filled the room. On the top of the nightstand, there was a Bible, pad of paper, and pen.

On the floor, in front of the bed was a large box with the flaps folded into each other to keep it closed. Mrs. Williams said, "Now Al, there are some clothes in this box. And, you can have whatever you need. I'm pretty sure most of the clothes should fit." It was at this point that Al remembered that up until his time in the hospital, he had been wearing the same clothes. The social worker at the hospital had been able to find him a sweatshirt and matching sweat pants for his discharge.

It didn't take long for Al to go through the box and find a couple of pairs of blue jeans, three shirts, underwear, and socks. Putting the clothes on the bed, he headed to the shower. Soaking in the comfort of the hot water time slipped away. The heavy rap on the door brought him around. Reverend Williams asked, "Are you alright in there? You need to save some water for the rest of the neighborhood."

Al sat on the edge of the bed and kicked his grungy pants. When he did, his wallet came out of the pocket and spilled out a few scraps of paper. When he picked up the scraps, he saw the writing on two or three was worn and smudged. Crinkling up the scraps, he tossed them into the wastebasket. The last scrap brought back an instant message and conversation. On the paper was a phone number and the name, Ray.

9

Battling the Forces of Darkness

For the next week, Mrs. Williams pampered Al. He woke each morning to the smell of coffee, strong and black. Breakfast was usually eggs, toast, and more coffee. A few mornings she went overboard with eggs, grits, biscuits and gravy, and coffee. Lunch was light, usually fruit and salad and fresh bread. Reverend Williams was home for dinner early, around four thirty. After eating, the Reverend and Mrs. went down to the Agape Station.

During the week Al had a follow-up appointment with the doctor who first saw him. Everything seemed to be progressing well, and the doctor agreed that Al could get a little more active. He had been away from the Agape Station since his emergency surgery and was looking forward to getting back to see friends.

The day of Al's doctor appointment, Reverend Williams said, "A lot of the regular folks have been asking about you. They want to know when you're coming back for dinner and the service. Some of those dear ones have been praying for you every day. I probably shouldn't say this, but I'm going to. Some of the dear ones there would put many so-called fine Christians to shame when it comes to praying for their friends and families."

Al replied, "It's time I go and pay a visit then. I miss some of those people."

With a smile, Reverend Williams said, "Great, and I'll have

you take part in the service. You can give your testimony and tell the folks what God has done for you."

Mrs. Williams spoke up, "Don't you two think it's a little early to be doing that? I mean it has only been a short while."

Reverend Williams chuckled and said, "Now don't worry, I won't let him overdo it, and it might just be what the Lord wants him to do."

Mrs. Williams looked at Al and said, "I don't want to stand in the way of God or his good work, but be careful that you're not pushing yourself. You know standing in front of people and talking about the Lord can be a taxing thing."

When Al went through the old grocery store doors at Agape Station, he was surprised to see so many people waiting for him. It took him a full five minutes to greet everybody. Even a few people that he had hardly ever talked to shook his hand. Two or three of the ladies took his extended hand and pulled him in for a hug. He had no idea that such a mixture of people cared so much.

After a few minutes, he sat down on the old Naugahyde sofa and thought about what just took place in the old closed out food store, now giving out free eternal food.

Al's thoughts carried him back, and his heart reminded him, *These folks are by some people's judgment the dregs of society. Many of their lives have been destroyed by bad choices. They're just like me, walking around with their entire estate in a shopping bag, wagon, or push cart. Life has been hard and in many cases unfair to these souls. I guess I know what their life is like.*

He looked over at Old Joe who had lost three fingertips to frostbite. And there was Susie, surrounded by people, yet so alone. Susie was troubled; twice her dreams had sent her to the point of suicide. Both times it was the friends at Agape Station that told Reverend and Mrs. Williams about her. Both times the

Williams rescued her and cared for her, bringing her back to a level of functioning.

The doctors told the Williams that Susie was a paranoid schizophrenic, and without a caring community around her, she would have to be confined. To Al's surprise, he found out that Reverend and Mrs. Williams were Susie's custodians and guardians. Al thought, *Many people judge this mixture of humanity to be undesirables and misfits. People who judge them can't be any further from the truth.*

About an hour before the gathering sat down to eat, Al began to feel a bit agitated and the Mrs. Reverend could tell. She sat next to him and asked, "What's bothering you so?"

He said, "There are still things that bother me." Her gentle and sweet spirit confirmed in his heart that telling her this part of his life was the right thing to do.

He looked at her and went on, "I was going to be a dad. Sarah was gonna have a baby but thought it best to end the pregnancy. She told me she wasn't ready to be a mother."

As the words come out of Al's mouth, Mrs. Williams seemed to bear the words on her shoulders. She began to slump with her head bowed low.

Al heard her praying. It was not like other times. This time as she prayed, she was in a great struggle, battling a great hidden force, a force that even claimed her right to pray. "Precious Father," she said, "Giver of life, Author of creation, a great evil is befalling our land. You just heard your son talk of the life he fathered being blown out like a candle. I fear our land is coming to the edge of a great cliff, and if we take another step, we are lost. How can we be at the place where we say it is fine, our right, to kill a precious life within us? Father, please forgive Sarah for such a decision. I know her mind has been blinded by the spiritual influences of selfishness and ignorance. I know she wouldn't have destroyed her child if she had only known that her baby was a gift. Dear Father, forgive her."

Al listened as she was still praying in a whisper so that she could hardly be heard. Sitting close to her, he placed his arm around her shoulder as if to support her in her struggle with demonic forces. She continued to pray for ten or fifteen minutes, and when she finally looked up at Al, she looked tired and drained. Her face was wet with tears, and she hesitated to talk. "Dear Al," she said, "I'm so afraid for our land. We tell children they can't pray in school, that it isn't right to talk about God in public. And now our country is going to allow the killing of innocent babies."

In her whispered voice, she continued, "Mark my words, it won't be many months from now when killing the innocent unborn will be the law of the land. I've listened to young women who don't want to be tied down. I talked with women who have been victims of rape and abuse, and my heart breaks for them. I ask them to bring their child into the world and give their child as a gift to a childless couple. They tell me that it's a wonderful idea but that I don't understand. I'm not going to judge Sarah for what she did, that is over and past. Let's remember that the good Lord is the Giver of all life."

With the evening meal coming to a close, the volunteers began moving the chairs for the evening service. The music stand was in place, the microphone was set up, and the Reverend's prayer chairs were set. Al watched as Mrs. Williams moved to the piano. His love for the elderly saint was growing by the moment. Al thought she appeared to have recovered from the intense time of pleading with God. She began the service by playing and singing an old hymn about prayer, "Sweet hour of prayer, Sweet hour of prayer that calls me from a world of care."

As Al looked around, it seemed there were more people than he remembered. Reverend Williams gave his sermon on Jesus leaving the ninety and nine to look for the one lost sheep. He explained how all of us are like the lost sheep, and Jesus is looking for us and will continue to do so for as long as it takes.

Al listened more intently than ever, silently thanking Jesus for never giving up on him. He felt a strange movement in his heart as Reverend Williams continued. In silence he was experiencing deep within his heart that God loved him and accepted him as a son in his divine family. Overcome with peace and serenity, tears began to run down his cheeks.

After Reverend Williams' sermon, he introduced Al and told the gathering that Al was going to speak for a few minutes. He finished by saying, "Now and then the Lord allows certain people to come into our lives. We never know the circumstances or the purpose that the Lord has. At times we're in for a big surprise. Al coming to us was a big surprise and a true blessing. Now I've asked Al to come up here and speak for a moment about his life and coming to Christ."

As Al stood up and started towards the front, he attempted to clear his throat. At the microphone he tried to wet his lips, and the first sounds coming out were not words but merely noises.

He said, "Please excuse me for a moment. I've never tried to give a speech before. And, I guess you can tell I'm a little nervous."

Al stepped back and cleared his throat again. Stepping up to the microphone again he said, "I'm sure that finding this place saved my life. Walking through the front door of Agape Station those weeks back was the best thing that ever happened to me. God used this place to help me through some troubling times. My heart was broken when I first came here. I wanted to die by drinking. But here in this converted grocery store, I found peace in my life and Jesus Christ as my Savior."

At the end of that sentence, a few amens and praises to God could be heard. He continued, "I spent some time in the war taking pictures and writing stories. After I came home, I fell in love with a beautiful girl; she was like a wildflower, full of beauty and life. We had to part, and it was devastating. It was like my heart had been ripped out of me. After losing her, I lived in the lie and deception of booze. The bottle became my friend, my confidant, my companion that understood me and was there to help me."

He ended his testimony by saying, "I'm glad God never gave up on me, even in my darkest times. I can't begin to express the thanks and love I have in my heart for Reverend and Mrs. Williams." At this point, Al looked directly at the Williams and went on, "Your godly example helped me more than you will ever know."

Now Al was choking up. As he looked at Mrs. Williams, he had to clear his throat again and then said, "You are the most gracious and godly woman I have ever known. I believe the love of God finds perfect reflection in your heart." Mrs. Williams was using her tiny white handkerchief to dab at her tears. Al turned his attention to the people in attendance and said. "And, you, my friends, you have been an example of real friendship. I will always remember Agape Station and all of you."

Reaching into his back pocket, Al pulled out his wallet and took out a scrap of paper. He tried to hold it still in his shaking hands and said, "On this piece of paper is a phone number from my old boss. I think it's time for me to use the phone number and continue on with my life."

A very long silence hung in the converted old grocery store. Reverend Williams approached the music stand and hugged Al.

The two men, a godly giant and a new child in the faith, embraced for a moment. With moist eyes, the pastor of his flock pronounced the benediction.

Al found Mrs. Williams sitting in the general office area after the service. She was dabbing at tears with her lace handkerchief. Sitting next to her, he placed his arm across her shoulder. After a quiet moment, he said, "I'm sorry for just standing up there and blurting all of that out. I should have shown more respect and talked with you and your husband about what I was gonna say."

Fighting her tears she said, "I'm not upset over what you had to say. I'm just saddened that you're going to be leaving us." She hesitated and said, "You're like another son to me, another one of my boys."

Reverend Williams sat next to his wife and said, "So, tell me about the phone number."

"Some time back my old boss told me that when he retired from the city desk, he and his wife were going to find a weekly newspaper for sale. Somewhere up north he said. Well, it seems like he found a place and called to tell me that if I ever wanted a job, it would be mine. I was going through my old clothes, and this scrap of paper fell out of the pocket."

Reverend Williams put his hand on Al's arm and said, "God doesn't do anything by accident. He must have a plan for all of this."

Al stood at the counter and dialed the number. Shuffling his feet and tapping the countertop was evidence of his nervous anticipation. He looked puzzled as he hung up the phone. "Talk about strange. I was connected to an answering machine. It said, 'This is the *Lusus Naturae Weekly*, please leave a message.' What in the world is the *Lusus Naturae Weekly*?" Al's face was comical.

A moment later he dialed the number again. The same message played and this time instead of hanging up, Al identified who he was, telling the machine and the strangely named weekly, his phone number and that he was an old friend.

Al said to Reverend Williams, "Things don't make sense to me. They say I saved your son Joe's life. Most people would think it was by accident. I did what I did out of pure selfishness. And then, a month later, your Joe is killed. What is the purpose of all of this?"

After a moment Reverend Williams spoke up, "There are times when we need to stop asking all the questions and just listen. If you listen and pay attention to life's events, things might begin to make sense." Leaning from his chair and getting closer to Al, he said, "At times we just need to shut up and listen."

Two days later the phone in Agape Station's office rang. The voice on the other end asked for Al and remarked loud enough to be heard, "What the hell is an Agape Station?" The volunteer almost dropped the phone and then told the caller that Al would be right with him.

Moments later, Al picked up an extension in Reverend Williams' office and said, "Hello, this is Al."

The voice on the other end said, "This is Ray. How in the hell are you? I'm glad you left me a message. Sorry I didn't get back sooner, I was out covering a story."

Al said, "I was really surprised by the message. What in the world is a weekly paper doing with the name, *Lusus Naturae?*"

Ray laughed. "The paper has had that name since the turn of the century, maybe before. Remember your Latin?"

Al shot back, "Of course I remember. What in the world can be weird or freaky about a tiny town near Canada?"

After a few more minutes of pure jabbering, Ray asked, "Are you interested in coming north to the land of pure water, virgin pines, and a different life?"

Al explained to Ray about the past few months and what he had been through. After a minute or so of thought, Al said, "Give me two days, and I'll call you back with my answer."

After Al hung up the phone, he found Reverend Williams in the outer office. The look on Al's face must have spoken volumes. He got up and walked Al back into his office. Without any hesitation he said to Al, "Let's talk. I don't want you all concerned and worrying about my wife. She's a powerful woman, a woman of great faith and prayer."

Al looked stunned at the words. "How did you know what I was thinking?" he asked.

The reverend said, "I've been around the block a few times. I know the Lord is alive and working inside your heart. Remember we've been praying for you from the first day you came in the door, dirty, lost, and in need of love."

Al asked Reverend Williams, "How do I know what the right thing to do is? How do I know the voice of God?"

"At times it's hard to understand the voice of God. Some people look for signs from God. Other people think God will openly talk to them. I have found that when I look at the circumstances that surround a situation and pray earnestly about the options, the Lord has a way of giving me light."

Shifting his position, Reverend Williams continued, "Now, Al, take this place. We've told you about Joey wanting to have a place of love and redemption. It was just days after we buried him that it was plain to me and the Mrs. what we were supposed to do. I was happy being a pastor in the country. I loved the folks there, and most of them loved me. You see, son, in our heart we knew that this was the right thing to do."

Al was focused on the words of wisdom coming from a godly man who had witnessed the blending of faith and real-life decisions.

Reverend Williams continued, "You'll do the right thing if you clearly look into your heart, understand your passion, and then the direction you sense is the right thing. Your sense of the right thing is the right thing. Commit it to God. He cares for you, and he has brought you this far. He is not going to leave you alone; and if you make a mistake, big deal, every person who does something makes a mistake. The only person who never makes a mistake is the lazy slug that does nothing."

The following day Al called Ray and told him that it would take him a few days or even a week to get things together for the trip north. Al could sense a kind of relief in Ray's voice when they talked about the details. Ray ended the conversation by telling Al that he would never regret the decision to come north.

A few minutes later, Al approached Reverend Williams to tell him of his decision. Feeling like he had cotton in his mouth, he attempted to speak.

Reverend Williams interrupted, "Now, son, I know what you want to say, and I know what your decision is. My dear wife knows as well. Remember I said that we've been praying for you. I believe that God has work for you. He has his hand on you for a reason. You went through your own personal hell. I do not understand the reasons, but God does, and eventually you will too. And tonight we will be back here for a special dinner, as our way of saying, God speed to you."

After the meal, the front of the hall was arranged in the usual way with the piano in the front with the music stand/pulpit and microphone. The same dog-eared song sheets were passed out as the Mrs. Reverend warmed up with the melody of "Amazing Grace," and then "The Old Rugged

Cross." After the group sang a couple of hymns, Reverend Williams came to the pulpit and read from the fourteenth chapter of the Gospel of John.

At the end of the reading, he prayed and asked God to remind them that his promises are for all who believe them. And then he told them that even though Jesus had to leave the disciples, he didn't want them to worry about their future. A new home was waiting for all who loved Jesus, and he was the one fixing up the place just for them. Al felt a small tear in the corner of his eye as he thought back to the cabin and the massive pine bench. A cabin by the water would be glorious.

Nearing the end of the service, Reverend Williams seemed to be filled with joy. He said, "Someday King Jesus is going to return to this old earth and make all things right, and peace shall reign."

No sooner had those words left his mouth, Mrs. Williams began playing, "Soon and very soon we are going to see the King, Soon and very soon we are going to see the King." Most of the folks in the gathering didn't know the song, but they sure enjoyed Reverend Williams singing. He was as joyous as they had ever heard him.

After that song Mrs. Williams began to play and sing, "Some glad morning when this life is over, I'll fly away." Most of the folks knew that song, and they began singing, clapping, and smiling. Al was smiling as he watched his friends, some dressed in rags, unshaven, unwashed, and uncaring about the world outside Agape Station. And he thought, *How great it would have been to witness this wonderful, godly black preacher with his rural congregation.*

It took a few minutes for things to settle down in that converted grocery store. The blessing and glory of God lingered for some time. Even then, Al was looking around at the gathering, and most were still smiling and enjoying the afterglow. With a wave of his hand, Reverend Williams got their attention and brought the focus back to the front of the hall. He said, "Folks, I need your attention. Now listen up. Not that long ago the Lord brought a man into all our lives. Al, come on up here."

As Al walked towards the front, Sweet Pea got up and wrapped her arms around him. In the embrace, Al said, "Dear Sweet Pea, I'll always hear your singing, and I know he's watching over all of us."

As she sat down, it was easy to see her tear-streaked face. With his massive arm around Al, Reverend Williams said, "It's time for Al to go out and accomplish what the Lord has had planned for him." Al tried to look away from his father in the faith, but when he did, he caught a glimpse of the gentlest eyes he had ever looked into, Mrs. Williams. She was smiling such a wonderful smile, even as tears ran down her cheeks.

After a moment, Reverend Williams asked the folks to stay in their seats because he had one more thing planned. At that, Ben wheeled out a cart with a large cake on it. The lettering on the cake read, "God Bless Al," and underneath it read, "From all of your friends at the Agape Station." Ben said, "Al, thank you for coming into my life. God has some pretty weird ways of doing things. You have helped me make some decisions. With God's help, I want to become a journalist. Now you need to cut the cake."

Al's hand was shaking as he held the knife. Reverend Williams broke the silence, "Come on now, son, cut the cake. We don't have all day."

The chuckle from the group helped Al relax, and he cut the big sheet cake into pieces. After cake and coffee, dozens of Al's friends came up and wished him well. He was moved as he watched folks stand in line to greet him with a handshake or a hug. Many of them were fighting back tears as they wished him well.

Later, Al and the Williams sat in the office area and talked about the evening and Al's future. At a time when it was quiet, an uncomfortable time, when the heart is talking and voices are still, Reverend Williams motioned to his wife and asked, "Would you please go into the other office and get the box?" Al looked puzzled as she got up and came back carrying an old Dutch Masters cigar box.

Mrs. Williams stood in front of Al, holding the old cigar box. One of her hands was under the box, and the other was across the top. Then she said, "All of your friends gathered up a gift for you." Stretching out her frail hands, Mrs. Williams handed Al the old cigar box. Al's hand rested on hers for a moment, and they both sat down on the squeaky sofa.

Reverend Williams said, "We're not really sure how much the trip north will cost, but this should help." Al opened the old cigar box to find a mixture of coins and paper money. A few folded and crumpled bills were atop the coins. As Al held onto the box, his hands shook, and his lip quivered when he tried to talk. Mrs. Williams took Al's hand, causing the cigar box to slip onto his lap.

Reverend Williams said, "I didn't count the money, but tomorrow we will go to the bus terminal and find out how much the ticket is."

Back at the Williams' home, Al sat on the edge of the bed, with the cigar box next to him. He opened the box and turned it upside down. He pulled the bills out and very carefully, almost cautiously, straightened them out and positioned each one facing the same way. After he had each bill straight, he counted them, nineteen dollars in all, a five-dollar bill and fourteen single dollar bills.

He touched each bill, and his heart was filled with wonder at the sacrifice his friends had made for him. How could they freely give away a sandwich, cup of coffee, or a bottle of cheap wine? He counted the coins, and they totaled nine dollars and forty-seven cents. Sitting on the edge of his bed, he stared at his gift of pennies, nickels, dimes, quarters, dollar bills, and the solitary five.

The next morning, Al had breakfast as usual and then headed out the door with Reverend Williams. They were on their way to the bus terminal to find out how much Al's ticket would be. When they got to the terminal, Al and Reverend Williams approached the ticket counter. Al asked, "Could you please tell me the cost of a ticket to Salmon Stream Crossing, Maine?"

He no sooner spoke his destination, and he could hear Reverend Williams chuckling and mumbling, "Salmon Stream Crossing, where in the world is that?"

The ticket agent said, "Sir, the bus stops just north of Bangor. You'll have to take a regional bus from the last stop to Salmon Stream Crossing."

At that comment, the good reverend was outright laughing.

The agent said, "The ticket price will be thirty-nine dollars and forty cents and that includes the regional bus to Salmon Stream Crossing. The fare price also includes a bag lunch at the Pigeon River Crossing stop."

The still snickering reverend turned his back on Al and mumbled, "A sack lunch at Pigeon River Crossing."

Back at the Williams home, Al went into his bedroom and closed the door. Mr. and Mrs. Williams were in the living room. Mrs. Williams asked, "Well dear, did you find out how much the ticket cost?"

"Yes dear," Reverend Williams replied. "It is a little more than what he has. I think that's why he went into his room."

After a moment Mrs. Williams asked, "Did you ever pay him for all the work he did on the newsletter? I'll bet he put in well over forty hours, writing the first letter, organizing all the names, and making those mailing labels. That was a lot of work."

The massive man of God smiled and reached for Elizabeth's delicate hand. "You know," he said, "you're right."

Using his booming preacher voice, Reverend Williams said, "Al, would you please come into the living room?"

A moment later, Al walked in to find a big smile on Reverend Williams' face. He said to Al, "I'm sure glad the Lord blessed me with such a wonderful woman."

Al seemed a little surprised until Reverend Williams continued, "I never did pay you for the work you did on the newsletter." At that, he pulled out his wallet, drew out two twenty-dollar bills, and put them into Al's front shirt pocket. He said, "This is for services rendered. I'll mail you a receipt, so please sign it and send it back to me." The look between the two men spoke volumes of their trust and love.

Later that evening, as Al was putting his belongings in order, there was a gentle knock on his door. He opened the door to find Mrs. Williams holding an envelope and a small oak box.

"Come in," Al said, "I was just getting things in order. Please sit down." She seemed nervous, and her hands were fidgeting with the envelope and box as she sat.

After a moment she looked up at Al. "Dear Al," she stumbled, "I've been really burdened for a while. And I've been wanting to ask you, no, not wanting to ask you, I need to ask you this question: How have the dreams and nightmares been? Are they gone? When was the last time you had one? I have been asking God to heal you. I know He can if it is His will. Do you want to talk about it?"

Al was smiling at her, and within a second she was up from the chair and hugging her heart adopted son. As they were hugging, the oak box she was holding poked Al in the stomach. As he flinched, Mrs. Williams backed up.

Seemingly embarrassed she said, "I'm sorry for being so forward, please excuse me." She sat back down next to the nightstand.

Al smiled at her and said, "I haven't had a headache or nightmare since the surgery. I remember that the doctor said I might go weeks, months, or years before I have another."

Holding out the envelope to Al, she asked, "Would you please take this? There's something in it I want you to read."

Instantly Al recognized the air mail envelope and stamps and the military base address. It was addressed to Reverend and Mrs. Williams. The pale blue envelope with its red and dark blue bordering was smudged and worn.

She said, "That's the last letter my Joey wrote to us. He wrote it just three days before he was killed. There's a part of the letter I want you to read."

Al said, "No, I don't think I should be reading your son's letter. It's far too private for me to read."

She replied, "The man who saved my son's life is now part of our life. Please do this for me."

Al opened the envelope with the care that what he was holding in his hands was close to holy script and took out the letter. The salutation jumped out at Al. It read, "Dearest Mum and Pa." Instantly Al recognized the intimacy and tried to hand the letter back to Mrs. Williams. She refused his offer and said, "Skip down to the middle of the page where it starts with, 'I know God has a plan.'"

Al found the sentence and began to read what followed. Besides the intimacy of the letter, Al noticed that her son had printed it. Al thought, not too many young men have the patience to print their thoughts. The letter went on, "I know God has a plan for my life, just like he does for all life. Living among the people here, knowing their struggles and trials, I believe that I am a much better man for being here. Yes, I have witnessed far too much death and brutality, so do most people living here. But I have also seen the hand of God. The reporter who saved my life, he had no idea what was going to happen that day. But God used him for my benefit, and I believe in some time to come for the good of many more people. I wonder how he's doing."

At the last line, Al's hands were trembling, and his tears were flowing freely. The bedroom door opened and Reverend Williams, standing at the end of the bed, understood within seconds what was taking place. Al's trembling hands held out the letter to Mrs. Williams. Taking the letter from his hands, she held it close to her chest as if she were cradling her newborn son. Slowly she folded the thin airmail paper and slid it back into the envelope. As if she were saying goodbye, her frail fingers tucked the flap inside. Quietly she glanced up at her husband and placed her hand on top of the letter.

A moment later she handed the letter to her husband. Still holding the box, Mrs. Williams ran her fingers over the grain of the wood. Al was thinking that he knew what was in the box. He was sure it was an item that opened the soul, and he was right. Mrs. Williams opened the box and nestled within red velvet were two medals. Al recognized the Purple Heart with the Patriot. The second medal he wasn't sure about.

Reverend Williams spoke up and said, "There's more to the story and Joey's last days. There are some things about the attack that you might not be aware of. I'm not sure if you knew that the woman behind the little girl was her mother. The blast that killed the little girl almost killed her mother. Joey was able to recover his senses enough that he ran out and dragged the mother to safety."

Al was gripping the mattress as he sat on the edge of his bed. Reverend Williams continued, "Later, after she recovered, Joey learned that she was raised by the Catholic sisters who ran an orphanage two miles away. The mother worked at the orphanage, helping with the children and preparing meals. Her little child that died was with her every day at the orphanage."

Reverend Williams continued, "Our Joey was so moved by the life of the little girl's mother that he spent time at the orphanage. Every moment that Joey could get away, he was there. He loved to be around the children and brought them treats. He told us that the kids loved chewing gum and laughed at each other when they tried to blow bubbles."

Al's attempt at a chuckle did little to the somberness permeating the room. Reverend Williams continued, "The day that our son died, he was at the orphanage. He had been there for a couple of hours helping build a bamboo chicken coop. While they were working, the village was attacked, first with mortars and then small arms. Our Joey ran to the main building and helped the sisters get all the children safely down into a tunnel."

With tears forming in the corners of his eyes, Reverend Williams continued on, "While he was running and directing the villagers to safety, Joey was trying to get the girl's mother to the tunnel when both of them were killed."

When Al fidgeted, the noise from the squeaking mattress did little to disguise his emotions. A view from heaven would find three souls, a recovering reporter, and his godly pastoring friends, frozen at the moment. They were almost eyewitnesses to the ending of two lives. The lump in their throats and tears in their eyes made the strength of the three as iron.

Al spoke, breaking the holy silence, "You, my friends, will

never be able to understand what your love and friendship has meant to me. I don't pretend to know the ways of God. But I do know this, God used the two of you to save my life. I have no idea where I might have ended up if it hadn't been for your love and acceptance."

Clearing his throat, Al continued, "Drinking almost killed me, and a broken heart almost killed me. I was lost and in need of love, and you gave it to me. I don't know what living in the north is going to be like, and I don't know what working on the paper is gonna be like. But I promise the both of you, right here and right now, I will look for God in every situation; each morning I will look for Him, and each night I will thank him."

Early the next morning, the smell of coffee and frying bacon brought Al to his senses. His bag was packed, and he had everything ready to head to Salmon Stream Crossing. He walked out of his room, bag in hand, and closed the bedroom door for the last time. Going into the kitchen, he found Reverend and Mrs. Williams dressed and sitting at the small breakfast table.

Mrs. Williams said, "The eggs will be done in a minute, pour yourself a cup of coffee and have a seat." Al poured his coffee and sat down next to Reverend Williams. The smell of coffee, bacon, and eggs always brought a sense of "alrightness" to Al. He could never explain it; it just was.

The three members of the family joined hands as Mrs. Williams prayed, "Dear Lord, we thank you for the blessing of food. We thank you for the blessings of family. Dear Lord, please watch over our Al as he heads off to accomplish your purposes for his life. We love him, dear Jesus, just like our own. Amen."

It was quiet until Mrs. Williams said, "Now I didn't cook that bacon and those eggs for you boys to just look at them." Al moved in on his eggs, basted in the bacon grease and heavily

peppered. The table was silent as Al and Reverend Williams de-
molished the precisely placed bacon, eggs, and toast. Mrs.
Williams paused a moment as she watched the two grown men
enjoy the food she prepared.

Almost done, Reverend Williams said to Al, "You know, Al,
Jesus only had bread and wine at his last meal. Just look at what
you have."

Much to their surprise, Mrs. Williams broke out in such
laughter that she covered her mouth and turned away in embarrassment.

Al said, "If Jesus only had bread and wine, he sure missed
out on one of the best breakfasts any man could have."

10

Revealing the Reverend's Heart

Going out the front door, Al looked around at the flowers and neatly cut grass. "I'm going to miss your flowers, Mrs. Williams," Al said as he put his bag in the trunk of the car.

As they headed to the bus station, the stillness in the car was almost absolute, except when Al or Reverend Williams shifted in their seat. The rhythmic noise from the tires on the concrete seemed loud as it invaded their silence. The twenty-minute drive to the bus depot felt like an hour.

As they approached the station, Al broke the silence. "So, when are the two of you going to come up to Salmon Stream Crossing and pay me a visit?"

Reverend Williams chuckled and said, "I suppose we might try someday, probably the first black preacher ever been up to Salmon Stream Crossing." The three of them chuckled as they pulled into the parking lot.

At the counter, Al paid for his ticket and placed the suitcase that was given to him on the trolley. The ticket agent told him that he had fifteen minutes before departure. A few other travelers were entering and milling about.

Al snickered and said, "Wonder how many folks in here are heading to Salmon Stream Crossing?" Before the other two could answer, he finished, "Probably none."

Mrs. Williams reached out and took hold of her husband's

hand. "Well, we'd better be going now," she said hesitantly.

Reverend Williams said, "We're gonna pray in a minute, but there's something you need to hear from me." Al could see the tears beginning to form. "You know, you saved my son's life. I know that you didn't even know it at the time, but that doesn't change what God allowed to happen. You saved his life so he could save the lives of all those precious children in the orphanage."

Neither Al nor Mrs. Williams could look at the massive preacher choking back soul cleansing tears. He continued, "Nobody but God knows this, but I was mad at God for allowing my Joey to be taken from us. In Joey we saw the promise of God touching the lives of our dear people. When God allowed him to be taken, I was mad, mad at God and mad at the world."

As the words were penetrating the souls of Al and Mrs. Williams, Al watched the wife of this massive man of faith choke back her own pain.

"Al," Reverend Williams said, "That time of being mad at God ended when you came to us, and I began to understand His ways. You are my son now. You'll always be a part of us, and I hope we'll always be a part of you."

With their arms around each other and their heads bowed, Reverend Williams began his prayer. "Dear God, our heavenly Father, Creator, and Sustainer, please guide our dear son. May his travels be safe and please guide his footsteps. Honor his love for you, God, by blessing the work of his hands. May your Kingdom be blessed and enlarged in mighty ways. For we pray in the mighty and powerful name of your Son, Jesus Christ."

It took a moment for Al to compose himself and turn towards the bus. As he did, Mrs. Williams reached out to give him a hug. He bent down and kissed her on the forehead. As he did, she whispered in his ear, "I will always love you." When she finished, she tucked a paper bill into his hand and said, "See if you can find a good breakfast up there in Salmon Stream Crossing."

Turning to Reverend Williams, the two men embraced. After a moment they held each other at arm's length, neither speaking a word. A grin appeared on the face of Al's father in the faith, and he said, "So off to Salmon Stream Crossing, God speed and his blessings follow you." He turned and began to walk away from the bus, leaving Al and a large part of his heart. Turning, he embraced his wife, taking her hand in his as they walked out of the terminal.

Al moved to the back of the Travel Cruiser. Knowing it was going to be a very long trip, he hoped the blue and gray bi-colored seat was comfortable. He watched a few more people get on the bus, and then he heard the release of the air cylinder that controlled the heavy door and the brakes. The large mover of people and dreams headed out of the terminal. As the bus was pulling out, he saw his dear friends standing near the road and raising their hands. Al pressed his hand against the window, turning his head away.

The first few hours were uneventful as the bus headed northeast on the freeway. During the quiet Al found himself lost in memories of the past months. Images and thoughts of Sarah brought smiles and tears. His heart replayed walking the beach and eating seafood at the little dive of a restaurant. Emotions were moving him just as the waves did on the coast. His heart broke again as the words of their parting were replayed in his mind.

The emotional stress of the past days was taking effect. Just before dozing off, his mind went to the past weeks with the depth of depression and despair, nights soaked in booze, headaches, and the god-awful images of the little girl vanishing in the red mist. His mind wandered at the various events and places he found himself. The thought of the extended hand with the cup of coffee brought fresh tears to his eyes. *Ben, what a wonderful young man,* he thought. *If it wasn't for him where would I be, or what might have happened? He was the one who pointed me to Agape Station and salvation.*

Four hours into his journey, the bus pulled into a small town. The sound of the air brakes and door roused Al from his nap. A fellow traveler got off the bus, and another one boarded it. The new passenger, an elderly woman, walked down the narrow aisle. Al noticed the old style black leather tie shoes. She took the seat across the aisle from him.

As she sat down, she smiled at Al and introduced herself as Edith. Al spoke to her, "Well, Edith, my name is Al, and how are you doing this day?"

"Why," she said, "It's so nice to meet you and thank you for being so polite. I'm on my way north to visit my daughter, son-in-law, and grandkids. I just lost my husband; well, it has been a few weeks. I just needed to get away and visit my family."

Edith reminded Al of Aunt Bee. Her dress came down below her knees, and her shoes were black leather tie-ons. Her hair was in a bun on the back of her head, and she was wearing a sky blue hat with a small flower print. In that instant of recognition, he imagined Aunt Bee was before him, holding out a plate of her cold fried chicken.

He must have seemed in a daze because he was startled when Edith spoke again to him. "I'm so sorry," she said. "Did I disturb your thoughts?"

"No," he said, "you just remind me of a very wonderful lady in my life. I was just thinking of her and the best cold fried chicken I have ever had."

"Oh, she must be a wonderful person," Edith said. "Have you seen her lately?" Al hesitated a minute before he could answer her. "No, I haven't been able to see her for a while, but I would love to have the chance."

Edith said, "I'm sure that one day you'll see her again. Special friends have a way of keeping us close." At that, she settled in her seat and seemed to doze off. Al couldn't really tell if she was sleeping or just resting, he only remarked to himself that she was a very peaceful and gentle soul. Moments later he closed his eyes, and the bus continued north to a new land.

The noise of the air brakes startled Al from his dozing. The cruiser stopped, and the driver spoke over his microphone that the bus would be there for thirty minutes for fuel and new passengers. He said there was a diner next to the bus stop if they wanted something to eat. Al got up from his seat, and when he did, he woke the kindly grandmother.

Entering the diner, Al turned to find Edith right behind him. He asked, "Would you like to join me? We can sit at the counter or a table?"

"Yes, I would. The counter is just fine," Edith said. The young waitress came from the other end of the counter and began to ask Al what he wanted. Edith spoke up, "Oh excuse me for being forward, but I think I know what my friend wants. I think he likes his coffee strong and black, along with a piece of peach pie, if the crust is made the old fashioned way with lard."

Al turned his head so fast to look at Edith that he almost fell off the stool. He asked, "How in the world did you know that was the way I liked my coffee? And, what about peach pie, with the crust made with lard, was I talking in my sleep or something?"

Edith smiled at Al's remarks and just very politely said, "I could just tell by looking at you, you're the kind of young man that likes the basics in living, and nothing's more basic than strong black coffee and peach pie."

The two sat quietly for the next few minutes. Al drank his first cup of coffee and ate his pie while Edith sipped at her English Breakfast Tea and nibbled at her piece of rye toast. When Al was nearly finished, Edith turned on her stool, looked right at him, and said, "You know, Al, I can see in your eyes a great love, but I also see seasons of great pain and suffering."

Al moved on his stool as Edith continued. "I don't know how to tell you this, except straight out. I am a child of God, and he has given me the gift of looking into the souls of people. I see great love in your eyes and great pain. You must always remember that your life matters. Your life matters to God and untold numbers of people. When I told you I can see love in your eyes, I know that it is the love of God. His love mixed with your pain will change the hearts of men and women."

The air horn on the bus blasted the message that it was time to depart. Al got up and put a dollar on the counter for the waitress and walked over to the cash register. He turned and asked Edith if she would allow him to pay her bill.

She answered, "Why yes, that would be very nice of you, thank you so much." When he finished paying her bill, he looked around to find her. He was going to walk her back to the bus. He watched her walking away from the bus. Running to her side, he asked, "What are you doing walking the other way?"

She smiled at him and said, "Son, I have reached my destination. My family is waiting for me just down the street."

"Alright," Al said, "It was a real blessing to have met you. I'll be on my way." Walking up the stairs on the bus, he headed back to his seat. As he sat he was thinking, *How did she know I liked my coffee black? And, how in the world did she know about peach pie and the crust made with lard?*

As the bus pulled away, Al tried to get a glimpse of Edith walking down the street towards her children's home. As he looked, his face was one of amazement. The only dwelling there was an old clapboard home, the windows boarded and the yard overgrown. Al closed his eyes and whispered a prayer, "Dear Lord, help me in the days ahead."

The next hours were quiet as the bus entered the heavily wooded regions of the Northern Adirondacks. Al spent what seemed like hours gazing out of his window as stands of white pine and silver maples came close to hug the highway. An occasional river or stream would be added artwork to the living canvas before his eyes. He had not been this far north before, and his eyes fed his soul as the forest and mountains spread before him like a great feast. A peace and sense of rightness filled his heart and brought tranquility and a sense of contentment.

Two hours after dark, the transporter of dreams and souls pulled into the depot, the end of the line for the big cruiser. When he stepped out of the bus, his senses were filled with the fragrance of pine. The cool evening air mixed with pine was close to enchanting.

Walking towards the depot, Al waited for the trolley to bring his bag. The depot was old and large with large lights hung by chains high above the travelers. The terrazzo floor was worn almost colorless by the thousands of shoes that skidded, shuffled, or slowly walked across the hard stone surface.

Finding a bench near the front windows, Al sat and waited for his bag until the bus driver came through the door. Walking towards Al, he said, "Excuse me, sir, aren't you the passenger going north to Salmon Stream Crossing?"

"Why yes I am," replied Al. "

Well," the driver continued, "you're welcome to stay in the station until the morning shuttle or just down the street at the

Pine Motel. They have decent rooms. The shuttle arrives here around nine, give or take. And if Jimmy is driving, lots of luck." He was chuckling as he turned his back on Al.

Al remembered the bill slipped into his hand by Mrs. Williams. Pulling it out of his pocket, he decided the twenty-dollar bill seemed like the perfect gift. The Pine Motel was a quaint series of small cabins made of half pine logs and a picture window in the front. Al found the office and went in. A man was sitting on a large chair smoking his pipe and watching a small television.

Al said, "I'd like to stay the night. I'm heading to Salmon Stream Crossing in the morning."

With his pipe still in his mouth, the man said, "Going north are ya? Wonder if Jimmy is the driver."

Al said, "You're the second person in five minutes who has mentioned Jimmy. What is up with that? How much for the room?"

The old man replied, "You'll see about Jimmy. The room is fourteen dollars and ninety-five cents." Al gave him the twenty and put the change in his pocket.

The door to his cabin gave in with a squeak as wood against wood resisted his entrance. The room was dark with the walls paneled with tongue and groove knotty pine. Two chairs were pulled up to the small table that doubled as whatever was needed. When he tossed his bag on the bed, the steel springs squeaked in response.

Perched on the edge of the table, within reach of the bed, was a big wind-up alarm clock. The bathroom was at the back of the room and a flimsy shower.

Al looked around and mumbled, "Shouldn't expect much more for the price. The place smells clean, not quite like Mrs. Williams' though."

He wound up the big clock and set it for 6:30, thinking that ought to give him enough time for coffee and something to eat.

The cool evening combined with the humidity had left the morning grass wet with dew. Al stepped out of the cabin and was greeted with a sparkling display of dew on the grass, blooming flowers, and the ferns with their long, triangular shaped leaves hanging wet from the moisture. The morning sun caught the leaves rising and falling in the morning breeze. Al thought, *If Salmon Stream Crossing is anything like this, it's gonna be beautiful.*

Just down from the motel, Al found the little diner. Taking a seat by the front window, he looked about the place. A row of tables stood in front of the windows, and old, chrome spinning stools lined the front of the counter. An older man approached him and asked, "What can I get for you, young man?"

Al answered, "Black coffee and crispy rye toast."

"Rye toast," the old man said. "We don't get too many folks asking for rye toast." As he set Al's mug of coffee on the table, he asked, "Traveling north?"

Al didn't know if it was a question or a statement and answered, "Yeah, I'm heading up to Salmon Stream Crossing; know some folks up there that run a small paper. I'm going to help 'em out."

The old man snickered and said, "Well, I'll be and rot my socks, you gonna go up there. I've heard of some pretty strange things goin' on up in the Crossing."

With that verbal puzzle sinking into Al's head, the man turned and left. He went over to the counter and came back with Al's toast and the coffee pot. He refilled Al's cup and returned to the counter. Al could still hear him mumbling about Salmon Stream Crossing and the strange things that happened around there.

With still an hour or so to wait, Al decided to take a walk around the diner and the few streets that came up close to the bus depot. The houses seemed old, probably built around the turn of the century. Most were two stories, clapboard style with stairs that led up to the front door on the left. Many of them had big front porches decorated with flower planters, and seasonal chairs and tables. Al thought about the tall stairs and porches and had images of high snow banks in the winter and lemonade in the summer.

He continued to wander for a while and chatted with a few people walking in the early sunshine. As he headed back to the depot, he thought it still might be a half an hour or so before the shuttle arrived. The depot was set back from a large horseshoe drive. This would allow the buses plenty of room to drive in and out.

The morning was still cool, and the smells of the night and early morning lingered. As he sat on a bench, an elderly couple walked past, looking at Al. The man nodded his head, kinda like saying, "hello, but I don't talk." The lady just smiled, and the couple kept walking. *Polite, but cautious,* Al thought.

He hadn't been sitting on the bench for much more than ten or fifteen minutes when an older van pulled in. It was a big one, and Al thought it would hold at least eight people. It was off white, with most of the rear wheel wells rotted out, along with parts of the front fender. The letters on the side of the van spelled out to Al that this was the regional shuttle. When the van stopped, a young man jumped out of the driver's seat. An old military fatigue cap was keeping his long hair out of his eyes, and his jeans and flannel shirt looked like they were well worn.

"Hey, you Al? I'm Jimmy." Before Al could get up from the bench, the young man was right in front of him. "I'm Jimmy, from Salmon Stream Crossing. You gotta be Al, right, nobody else around here."

Al replied, "Yeah, I'm Al, and I already know your first name is Jimmy." Al held his hand out, and his first introduction to Salmon Stream Crossing grabbed his extended hand and shook it with gusto.

A torrent of words spilled out of Jimmy's mouth, "Well, I'll be, face to face with a real-life hero and newspaper reporter. The folks up home are really looking forward to meeting you."

Al stood there, trying to take in this first impression. Jimmy seemed to know only one speed, fast and somewhat reckless. In an instant, he had grabbed Al's suitcase and tossed it on the first bench seat. In one motion he had the front passenger door open and was swinging his arm like he was trying to sweep Al into the van.

Al got in the front seat and fastened his seat belt. Jimmy looked at Al and said, "You big city fellers wear them seat belts. I don't ever wear 'em. I want to be able to jump out if I have to." Bouncing on his rear on the driver's seat, with one fluid move of his right arm, he shifted the van into drive and hit the gas. "Man, I can't believe it! You're really coming to the Crossing. Are you going to live in town? Where ya gonna stay? I know a place where rent's cheap. Oh man, I still can't believe it. Ray has been talking about you."

Al's head was shaking as Jimmy finished. Turning just a bit in his seat, he looked at Jimmy, already liking the kid. "Jimmy," he said, "do you always talk as fast as you drive? Do you have only one speed, that is, pedal down and hang on?"

Jimmy snapped his head around so fast it startled Al. "Aw man, I'm sorry. I did it again. Ray warned me that I better get control of myself before I met you. Forgive me, man, I didn't mean no harm."

The van headed northeast on the two-lane road. Massive pine trees came within ten or twenty yards of the highway. It seemed to Al that every five or ten miles a stream or river was visible as it cut through the forest. The view was beautiful, and each mile added to its beauty in Al's mind.

As the van was approaching the top of a steep grade, Jimmy looked over at Al and said, "I'm gonna pull over for a minute 'cause you just gotta see this. This is why I love living up here." Jimmy pulled the van over onto a small road right next to the highway. Al got out, and Jimmy was already standing next to a knee-high guard rail looking east.

Standing at the rail, Al felt that his senses were captivated. The smell of the pines was fresh and clean. Trying to drink in the view, he was close to the rusted guard rail where the ground dropped at least a hundred feet. The tops of the pines on the forest floor seemed to be almost within reach. Stretching out before them was a sea of green as the pines filled their view. Just to the left, Al could make out what looked like a couple of buildings.

In a second Jimmy ran to the van and came back holding a pair of binoculars. "Here, Al, use my binoculars," he said.

After adjusting the binoculars, Al recognized the bright white steeple of a church. Another building, rotunda in style, was flying a flag. Jimmy, almost as giddy as a child waiting to invade his Christmas surprises, was at Al's side.

"See why I love it here, see why, oh man!" Jimmy blurted.

Back on the road, Al asked Jimmy, "So Jimmy, what's up at, what do you call the town, The Crossing?"

Jimmy seemed surprised and asked Al what he meant.

"You know," Al said, "What is life all about? What do people do in Salmon Stream Crossing?"

"Well," said Jimmy, "the pulp mill is still running. I guess maybe a hundred folks work there. And then there is all the work around that, you know, woodcutters, truck drivers, ya know, that kind of thing. And, and, in the nice weather lots of folks come up from down below to fish and go camping, stuff like that."

"Okay," said Al, "that seems pretty normal for a small town in the north. So, what about the newspaper, what's that mystery about?"

Jimmy seemed confused, almost as if he had never heard of the mysteries and the odd name of the newspaper. Jimmy's silence told Al that he didn't want to talk.

Al decided to change the subject, so looking at Jimmy and his cap, he asked, "So tell me about the fatigue cap you're wearing, anything special about that"?

Jimmy looked at Al and in very subdued words said, "It was my brother's; now it's mine. It's my brother being with me when he can't."

Al recognized the pain in the voice of his new friend. Responding to Jimmy, he said, "I'm sorry, Jimmy, sounds like your brother is special."

"Was special," Jimmy said. "Now he's dead." The pain seemed fresh with his words.

Al responded, "I'm really sorry, Jimmy, if you want to talk about your brother anytime, I'll always listen."

The next thirty miles were quiet, and Al was quick to notice that Jimmy was hardly able to sit still in the driver's seat. He really wanted to get Jimmy talking again; he felt that he might have offended him by the questions.

"Are we getting close, Jimmy?" he asked.

Jimmy shifted his weight and smiled at Al. "Yep, we're getting close. We should see Bert's fishing sign just up the hill and around the corner. After that, it'll be just a few more miles.

We'll see the plant before we get into town."

Al asked, "The plant, do you mean the pulpwood plant?"

"Yeah, the pulp wood plant," Jimmy said. "You know, Al, if you're gonna live up here with us, you'd better understand us a bit better."

Al thought Jimmy was probably right.

Around the bend was the sign for Bert's fishing. The sign looked like it had been painted on plywood. It had bold lettering that read, Bert's Fishing-Boats-Bait, in smaller block letters, it read, Best Speck Fishing Around.

Al took in the sign as they went past, and Jimmy was quick to chime in, "Gonna have to get you to meet Bert. He's one likable fellow that Bert is."

At the top of another steep grade, Jimmy slowed the van, not to a stop but letting her coast near the crest. Looking out no more than two or three miles, Al could make out the pulp mill and the town of Salmon Stream Crossing.

If there ever was a town that would be the perfect postcard, it was Salmon Stream Crossing. The town sat in a valley with Salmon Stream cutting right through the heart of it. One half of the business district was on the east side and the other half on the west side of the river.

The residential streets ran up both sides of the valley. The folks living on the east and west sides of the valley had a great view of the town and the road that headed north. The bridge that connected both halves of the town was an old steel girder type. It was built close to seventy years earlier when the original wooden bridge almost collapsed.

As Jimmy headed down the hill into town, Al was taking in as much as possible. The side streets that went up each side of the river valley were picturesque with most homes looking well-maintained with lots of flowers and neat lawns.

Al said to Jimmy, "The town looks really nice, well-kept; people must take a great deal of pride in this town."

As if turned on again, Jimmy looked over at Al and said, "Well, they sure do. I tell you this, never was a town that looked better than the Crossing. Everybody in town takes real good care of things: the streets are clean, and there's no garbage blowing round 'cause folks wouldn't stand for it."

After a few minutes of silence between them, Jimmy continued, "Ray told me to bring you straight to the paper. It seems like he's really looking forward to you getting here. He's not well, ya know. I mean you must know that, right, you did know that, right?"

Al was startled at Jimmy's statement, and the look on his face told Jimmy that he didn't know.

"Oh man, I did it again," Jimmy said. "I opened my big mouth and said what I wasn't supposed to."

Al responded, "No, Jimmy, that's okay, I kind of knew something was going on. I'll wait for Ray or Gracie to tell me. I won't let on that I knew."

Jimmy crossed the bridge, and Al looked down at the river. "So, Jimmy, what's the big mystery about the river? Seems like this river and parts around here have been talked about for a long time."

When Al looked back from the river, Jimmy's frightened face was looking back. "I don't know, don't talk, don't think 'bout that stuff. You're gonna have to talk to Ray 'bout stuff like that," he said.

Al realized that he had touched another nerve with his young friend. The look on Jimmy's face was giving out a strong message of fear or pain. Jimmy's inability to put a sentence together told Al even more about the stress Jimmy was under.

He tried to calm him down by saying, "Hey, thanks, Jimmy,

for showing me all the cool sites on the way. That stop by the edge of the road was great."

His words began to work and Jimmy seemed to settle down.

11

Meeting Ray

A block after crossing the bridge, Jimmy made a left turn and parked next to an old, red brick building. The front faced the main street, and the building was long and narrow. No sooner had Jimmy put the van in park than he was out the door and ran to the front door of the paper and threw it open.

Al was still getting out of the van when he could hear Jimmy say, "I got him, Ray. Got him, Ray. He's here."

Al went up the three old concrete steps and stepped into the front reception area of the *Lusus Naturae Weekly*. Entering, Al thought, *One of the first things I want to know is, why such a crazy name for a newspaper?*

Stepping into the reception area was like going back in time. On the wall to Al's left, about six feet from the floor, was a framed New Year's edition of the paper. The frames went along the wall as far back as Al could see. Underneath the frames, just inside the door, was a very old counter. The sides were made of old glass, and the frame and top were oak. It was easy to tell that it was old, very old. The nicks and gouge marks told of years of use and hundreds of stories coming across the countertop. Al said to himself, "I wonder what stories these counters could tell."

As he was standing in the entry, Ray came out through the doorway from the back. Instantly, Al was back in DaNang, re-membering their first meeting. Ray looked the same, white shirt with the sleeves rolled up, cigarettes and Bic pen in his front pocket.

Al made the first move and reached out and took Ray's extended hand. "Why Ray," he said, "you don't look any better than the last time I saw you."

Ray replied, "Well, let me tell you, you look a hell of a lot better than the last time I saw you. If I remember right, you were lucky to be alive." Ray turned and hollered out, "Hey, Gracie, come on up front. Al's here."

Coming from the back, she walked right to Al and kissed him on the cheek. "So glad you made it up here," she said. "How was the bus ride, and how was Jimmy's driving? I told Jimmy before he even left that he better drive safe and keep his eyes on the road. He has a tendency to talk fast and drive the same way."

Jimmy looked like a scared deer caught in a car's headlights, and Al bailed him out saying, "Naw, he was just fine. We had a good trip, and things went well." Al smiled and looked at his new friend, Jimmy.

Ray looked at Jimmy and said, "Thanks for getting him here safe. You'd better get the van back to the garage."

Jimmy had been standing next to Al, holding his fatigue hat. "Why, yes sir, Ray," he said, "I best be getting it right back" and quickly went out the front door.

Ray said, "Let me show you around; this place is going to be like home."

First Ray took Al around the old office and remarked about the front page pieces hanging on the wall. "We have the New Year's piece going back to 1904. That was the year after the big fire. Seems a fire started in the north and swept down through town in a matter of two days. They say the fire was so hot that the embers from the pines jumped the river and just kept going."

In the back room, Ray said, "This is where the money is made or lost. Over there is the old Kelsey Excelsior. We use her for small specialty jobs. Yeah, I know, it's an antique, but she still prints some beautiful stuff. Just cuz she's old, doesn't mean she's not still got it, right Gracie?"

Al didn't know if he was supposed to laugh or not, so he decided it was best to hold it back.

Gracie shot right back, "I don't really know, honey, what you are talking about. You're the one that needs the plumber, the roofer, and the electrician." At that comeback, Al couldn't hold back his chuckle.

In the center of the room was the main printing press. It was set so the paper coming in from the back door could be brought right up to the feed end of the press. The machine, produced by Vandercook in Chicago, was one of the last models produced in 1956. Ray spoke up as Al was looking the press over, "Won't be long and electronics will be taking over the business. I don't want to be around when a pressman doesn't need to get his hands dirty."

"I don't know," Al said, "seems to me you're so far north that it might just take the modern world ten years or so to get up this far!"

"Okay, okay, enough of the snide remarks," Ray shot back. "Let's go next door and have coffee and catch up." Turning to Gracie he said, "Al and I will be next door for a while. I expect we have a lot to talk about."

As they headed for the front of the building, Gracie came close to Al and said, "Only believe half of what you hear."

They headed out the front door and not twenty feet away was The Coffee Cup. An old neon sign in the window was flickering its "open" message. The sign on the front door said, "Open unless fishing."

Al laughed at the sign, and Ray simply said, "That's why I have a key."

The front door gave way with a push, and the bell hanging overhead jingled their entrance. "Just have a seat, be right with ya" came a voice from the back.

Ray spoke out loudly, "Just me, got a friend here. I'll get the coffee; keep doing whatever you're doing."

Again the voice from the back said, "Thanks, Ray, be right up there. I gotta meet this friend of yours."

A moment later a wiry older guy walked through the swinging kitchen door. He was wearing a white shirt and an apron around his neck. On the front of the apron were the words, Chief Cook and Bottle Washer. He was wearing a white paper hat, pointed in the front and back.

Al noticed his neatly trimmed mustache and the tattoo on his arm. The anchor tattoo was a dead giveaway of the man's service in the navy. Before Al could even reach out to shake the man's hand, he was shaking Al's, telling him, "I'm Chuck. Real name is Charles; only enemies and bill collectors call me that."

Ray explained, "We're just gonna be here for a while, got some catching up to do."

Ray and Al sat on the chrome swivel stools at the counter. Sipping at his coffee, Ray said, "So bring me up to speed."

Al asked, "Do you really know what happened to me?"

"No, I guess I don't really know the details. I do know that you got your brains jarred pretty good."

Al grimaced. "When the fighting began, I headed for a bunker just down the street. The artillery started moving towards us, and people were running from the markets screaming. There was a marine next to me, Pfc. Williams. Next time I looked down the street, a small child was running towards us. She was screaming and crying. I could see her tears and her dirty white shirt. I was going to get the camera so I could get some shots of her running. Pfc. Williams told me he was going to run out and grab her."

At this point, Al was staring down into his cup. With his voice just above a whisper, he said, "I was sure I could get some fantastic shots. You know what I mean—the photo of a lifetime. An explosion knocked me back, and in an instant, that poor little girl vanished in a red mist." Al's words, "vanished in a red mist" were so quiet that Ray almost asked him to repeat himself. He didn't because he knew what he just heard, and it was no mistake.

Al continued, "I found out that the marine, Joey Williams, says I saved his life. At least that's what he told his mom and dad. He said that if he had gotten around me, the blast would have killed him."

Ray pulled his cigarettes and Zippo lighter from his front pocket. The Zippo was tucked into the plastic and paper of the pack.

As he lit the cigarette, Al remarked, "You still smoking those unfiltered things?"

With a chuckle, Ray said, "Yeah, the local doc around here says they'll kill me. But what the hell, I'm gonna die someday, anyway. The medical people were really good about keeping me informed until you left the hospital. But once you got back and started working, I got busy. I was transferred to the city desk in Philadelphia. Man, I loved that, but the stress was killing me. A man can't keep up that kinda pace forever. So, Gracie convinced me it was time to take it easy. We always loved the north and found out that this place was for sale. So, here we are in Salmon Stream Crossing."

As Ray was talking Al noticed the shake in his hand and that he seemed almost out of breath. "You okay," Al asked.

"I'm fine," Ray said, "just need another smoke."

Ray asked, "What happened later on, after you came back, I mean, you know, with your injury?"

"I started having bad headaches. I never knew when they would hit me and for how long they'd last. And, then the nightmares started. I would have dreams where every second was playing back in slow motion. I could hear the explosions; I could see the little girl, her tears, and the dirt on her white shirt."

By this time Al was having difficulty talking, and Ray cut in, "You don't have to tell me again."

Al's voice trailed off, "Dear God, Ray, she just vanished right before my eyes."

Al continued as Ray emptied his cup, "After I recovered I began the Northern Virginia gig. I went to D.C. to cover a protest. That's where I met Sarah. She was at the protest, and we hit it off over coffee. It didn't take long, and I was in deep. I fell for her really bad. All I had to do was close my eyes, and I could see her hair blowing in the breeze. And she always smelled like lilacs. We spent a lot of time together. The weekends on the coast were the best times in my life."

As he was talking about Sarah, it was easy for Ray to see just how much Al cared for her. Al asked, "Ray, do you believe in heaven?"

Ray sputtered and asked, "Well, I guess, I would like to think of such a place. We've both seen hell. Why do you want to know that?"

Al responded, "Sarah was going to have our baby. She decided she wasn't ready to be a mother, so she ended the pregnancy. I believe I have a baby waiting for me in heaven."

Ray's shifting on the stool told Al that his friend was uneasy, but Al continued, "After Sarah and I split up, I was in bad shape. I left the paper and was pretty much drunk for weeks. I found myself sleeping in an alley. Some kid told me about the mission. You know, the place I called you from, Agape Station. That was the exact place God wanted me."

The door from the kitchen swung open, and Chuck walked to the counter. Seeing the empty cups he said, "Let me fill 'em for you guys, and I got more work to do. Just thought I best check on you two."

As Chuck went back through the door, Al said, "God wanted me to stop running from my guilt and past. I have learned to trust the Lord."

Ray looked at Al funny when he used the word, Lord. He asked, "What do you mean, Lord? Like, Jesus Christ?"

"Yes, Ray, that's exactly who I mean," Al said. "Jesus Christ has forgiven me and has given me a real sense of purpose. If I were to tell you everything that happened, it would seem incredible. I know the Lord wants me to be here, right now, with you and Gracie."

To say that Ray was bewildered would be an understatement. Looking Al right square in the face, he asked, "After all you been through, and all the crap you've seen, you mean to tell me that you believe in God and Jesus and all that stuff?"

With their eyes still locked, Al responded, "Yeah, Ray, I do believe. I can tell you this without a doubt in the world that if it hadn't been for God and the folks at Agape Station, I would be dead. Yes, plain and simple, no crap, just dead."

Al twisted in his chair and continued. "Because of guilt, I was trying to drink myself to death. Whiskey was my best friend, my confidant, my counselor. That glass shrine listened to me and never argued back. I survived; that little girl didn't. I fell in love with a wonderful woman and felt guilty for the choice she made. I know that doesn't make sense. It was her choice, but I could have tried harder to make her understand how I felt."

"Damn, Al, I didn't know about all of that," Ray said with a frown. Feeling uneasy, he changed the subject. "So tell me, my friend, what do you think of our little town?"

Al set his cup down on the counter and asked, "How about you show me around?"

The two men got up and headed for the door. Ray hollered as he walked out, "Chuck, I'll cover the coffee later."

From the back, they heard Chuck's reply, "You bet you'll cover it later, you cheap old fart."

Ray and Al chuckled and headed down the street.

Al said, "So tell me about downtown here. All the buildings on this side seem the same."

Ray said, "Yeah, it was the fire of '03 I told you about. She burnt everything, right up to the river. A couple of folks still remember '03, that's what they call it, '03. Chuck's dad, near 90, still remembers '03. And to this day he can't tell what put the fire out. He says it should have burned everything for hundreds of miles, but something stopped it right at the river."

About half an hour later, the two men went through the front door of the paper to find Gracie waiting for them. She said, "If this is any idea of the kind of work I'm going to get out of you two, you got another thought coming."

Al was as quiet as a stone at her remark.

And then she smirked and said, "Al, I'll show you your place. When we bought the paper, we bought a couple of small cabins just down the road. I wanted them in case I ever had to kick Ray out 'cause I couldn't have him out in the cold."

Ray snickered at her comment and said, "Yeah right, best dog house around."

Gracie continued, "They're just down the road, almost at the end of town. Each one has a bedroom, small bath, and open kitchen/living room area. Not big, but it should be pretty cozy."

Gracie and Al left the office and headed down the street towards the cabins. Al looked at Gracie as they walked and asked, "So, Gracie, how is Ray doing? No stories. No bull. How is he?"

Gracie stopped for a second and looked at Al and said, "What I'm telling you is between us. Ray would be as mad as a hornet if he knew I told you this. The doctor told Ray that his ticker is in bad shape; he needed to quit smoking, lose weight, and eat better."

Al looked straight into Gracie's eyes and spoke quietly yet firmly, "Gracie, God has done a wonderful thing in my life. I know I'm here for a reason, and it might not be just to help the both of you."

Gracie responded, "When I first met you at the office, you sure weren't the person Ray told me about. He had some wild stories of the two of you."

They both chuckled. Al said, "Some may be true, and some may be just the rambling of a newsman."

In less than five minutes, Al was in the cabin, and Gracie was on her way back to the office. It didn't take much for Al to get things in order. The bed was comfortable, and like most small cabins, the stand next to the bed did double duty as a nightstand, telephone stand, and two-drawer chest. Sitting on the edge of the bed, he opened the bottom drawer. In a flash, he was remembering how many times he opened a drawer to pull out a bottle. He smiled as he closed the drawer, glad and thankful that a deadly chapter in his life was over.

After settling in, Al met Ray at the office, and they headed through the back room.

Ray said, "Getting to the house is easy. I just go out the back door and right in front of my nose is the house."

"Pretty nice being so close, Ray. I'll bet you don't spend much on gas and parking."

Ray piped up, "It has its advantages and disadvantages. Everybody in town knows where we live, and we can't put a closed sign on the front or back door. Oh, I guess we could, but folks wouldn't take it very good."

They walked up the stairs to the back porch and entered the kitchen. Gracie had her back to them when they came in. She said, "Dinner will be ready in a few minutes. Ray, why don't you set the table while I show Al around the house?" She continued, "The laundry room is through that door. Whenever you need to use it, the door is always unlocked." Leaving the kitchen, she showed Al the dining room and then the living room.

It was no wonder Ray needed to lose weight—Gracie was a fantastic cook. They sat down to meatloaf, mashed potatoes, green beans, and rolls.

Al asked Gracie, "What did you do to make the green beans so fabulous? They're the best I've had in a long time."

Her reply to Al was one word, "Bacon. I cook the beans with small pieces of bacon to add flavor."

The meatloaf was just the way Al liked it, just a bit crunchy on the edges. They finished dinner with coffee and a piece of German chocolate cake. After a moment of quiet, Gracie broke the silence, "When I cook, others do the cleanup." With that said, Ray and Al cleaned the table and worked over the sink for a few minutes.

As the sun was inching down in the valley, the reflection off Salmon Stream River was enchanting. It appeared as if thousands of diamonds were dancing on the surface. The evening was cooling off as Gracie, Ray, and Al sat on wicker chairs on the porch. As folks walked by, Gracie or Ray greeted them and exchanged small pleasantries, mostly about the weather. Al picked the chair near the far end of the porch, somewhat hidden behind a massive spruce tree.

Al asked, "So, what's with the name of the paper? I never did get that figured out. I know enough of Latin to know it means something mysterious or weird, even freaky. Who in the world gave it that name?"

Ray said to Gracie, "You give him the short answer, and I'll tell him all of it later on." At which time Ray lit another cigarette.

Gracie adjusted herself in her chair to see Al a bit better and said, "Going back a couple of hundred years seems that this entire area has a history of strange events. Most of them are connected to the river. The old-timers tell stories of things they can't explain. The library has local history books going back to the time of William Rogers. And they tell stories that are pretty hard to understand."

Al sat up in his chair a bit straighter as Gracie continued, "Some even say the Native Americans recorded strange things along the river."

Al asked, "What do these stories all have in common? What ties them together, anything? Or are they just different random events?"

Gracie looked at Ray, and he nodded. Gracie responded, "Seems that all the events have to do with people, young and old alike."

Al noticed that Gracie was obviously nervous about the conversation. He asked her, "So, what about people, and what is the rest of this about?"

"People just vanish," Gracie said in a serious tone.

Al's response was quick. "People do not just disappear. There is always some evidence, clue, or hint as to what happens."

This time it was Ray's turn to chime in. "Listen, Al, I'm as big a skeptic as they come. A stinking Martian could walk up to me, and I'd laugh in his face. But some of the stories seem very real and believable. I can't honestly say it's all bunk."

Al asked, "What about bodies? Do people drown and their bodies are never recovered? Have there been reports of accidents that are unexplainable?"

Ray answered slowly, "Yes, we've had drownings. But those have been of victims known to be swimming in the water or in a boat fishing, stuff like that."

They looked at one another in silence and sat quietly until they called it a night.

12

Unanswered Prayers

Al spent the entire week with Ray learning the dirty side of the newspaper—how to use both pieces of equipment. Most of the time was spent on the big press that ran the weekly paper. Al was beginning to understand that it was a hard business to run and make a profit out of it.

At the end of the week, Ray, Gracie, and Al sat down together in the front office. Ray said, "Al, I talked things over with Gracie, and we think it's time to divide up some of the evening and on-call work. Most of that stuff is mundane calls from neighbors to the police, usually over barking dogs and stray cats. You and I will rotate on council meetings and late night fire and police calls."

On Monday, Al was introduced to the town council. He had met a few of the members at the news office. The mayor of the town, a man by the name of Larry, was a pipe smoking, smiling, and friendly guy. Larry invited him to go fishing any time he wanted. "I'll show you the best damn spec fishing anywhere."

The next morning Al said to Ray, "The council meeting was a yawner, but I met the mayor, and he invited me to go fishing."

Ray was fast to respond, "If Larry invites you to go fishing, you best take him up on the offer. Not only will you have great fishing, Larry will also fix you the best shore lunch in these parts. No fooling, take the offer."

Al laughed and quipped back, "Yes, I will, when I can get my boss to let up on me a bit."

The paper run kept Gracie, Ray, and Al working past ten. It was late when Al got back to his cabin. He had found a lamp, small table, and a decent, comfortable chair that he put near the front window. Stacked near the window was close to twenty years of newspapers. He convinced himself that he was going to get caught up with the community and the mystery surrounding the river.

That night Al was working his way through the papers when he picked up a copy almost twenty years old. The headline declared a missing woman, and the accompanying article reported that a woman from a local care facility was missing. According to the report, the woman suffered from dementia and just wandered away—no trace, no evidence, no hint of foul play, just vanished.

Close to midnight, Al was just beginning to doze when flashing lights caused his stomach to tighten and fear gripped him by the throat. Within minutes the flashes of light were committed to their mission of pain and panic. Even as he squeezed his eyes as tightly as possible, the brilliant lights continued on their wicked path.

Soon the pain was consuming. Waves of nausea were in concert with every pore on his skin pumping out perspiration. As he crawled to the bathroom, he looked wretched and pathetic. After emptying his stomach, he clung to the varnished knotty pine walls. He made it back to bed only to find the taunting cries of an infant and a tear-streaked little girl begging for rescue. As she begged for rescue, Al was begging his God for rescue and relief.

Early the next morning, Al was at the back door of Ray and Gracie's place. As usual he knocked once and then went in.

Taking his laundry right into the laundry room, he was hoping to escape Gracie's eye. He put the sheets and linens from the night before right into the washer. As he was finishing up, he heard Gracie in the kitchen.

He came from around the laundry room door and said, "Good morning." It must have caught her by surprise. Startled, she turned around and dropped a glass in the sink. "Dear Lord, Al, you scared the daylights out of me," she said. In the very next breath she said, "My, you look terrible, is everything alright? You look like you've been sick. Come on into the kitchen and let me get you some coffee."

Working on the second cup, Al began to feel better. Gracie was busy finishing up things in the kitchen, and he was glad that she didn't press him about how he was feeling. Looking into his cup, he asked Gracie, "Ray at the office, or running errands?"

"He had to go to the post office and then he was coming back. Hard to tell how long, he could be anywhere. Been times when he was talking somewhere and forgot what he was supposed to be doing."

Al chuckled as he finished the last of his coffee. Afterwards he went to the office. and spent an hour cleaning the press and getting the stock area cleaned up.

Ray's voice interrupted him, "Hey Al, you in the back?"

Al shouted back, "Yeah, what's up?"

Ray hollered back, "Meet me next door, and I don't mean in an hour."

The front door of the diner squeaked, and the bell jingled as Al went in. Ray was at a table near the back, not his usual counter seat. A cup of coffee was waiting for Al. Ray was looking a bit unusual, and Al was trying to figure out what was going on. Trying to lighten things up Al said, "I wonder what would happen in the coffee world if news people stopped drinking it?" He chuckled at his own joke, but Ray didn't respond. It was easy for Al to see that something serious was on Ray's mind.

Holding his cup in both hands, Ray was direct. "Was last night the first time since the surgery that you had the headaches and the dream?"

Al sat back in his chair and glanced down into his cup. He looked up at Ray and responded, "Yeah, it was the first time. I don't know why it was last night. I thought it might be that I was just really tired or something."

"What something?" Ray shot back.

Al said, hoping to diffuse the emotional bomb, "The doctor told me that they could come back at any time. It could mean a couple of things, he said. The doctor said it could be the tumor is active, or it could mean I just did something to aggravate it."

Ray almost spilled his coffee at Al's remark. In an instant he poured out, "How in the hell do you aggravate a tumor? Aggravate a tumor, I never heard of such a thing. What are you supposed to do, walk around with a helmet on?"

"Listen, Ray," Al said, "my life has been in God's hands, and it still is. God never promised me that I would be pain-free or even tumor free. I know that he cares about what's going on. When it comes right down to it, my life is in his hands."

Al could sense Ray struggling with what he'd just said. After a moment of silence, Al got up and brought the coffee pot back and refilled their cups. "Listen, Ray, what's the real problem here? You knew what happened to me; you knew about the dreams and the headaches. Why does this eat at you so much?"

Ray's cup was jittering on the chipped tabletop as he fumbled with it and searched for the right words.

Al spoke up. "Ray, my friend, do you think for a second that

I hold you responsible for what happened to me? Do you feel guilty about what happened? Remember, I asked for the assignment. I was the one who wanted to go and make a big name for myself. That was all me, not you."

As Al finished, Ray moved a bit in his chair and looked at him. He was clearly at a loss for words and choked up. Clearing his throat, he said, "Al you don't know how many nights I've tossed and turned with images of you strapped down inside that plane. Knowing that you were working for me, I felt responsible."

Al had no doubt that this had been eating at Ray for some time. As he talked with his friend, he was also asking God for wisdom and the right words.

Al began, "I can honestly tell you that I never once held you responsible for what happened. You had no idea what could take place from one day to the next. I knew it then, and I know it now. God has a way of working things out for good. It might be hard to see how it's going to happen when you're in the middle of it, but I know that this all worked out for my good. Just think of what life might be like, at least now you have me around. I might even let you teach me how to fish."

Al's humor helped, and they finished their coffee. As they left the diner, Ray told Al that Gracie was expecting him over for dinner. Ray added, "Don't be a minute past six. Gracie is worried about you, and I promised her that you'd come."

Al chuckled and said, "Sure of yourself, aren't you? Sounds like you make some pretty big promises. Good thing for you, I love her cooking. Yeah, by the way, what is she making for dinner?"

Ray's cryptic nature emerged. "Listen, young man, didn't your parents teach you anything? Beggars can't be choosers, and you never look a gift horse in the mouth."

Al was at their back door fifteen minutes early. As he came in, Gracie was in the kitchen getting ready to pull some plates off the shelf.

Al asked, "Where's the boss? I want him to know I'm early."

"Oh, the boss. He's in the living room, napping on his throne."

Gracie's humor was obvious. Al stuck his head around the corner of the living room to find Ray asleep with his head back and snoring. Al retreated to the kitchen and helped set the table and plug in the electric percolator.

When he sat down at the table, Gracie hollered out, "It's on the table, Ray, and we aren't gonna wait forever."

Ray came to the table as Al jabbed at him, saying, "Telling me not to be late, and you're asleep in a chair. Last time I listen to you."

After a wonderful dinner of scalloped potatoes and roast pork chops, the two men did the cleanup and then sat down for coffee. Ray looked out over the top of his cup and asked Al, "Has Gracie asked you about last night or this morning?"

Al said, "No, she hasn't. Does she want to talk to me? You know I'd rather not. It's just stuff she doesn't need to know about."

"I agree," Ray said. "But she does deserve some information. She ought to know a little of what goes on."

As Ray and Al sat at the kitchen table, Gracie walked past.

Al said, "Excuse me, Gracie, would you sit down for a minute? Out of respect, I owe you an explanation."

Gracie responded, "Listen, young man, you don't owe me a thing." Her tone was so gentle that Al didn't read anything but sincerity.

Al continued, "Okay, I want to tell you a little about this morning. Since coming back, I've had severe headaches. The doctor told me they were from the injury and a subsequent tumor on my brain. Along with the headaches, I've had bad dreams. So when they happen, I look like I did this morning. I hadn't had one in a while, but last night they came back. I might not have another one for weeks or months."

13

Investigating the Mystery

The phone on the stand rang once, and Al picked up the receiver. Ray was on the phone and told Al to get dressed and be ready to go in five minutes. Without so much as asking why, Al told him he'd be ready. Almost exactly five minutes later, Ray pulled up in front of the cabin and honked the horn once. Even before the horn ended, Al was out the door. He climbed into the front seat of the old four-wheel drive, and they headed north out of town.

Al asked, "So, what's up?"

"Well," Ray answered, "I just got off the phone with the sheriff up in the town of Wausoneke. It seems like an elderly man went missing. They found his car by the river and no trace of him."

"Wausoneke," replied Al. "Where in the blue blazes is Wausoneke?"

Ray frowned and said, "What do you mean? You've been reading all the old papers, haven't ya? It's up on the river, close to fifty miles north of here. Over the years it's been the spot of a few of the strange occurrences. We're going to meet the sheriff at the river, take pictures for him, and wait around a while. Sometimes they call me to show up and just take pictures. Their cameras are junk. They know a professional when they see one."

An hour later, Ray pulled the four-wheel drive up next to

the patrol car. The sheriff was standing down by the river, tossing rocks into the swift current.

With the wind picking up, Ray hollered out, "Hey, Bill, don't shoot me."

The sheriff turned around and shouted back, "Now tell me, Ray, it's dark out. How the heck did you know it was me?"

Laughing Ray said, "I guess it could have been another officer if he had stolen your cruiser. You're the only sheriff who drives car number 21, aren't you? I get paid for paying close attention to details. Who knows, someday you might be famous around these parts."

Bill laughed and said, "For an old fart, you're pretty observant."

Ray got his camera out from the backseat while Bill met up with them. He asked Bill, "What kind of shots do you want?"

"Well, since we don't know much about the guy and what might have happened, you better take plenty."

Ray began by taking photos of the car from all angles and then from the riverbank. He had Al and the sheriff stand in front of the car with their arms outstretched to show the approximate distance from the vehicle to the water's edge.

After a couple of minutes, Ray was done with the outside. "What about the inside, Bill?" Ray asked.

"Let's take a look and see," Bill said. Pulling out a large flashlight from his belt, he illuminated the inside of the car. "Not a thing in this car, not a gum wrapper, cigarette butt, napkin, nothing, nothing at all. I don't recall ever seeing a car so clean on the inside."

After taking pictures, the three men stood against Bill's cruiser. Bill said, "I'm waiting for a message back from downstate. We ran the plate, and the car is from downstate, so we sent a local officer over to the address."

Ray asked, "What else is happening around here?"

"The woods up here are as dry as I've seen them in years," Bill said. "I'm telling every camper and fisherman to be careful with fire. An accident or a careless person, and a fire could be down to the river in no time."

The radio in Bill's patrol car crackled and ended the conversation. "Yeah, this is Bill, what do you have for me?"

"Yeah, Bill," the voice on the radio squawked. "The local police tell us the house is empty. They went in and found a cup still filled with coffee on the table. Bread and toaster were still on the counter. They said it was very strange, almost spooky. And you know cops don't talk about stuff being spooky."

"Damn," Bill said, "that's what I was afraid of."

The three men walked up and down the riverbank, looking for any sign of the elderly man. The river was swift with deep pools and trees hanging down into the water. After an hour, Bill got back on the radio and asked the office to organize a search that would begin at sunrise. At the end of the radio conversation, Bill said, "You'd better have the hounds come down as well. There should be some scent, and they just might pick up on the old man."

Turning from his patrol car, Bill said, "I bet the old guy came down to look at the river, slipped, and went in. Now he's probably stuck under some logs or floating downstream. It's gonna take a few hours to get the search team ready. You two ought to just go home."

Ray said, "We'll stick around and help out a bit. Besides, if you find the old guy, I want to be the first to have the story."

Bill chuckled as he said, "Things are kinda quiet down in the Crossing. Anything for a story. I think the diner opens at five, just a couple of hours from now."

Al said, "You two can talk all night. I'm taking a snooze in the back seat." The back door creaked as Al opened it and crawled in.

Bill said to Ray, "Young kid, hey, can't take this nightlife?"

Ray stiffened and answered, "He's a great kid, been through some pretty rough stuff. Got hurt pretty bad. I'm glad he's okay and up here with us."

Bill and Ray walked along the river bank, and the talk turned to fishing for big specks. Bill, born and raised on the river, argued that the very best method to catch a trophy was to float a big worm just off the bottom on a light line. Ray argued that casting bright spinners with feathers on them, down in the deep holes would work best. At the end of the debate, Bill had evidence of success, and Ray didn't.

Around five the two fish yakkers knocked on the car window. Al stirred and rolled down the window. Ray said, "Hey sleeping beauty, want some coffee? We're heading up the hill to the diner, supposed to open at five. Are ya coming?"

Al opened the back door and got out, trying to stretch and work out the kinks. "Drag me up north, make me sleep on the backseat, and now you want me to walk uphill for coffee."

Ray, looking at Bill, laughed and said, "Kids today, a lazy bunch I'd say. Gonna cry about walking to get a cup of coffee,"

Bill chuckled and said, "Yeah, I remember when I was a kid. Up here in the winter, I had to walk to school, and it was four miles uphill both ways."

Al heard the remarks and shot back, "Yeah, that was probably when it was a one-room schoolhouse with an outhouse."

In the dark it was hard to make out the diner. Al could tell that it was really old. Getting closer, he could see the white clapboard was in bad shape—a few of the boards on the front of the building were cracked and split. The three-step entrance was old concrete that had pulled away from the front door by a couple of inches. First to the door, Al pulled on a rickety screen that stuck to the floor.

The inside was just as Al imagined or had seen before. On the left was the counter with round chrome stools and black padded seats. On the right side was a row of small tables placed in front of the bank of windows facing the south. Most of the tables would seat four. In the front, just to the right of the door was a large window that faced the road, and a larger round table was in front of the window.

As they walked in, the smell of fresh coffee assaulted their senses. Along with the coffee, Al took in the smell of bacon. His mind went back to Aunt Bee's cooking. She knew he loved thick, peppered bacon. He had forgotten about how well she took care of him. As he stood silent for a moment, Bee's presence filled his heart. He wanted to be able to talk to her again and tell her how his life had changed.

Ray interrupted Al's moment of reverie and told him to sit down. As he did, he looked over the counter on the back wall to see a sign proclaiming, River's Edge Diner. It had been cut out with a router, and the lettering painted black. The board looked like pine that had been whitewashed. Al thought the sign looked fitting.

A very petite white-haired lady came from the back room. She couldn't have been much more than five feet tall and probably weighed less than a hundred pounds. She said, "Good morning, men. I'll bring you coffee right away. I bet you young men like your coffee strong and black."

Her comment caught Al off guard. He asked, "Excuse me, did you say that we would like our coffee strong and black? How did you know that?"

She smiled at Al and said, "Now listen, young man. I've been waiting on and serving people for a really long time. You don't do this for as long as I have and not learn a few things. I could see it your eyes."

The three men sat and drank the first cup in silence. The woman refilled their cups and asked if there was something she could fix for them. Al, out of curiosity, asked her, "What kind of bacon were you frying when we came in?"

"Why," she said, "the kind we use most up here—thick cut and peppered; the other would be thick cut and maple smoked. Most visitors from down below prefer the maple smoked. Most folks from 'round here like the peppered."

Al was quiet, and his mind was working hard to remember the last place he had ever been that served thick cut peppered bacon.

The men finished their coffee, left more than enough to cover the bill, and headed for the door. The voice from the back called out, "Come back later. You can meet Rose. She's the owner, been here a really long time."

As they headed down the hill, the sun was just beginning to break and shine through the stand of giant pines. The three men stood on the edge of the road. The sun was to their right and the river right below them. The sight was fit for any calendar or magazine cover. Bill said, "God, this is beautiful country."

A few minutes later, two patrol cars and an old pickup truck pulled in alongside the other two vehicles. The old pickup had a plywood dog kennel that filled the back end. The two doors for the kennel were drilled with holes the size of a broomstick. As the old man got out of the truck, the hounds started their singing, begging to get out of their traveling lodge and start sniffing. Bill introduced the three newly arrived deputies and Willie, the owner of the hounds.

Bill asked, "Anything new from downstate about the owner of the car?"

A younger deputy said, "Nothing new, still waiting for another call from down below."

"Okay, Willie," Bill said, "let's get the hounds out and get started." Willie opened the first door on the kennel and put a long leather lead on the first dog. Before he could even move to the second door, the freed hound was pulling and tugging. With the lead on the second hound, Willie reined them in and took them over to the abandoned car.

Bill, about ten yards away, yelled at Willie, "Hey, Willie, how 'bout you introducing your hounds to our members of the press."

Willie shot back, "All right, make fun of my hounds, but they're the best in the north."

Bill responded with a smile, "They're the only bloodhounds in the north."

Turning to Al and Ray, Willie said, "Now don't make fun of my dogs. Both are males 'cause they have the best nose." Pulling the larger of the two away from the car, Willie introduced them, "The big boy here, he is Nuttin; the other boy, he's Butta."

Ray couldn't contain himself, and his barrel chest laugh echoed down the river. He replied, "I've heard it all, here we are a stone's throw from Canada, and we have a southern boy with hounds named Nuttin and Butta."

Willie announced, "I'm gonna let the boys work loose. That way I don't have to keep up with 'em. Gonna let 'em get the scent from the car and go to work."

Al asked, "Mind if I go along with you? I would love to watch Nuttin and Butta."

Willie worked the hounds upstream about a half of a mile, and they didn't catch a scent. Al walked with them, fascinated with the dogs. As the two hounds worked around the pines and cedars, their noses were constantly sniffing, and their ears were so close to the ground, it seemed as if they were sweeping it.

Al asked Willie, "What makes hounds so good?"

"Ya see how close to the ground they keep their nose, and how their ears seem to be flapping? Those big beautiful ears flap and stir up the scent, bringing it right up to their noses. These boys of mine are the best sniffers in the world."

After working the dogs upstream, Willie moved the hounds back downstream. As they worked their way down, Al stopped at the car, and Willie kept going. Ray and Bill were standing at the patrol car and having a smoke. Just in front of the vehicle, the bank dropped down a couple of feet. To Al's left, a fallen cedar bobbed up and down in the water's current. The water was dark below the cedar, and Al thought that it must be a deep spot. To his right, the river began a long and gradual bend, heading north. He told the two standing at the car that he was going to walk downstream for a bit and wouldn't be long.

Ray replied, "You better be careful; I don't plan on having to look for you as well."

Al was walking carefully along the bank of the river. The path worked its way around deadfalls, ferns, and young saplings springing up in the small clearings. Near the water, it was apparent where people fished. These cleared spots had an excellent opening to the river. Some of them even had small fire pits made with river rocks.

Back at the cars again, Al found Ray and Bill still engaged in small talk. The dogs had been silent, not a bark for awhile, and certainly not the low moaning or requiem-like barking that signaled they had done their job. About an hour later, Willie came back down a trail from the high bank section of the river that led up to River's Edge Diner.

"Not a trace, not a sniff, nothing, I mean nothing. Nuttin and Butta worked the whole area real hard, real hard, and not a thing. I've never in all of my days with these boys come up empty, cold nosed, I mean. It just doesn't make sense. They got his scent in the car, got it real good, and now, nothing. I'm telling you this, that guy just up and vanished."

Ray hollered over to Bill, "Al and I are heading back to town. If you get any more news, give me a phone call."

"Sure will," Bill said. "And if the old guy just happens to float on by, I'll let you know that as well." His chuckle revealed his history and shielded emotions.

Neither Al nor Ray laughed in return, and the meaning of their silence was obvious. Both men were quiet on the trip back to Salmon Stream Crossing. As Ray parked the four-wheel drive, he told Al that after a couple of hours rest, they would put together the information and write it up for the next edition.

That evening Al and Ray sat in the office and discussed the events surrounding the elderly man's disappearance. It didn't take them long to put a short article together for the paper. Ray decided that the headline would be: Elderly Man Vanishes; Hounds Find No Trace. The piece would give some of the details about the abandoned car, the dogs, and how many officers were involved.

On Monday evening, Al went to the town council meeting. He found a chair in the corner, sat during the very dull event, and recorded the usual business. The meeting was called to order; all in attendance stood for the Pledge of Allegiance. Then a local clergyman offered a prayer. The business of the town was discussed. The only item of interest to Al was the financial condition of the town. The treasurer reported that with all bills paid, they were able to have a sizable Rainy Day Fund. After the meeting, Larry walked up to Al, shaking his hand as he led him into a corner of the room.

"So," Larry said, "tell me the scoop about what happened up

at the river." The statement took Al by surprise, and he stumbled for a moment trying to gather up a response.

"It was a missing person's report," Al said. "They found a car down by the river and conducted a search. Not much more than that."

Larry's response was quick, "Now come on, Al, I wasn't born yesterday. There's always more to a story than what is public knowledge."

Al's response was quick and pointed, "Mr. Mayor, you know that there are facts that are to remain a mystery until the proper time. So, if I'm leaving anything out, you are well aware it is for a very good reason."

Larry chuckled and put his old English pipe in his mouth. With his arm around Al's shoulder, he told him, "You know, you're a pretty good guy. I was just prodding you. I'm gonna stop by on Wednesday and set a time for us to go fishing. I've been promising your boss for a while that we were gonna go."

Larry stopped by the news office on Wednesday just as he promised. Finding Ray in the office with his back to the door, he cleared his throat and said, "Not much of a way to greet a potential customer."

Ray with his back still turned, shot out, "I knew you weren't about to spend a dime."

Larry laughed and quipped, "Saw me coming, didn't ya?"

Ray and Larry agreed that Friday morning would be a good time to go fishing. Ray told Larry that they'd be ready barring any unseen emergency or major story.

Going out the office door, Larry said, "Now you boys just be ready at five. I'll have all the gear and be out in the front of Chuck's place."

14

Trout Fishing

Larry parked Old Gettem-Up in front. Before he could get out, Ray and Al were out the front door. Ray got in the front seat of the old four-wheel drive, and Al sat in the back. Next to Al on the bench seat was an assortment of three metal boxes. They looked like old tool boxes, banged up and rusted where the paint had been scratched away. Behind him were three plastic tubes, four inches in diameter. Larry put the four-wheel drive in first gear, and they headed out of town.

"Well, how do you like my Old Gettem-Up?" Larry asked. "I use her mostly for fishing and hunting. The old standard transmission and four-wheel drive takes me everywhere I want to go. She's perfect for getting to the holes where the big specks are."

Larry, out of breath, pipe clenched in his mouth, listened to Ray's barrage, "You got all of that out in one breath. What do you want me to answer first? You want to know what I think of Old Gettem-Up, or her abilities, which I know nothing about."

With that, Larry shot across the old seat, "I'd say you're kinda testy this morning. What's the matter, not enough coffee, or ya just not used to chasin' specks at five in the morning?"

After twenty minutes going north on the blacktop, Larry turned down a dirt road. The pines were growing closer to the edge of the road; in the predawn light, it was more like driving

151

through a tunnel. Five miles down the dirt road, Larry turned Old Gettem-Up onto a two-track. The sun was trying to bust through the pine branches that reached across the track and meshed like left and right fingers.

As they wound down the two-track, Larry tried to talk and hold his pipe in his mouth. With Al bouncing around in the back seat, Larry downshifted, going around a corner and slammed it into second gear when the track straightened out. They made their way along the track, and Larry, pipe clenched as always, laughed and said, "Old Gettem-up, what a gal, always gets me where I'm going."

Larry pulled Old Gettem-Up into a clearing and turned off the ignition. He got out and relit his pipe, and the smell of the tobacco was a sweet mixture of dark and light burley. Larry opened the back door and took out the three plastic tubes and the metal tackle boxes. When he opened the first tube, he pulled out a long flannel sleeve tied shut on one end.

Untying the sleeve, he announced to Al and Ray, "All right, boys, I'm about to show you a thing of real beauty, a piece of craftsmanship that's almost a hundred years old." He continued waxing eloquent and pulled out a two-piece split bamboo fly rod. "This here," he said, "is one of the best fishing rods ever made. It's made of young bamboo, split with absolute precision, and held with the strongest glues made."

Larry's fishing gear was worth bragging about, and the beat-up tackle boxes provided the perfect disguise for the treasures within. One tackle box contained an assortment of flies, everything from streamers, wet flies, nymphs, and dry flies. Another box contained a vast variety of spinners. Some spinners were silver while others were gold. Some spinners had bits of hair called "bucktails." The last box contained what most people would consider standard fishing gear—a complete inventory of hooks and sinkers. The hooks ranged from the smallest to some measuring an inch from the barb to the shank. The sinkers were tiny split-shot to ones weighing more than an ounce.

After showing off his arsenal of angling weapons, Larry opened the other tubes that held the fishing rods. One rod was fiberglass and the other a bamboo designed to hold a spinning real. Looking at what he assumed were two river fishing virgins, he asked, "Which one of you ever fished a river before?"

Ray piped up, feeling a bit challenged. "I've done plenty of fishing. As a kid, I fished all summer long. What's the big deal?"

Sensing a bit of blood in the water, Al kept quiet, waiting for the next slash. He didn't wait for more than a few seconds until Larry jumped on Ray's confession. With his pipe clenched and a bit of smoke snaking from the bowl, he said, "Fishing as a young whipper-snapper in some farm pond is not river fishing, believe me."

Sensing more blood, Al broke in, "All right, kids, let's get to fishing instead of this verbal jousting. I've done some river fishing down in the Blue Ridge. I never used a fly rod, but I'm pretty good with a spinning rod."

Ray and Al got their gear together and decided to use spinners and fish them into the deep pools along the bank. As they were walking, Ray turned to see Larry with waders on and adjusting some type of fishing vest. He whispered to Al, "Check out Larry."

Al turned to see Larry walking towards the river, fly rod in hand, hat perched on his head, and a net over his shoulder. The pockets of the vest were bulging, and chrome circles had what looked like surgical equipment hanging on them.

Turning to Ray, Al said, "Man alive, this guy really takes his fishing seriously. Hope he catches some fish. Wearing all of that stuff would be a waste of time if there aren't any fish."

There was plenty of room for Ray and Al to fish along the bank. The bend in the river provided a pool at least twenty yards long and out about ten or fifteen yards. The object was to cast upstream, let the spinner get close to the bottom, and then start the retrieve. As they discussed their tactics, Larry went upstream. As he passed, he said, "I'm gonna fish upstream near the flats, need to make sure we have fish for lunch. Don't know if I can depend on you boys to fill the frying pan."

On Ray's third cast, his spinner stopped dead in the water, and the rod jerked in his hand. With the excitement of a child standing in front of the Christmas tree, he shouted, "I've got one. I think I got one."

Al heard Larry chuckling as he got his line in and went over to Ray. The fish was moving Ray's line up and down the river. Al tried to encourage Ray, "Keep the rod tip up, and don't let him get into the logs. Keep him close and reel him in."

Ray moved the fish out of the pool and into an area where he had better footing. About a minute later, which must have seemed like an hour to Ray, Al slipped the net under Ray's first speck.

"Hey Larry," Ray exclaimed, "how many you got? Mine is a monster. My, this is a beautiful fish!"

"Good job," Larry said back. "Now you have to measure him. If he's over eighteen inches, put him back. Make sure you wet your hands before taking him out of the net. Now, my friend, catch a few that we can eat."

As Ray held the net, Al wet his hands and slipped them around the speck. Holding the fish, Ray pulled from his pocket a fabric tape measure. Placing the end on the tip of the tail, the fish measured a perfect nineteen inches. Looking up at Ray, Al said, "Looks like we have to let him go."

The fish was glistening in the early sun; his sides were a

dark blue with yellow-gold circles and a golden underside. The speck was a beautiful specimen of creative splendor.

They continued fishing in the deep pool for another hour. Sensing their luck was running out, they decided to move upstream past Larry. The footpath took them around a clump of cedars and into another clearing. Now they were about thirty yards upstream from Larry. As they prepared to cast, they heard Larry laugh and shout out, "Got you, you river runnin' bandit! I got you real good!" As he laughed, he was a sight, pipe clenched in the side of his mouth, talking and laughing at the fish. They watched as he worked the fish into the shallows on the river's edge.

As Larry pulled his net down from his back, Al and Ray were shocked at the size of the fish. A silvery and pink trout, looking every bit of twenty inches, filled the handmade net. Larry trumpeted out to his friends, the trees, and everything that was around, "A native rainbow, what a beautiful fish, she's just under twenty inches." As gentle as a mother with her newborn, Larry wet his hands, and with the forceps hanging from his vest, he took out the hook and released the silver and pink bullet.

Al cast his spinner into the headwater of the pool. Allowing it to drift to the bottom, he raised the rod tip and began his retrieve. Within a second, the rod tip bounced and then bent almost to the water. The fish on the end had no intention of letting go. Almost ripping the rod from Al's hands, the swimming bullet headed downstream. The power of the fish propelled it past Ray and almost to the end of the pool before Al regained control.

Al's words were filled with shock. "You better get Larry," he said.

Ray got his line out of the way and gave a loud shout to

Larry, "Larry, hey Larry, you better get over here. Al's got a real trophy on the line."

Larry understood and shouted back, "I'll be there in a second. Tell him to keep the rod tip high and don't let the fish get into the flats. He'll never keep up with him if he gets to shallow water."

Ray could hear Larry moving through the cedars with his waders rubbing and swishing against the branches. As Larry neared the clearing, Al was knee-deep in the water, near the up-stream section of the pool. The fish made a run for the far end, and when he did, he came near the surface. Both Larry and Ray watched the flashing blue and gold giant rip past them. Larry was hollering at the top of his lungs, "Hold on, hold on, you got you a giant. Keep that rod tip up. Man alive, you got a real trophy on."

The rod tip was almost bent in half as the fish ripped out more line. Al was trying to regain control of the fish when it darted towards him. As Al tried to reel in the slack line, the ex-perienced trout changed directions. With a snap, the line went limp. Ray stood still with his mouth open. Al was motionless too as he held the rod with the empty line floating on the top of the water in the breeze.

Ray asked Al, "What happened? Where did your spinner go?"

The three men just stood there in silence. Al was trying to catch his breath; Larry looked at the two men in disbelief. In a moment, Larry was grinning from ear to ear. "That's what specks are all about, boys. They tease you, and then they beat the snot out of you and leave you with your mouth hanging open."

Larry, walking away from Ray and Al, said, "I'm going back to Old Gettem-Up. If we're going to eat, and I intend to, I'm going to have to catch us some fish for the pan." I'm gonna change my method of attack and get us fish."

Ray and Al watched as Larry stood at the vehicle for a couple of minutes.

Larry walked down the first path, and as he went, he was turning over rocks. Al watched him as he would turn over a rock, reach down, and grab something. Then, he'd put whatever it was into a small plastic box. As Al and Ray continued to fish upstream, they had no idea what Larry was up to. Within ten minutes, Larry announced to himself, "I got us four fresh ones for the skillet. It's time to get fixing lunch."

Larry called the other two and told them it was time to do some serious eating. As Al was walking up the trail from the river, Larry said, "Go get the wooden crates from the back of Old Gettem-Up."

Larry had found an old firepit and went about cleaning it out. He pulled the stones out from around the circle and then arranged them into a rectangle, about two feet long and a foot wide. When Al brought the two crates and set them down, Larry asked, "Would you go find a few old pine cones and a couple of handfuls of pine needles?"

As Ray walked up to the firepit, Larry said, "Hey, Ray, how about getting us some widow-sticks?"

Ray looked puzzled and said, "Alright, Mr. Fisherman, we might be greenhorns when it comes to fishing up here but don't treat us like we're stupid. What the hell is a widow stick?"

Larry must have sensed Ray's sarcastic tone and apologized. I'm sorry," he said, "widow sticks are the dry pine branches and twigs near the bottom of the tree. It's an old term that meant even an old widow could find dry wood for a fire."

Larry struck the blue-tip match on a stone and put it into the pile of pine needles. As the dry needles flamed up, he added the pine cones, and within a minute the widow sticks. As Ray and Al went scouting for some bigger pieces of firewood, Larry took out the contents of the wooden crates. The first crate had two cast iron frying pans, a wrought iron cook grate, a piece of iron shaped like a Z with a slight arc on the top, an old camp coffee pot, and a brown paper bag. The second crate contained a small container of cooking grease, two plastic containers with cornmeal and flour, salt, pepper, old enameled plates, cups, forks, can of coffee, and a small thermos.

When Ray and Al returned, Larry built up the fire and went about preparing the trout. He said to Al, "Take the coffee pot down to the river and fill it up. While you're down there, give the redskins a quick wash, they're in the bag."

A couple minutes later when Al got back to the fire, he asked Larry, "Do you want them sliced or chunked?"

Larry's response was a jab, "I don't know how you boys do it down below, but up here we slice 'em so they get really crispy on the edges and soft in the center. It takes a hot skillet and a good touch. But before you mess with them reds, get the coffee going. We aren't about to eat without coffee. Over there is the can of coffee and a cup. Put two cups of coffee in the basket, and it should be perfect."

After getting the coffee started, Al went about slicing the redskins. Larry set the frying pans on the cooking grate, plopping in a couple of big spoons of shortening in each one. While they heated up, he mixed flour and cornmeal in one of the plastic containers. He poured heavy cream from the thermos into the other one. With the mixes ready, he prodded Al, "Better get a move on, the redskins take longer than the fish."

The sliced redskins sizzled and popped as they hit the hot grease. After a minute, Larry rained down salt and pepper on the potatoes and moved them down the grate to where the fire

158

was piled high with embers. With a supply of dry wood close by, he added a few more pieces to the other end.

After another five minutes, he used the sleeve of his sweatshirt to hold the handle of the redskin skillet. With an aluminum pancake turner, he flipped the potatoes and set them aside. He announced, "Now, those babies will be done just as the trout are ready to jump out of the pan and onto our plates." With his grandiose announcement complete, he took the trout, first dipping each into the cream and then into the flour and cornmeal mix. Each of the beautiful trout soon yielded themselves as a pleasant aroma to the cast-iron skillet.

Larry hovered over the fire tending the redskins and trout, and the coffee began to perk. After a minute of hard perking, with a bit boiling out of the spout, he set the pot back from the embers.

"What a time," he announced, "Fish, redskins, and coffee— all done at the right time. My friends, the basics of living don't get much simpler, and the blessings of living don't get much better."

Ray chimed in, "Very eloquent, Mr. Mayor. Sounds like a campaign speech."

Larry, with his pipe still in his mouth, bent over the fire, turned his head to Ray and said, "Man alive, a guy can't even make remarks about eating fish and drinking coffee with friends without getting accused of political pandering."

Larry hollered over at Al and told him to drop the tailgate on Old Gettem-Up and get the plates and cups ready. Al got the plates ready and brought them over to the fire, setting them on the crate.

Larry announced, "The best a man can eat will be ready in a minute." Then he turned over the redskins and set the pan back. He turned over the trout and mumbled to himself something about life, the river, and food. The rest, neither of the men understood.

"Grab a plate and enjoy," Larry announced.

Ray and Al had not been paying really close attention to the master chef as he utilized his culinary genius over the fire. When Al, plate in hand, was getting ready for his trout, his surprise was evident. "What in the world did you do?" he asked. "They still have the heads on. How we supposed to eat fish that are still looking at us?"

Larry started to laugh so hard he choked and had to take his pipe out of his mouth. "They may be staring, but they ain't seeing. That's the way we serve trout up here. You're respecting his contribution to your life when you have to look him in the eye."

By this time Ray was laughing so hard he started to cough. Between the laughing and coughing, tears were running down Ray's cheeks. He said, almost choking, "I guess if it were up to a vote, the eyes would have it." In a second all three men were laughing at the trout and their sightless stare.

The staring trout, however, didn't put a damper on the men's appetite. Three of the four trout were consumed quickly by men who seemed as though they had been starved. The redskins were divided three ways. Ray made sure the division was fair. The only sound, apart from a fork on a tin-enameled plate, was the sound of the river. The last fish was split in two as Larry gave in to the pleading of his friends. His smile over the food and his new friends seemed to satisfy him.

After they ate, the coffee was passed around for a second time. As Al and Ray sat on the tailgate, Larry went about cleaning up. The seasoned cast iron frying pans only needed to be wiped out with a cloth, or in Larry's case, a handful of ferns scrunched into a ball. According to Larry, any cook worth their salt never used a wet cloth on cast iron. In a matter of minutes the cleanup was done, and Larry put more wood on the fire and moved the old smudged coffee pot closer.

The men sat in silence, listening to the river and the breeze that started moving through the surrounding pines. The breeze coming down from the pines made the rising smoke swirl in a circle. The three men found themselves enveloped in a strange intimacy. The combination of cool breeze, bright sunlight, wood smoke, coffee, and shared laughter contributed to their earthy bond.

Larry finally broke into the orchestra of water and wind. "So, tell me, Al, Ray says you have had quite an eventful past. Everything from living on the street to a come-to-Jesus mission. What happened to you?"

Al was unsure at Larry's questioning. He didn't know at first if Larry were sincere or just creating a scene in which to mock him. Al responded, "Do you want to know? Do you really want to know what my life has been like, or are you giving me some fake interest?"

Larry felt a bit offended at Al's comment and shifted his position to look straight at Al. He replied, "In all sincerity, I would like to know."

Al began, "Okay, how much do you know? Did Ray tell you about the attack and my recovery?"

"Ray told me you had almost been killed and spent a few weeks in the hospital. And then you were working an office in northern Virginia."

Al said, "Well, let me pick it up from there. While covering a D.C. story, I met Sarah, who knocked my socks off. What a sight she was at the D.C. mall—prairie skirt, peasant blouse, and long brown hair. We fell in love, and she had me acting like an idiot at times. Her smile was my sunlight, and she always smelled like lilacs. She could brighten up my worst day. I felt that she was a person I could spend my life with."

Al shifted his position and paused for a minute before he continued, "She made a decision that broke my heart, broke a very deep part of me. We were expecting a child, and she ended the pregnancy. I went off the deep end. She moved west with friends, and I moved to Kentucky, Kentucky Bourbon. I was drinking myself into a state where I wouldn't have to feel, sense, or exist. I walked away from my job, my place, and ended on the street."

Al showed his discomfort by moving around again. Ray encouraged him, "Go on."

Nodding at his friend, Al said, "I sold my car so I could drink, and when that money was gone, I was in an alley. A young kid came out the back door of a coffee shop, gave me a cup of coffee, and told me about a street mission down the road. I made it to Agape Station, and that's where I met Reverend and Mrs. Williams. After being there a while, I learned it was their son who was next to me during the attack. He told his parents I saved his life."

It was evident to Al that Larry was sincere and really interested in his story so he went on, "When I landed on the streets, I wanted to die. I didn't have the guts to pull a trigger; the bottle would be much slower and a more painful way."

Ray interrupted Al, "I think you need to tell him about the headaches and nightmares."

Nodding, Al began again, "Guilt was eating me alive, and I had no idea how to deal with it. It was like a noose around my neck, just barely getting tighter each day. Yeah, I had dreams, the most horrible nightmares imaginable. They were always the same scenes, noises, and smells, over and over—a little girl vanishing in a red mist right in front of my eyes. And then I started hearing babies crying in the night. I couldn't control any of it. I was sure I was going nuts."

Larry moved to the fire and got the coffee pot. He refilled their cups and put the pot silently to the back of the iron grate. As he sat back down, he said to Al, "If you can, I'd like to hear more."

Al said, "Let me get back to finding Agape Station. I went to the mission because I was hungry, dirty, and had no place to sleep. I didn't just find food and a place to sleep there. The people at Agape Station were genuine, genuine in their faith and desire to care for people.

"One evening I was listening to a marine who was blinded in combat. He sang and talked about praising God because now he could really see what was important in life. He said that people have a choice in life to live for themselves or live for God. He told me that after his blindness, he was mad at the world and God. He said he asked Jesus Christ into his life and to remove his bitterness and anger. And, I'm here to tell you he was one of the most remarkable men I have ever met."

Larry said, "Tell me about the reverend and his wife."

Al grinned and said, "It's easy to talk about them. First, they told me that I saved their son's life in the bunker. The blast hit me and my camera and not their son, who was trying to get behind me to reach the little girl. He must have been an exceptional young man. Agape Station was his idea, and later when he was killed, the Williams' decided to leave a large church and begin the mission.

"I'm here to tell you this. Those two people demonstrated Christianity to me. They took me in and loved me. Our relationship was as close as a son with parents. One evening, I had come to the point where I knew I needed to find peace in my heart. I asked God, if He was real and cared about me, to forgive me of my sins and change my life. That evening I understood that Jesus gave his life for me, that he died for the forgiveness of all people, and I wanted to be included."

Larry asked, "Did the nightmares stop after you found God? I guess that's how I would ask, you found God, right? And did the dreams stop?"

Al responded, "No, the dreams haven't stopped. But I have peace in my heart, and I deal with the guilt when it tries to tear me down. I don't know why that little girl had to die. I don't know why Williams was saved only to be killed later. There are so many things I don't know, and that's alright. I understand more today, and I will understand even more later. You see, I needed to stop asking questions and seek peace within my heart. I stopped demanding answers and found peace."

For a moment the men sat in silence and then Ray spoke up, "Alright, I guess it's time to go. I have a newspaper to run, and there's work to do."

Larry and Al agreed, and Larry moved the pot off the cooking grate and dumped the remainder of the coffee over the hot embers. They hissed and spat for a second, and then Larry headed to the river to get some more water. Al put the pans and other stuff back into the wooden crates and carried them over to Old Gettem-Up, setting them on the tailgate. When Larry was done dousing the fire, he moved the charred pieces apart from each other and kicked dirt on them. With the coffee pot away, the crates were put in the back, and the tailgate shut.

The three fishermen traveled back to town without any conversation for a combination of reflection and tiredness had settled on them. The only noise seemed to come from Old Gettem-Up. The all-season tires whined on the asphalt, and the manual transmission objected to every change of gears. As they got close to town, Larry broke the silence and told his new friends that they would have to do it again before the weather changed. He pulled up in front of Ray's place and dropped them off, and then he pointed Old Gettem-Up down the road.

As Al and Ray started to separate, Al said, "That was a great time, and I hope we get to do it again. Right now, I'm going in to shower; I smell like smoke."

Ray responded, "Yeah, it was a great time. Old Larry, man, he can talk your arm off. But I have to hand it to him that was the best lunch I think I've ever had. I hope the night is quiet; I don't feel much like running anywhere tonight."

Al said, "Well, listen, if you get a call tonight, let me know, and I'll handle it for ya."

"Thanks, I just might let you do that," Ray said.

15

Tragedy Strikes

As the images of the fishing trip clung to Al, the scent of wood smoke went down the shower drain. While he was sitting in his chair in the cabin, his mind was fixed on spending time with Ray and now a new friend, Larry. His mind went back to the conversation around the fire. *God has been good to me,* he thought. A wave of emotion began deep in his heart. He was watching Sarah, eating pizza with shrimp and wild mushrooms and laughing while she tried to catch a shrimp before it fell out of her mouth.

In seconds tears were cascading down his cheeks. As Sarah's image left, Aunt Bee took her place. He thought of her love and the way she had taken care of him. He thought, *I never took the time to talk to her about the pain of what happened.* The last image was that of Mrs. Williams. He could hear her praying and weeping over Sarah. With his eyes still wet, he fell asleep.

He woke up on the floor with the sadistic strobe lights flashing across his eyes. He struggled on his hands and knees to the side of the bed. Exhausted and soaked with sweat, he crawled onto his bed. The lights continued their demonic rhythm as the pain descended, crushing his skull like a vice. He covered his head with his pillow, and the intense pain caused him to thrash around. Little moans escaped from under the pillow.

Now with nausea rising up in his throat, he knew he had only moments to try to get to the bathroom. He took one step and fell against the side of his bed, landing between the bed and the front window. Crawling to the bathroom, he just made it to the toilet as a flash of light and a shot of white hot pain pushed the contents of his stomach into the bowl.

Al showed up at the office after ten the next morning. Saturday at the office meant following up on advertising, returning phone calls, and making sure the press was ready for Monday and Tuesday. Al took his time in the back room making sure the paper stock was in order, and his printing partners were well oiled and clean.

Walking to the diner, he spotted Jimmy. Al really couldn't put a finger on why he liked Jimmy so much. Maybe it was the simple way he looked at life and got excited about the everyday stuff. He marveled at times how Jimmy would get excited over a bottle of soda or a piece of pie. Al liked the happy spirit Jimmy had.

He took the stool next to Jimmy and placed his hand on Jimmy's shoulder. "How are you today, Jimmy?" he asked.

Jimmy shot off the stool, taking his fatigue hat off in the air and grabbed a hold on Al's hand. "Why Al," he said, "it sure is nice to see you. So you and the mayor of our distinguished town went out fishing. That's what I hear, is it true? Did he take you up to the river? Did he take you in Old Gettem-Up?"

"Jimmy," Al said, "just slow down, and I'll tell you all about it."

"Oh man, I did it again. I get so excited about stuff; I'm real sorry, really I am," Jimmy said in his panicked tone.

Al took Jimmy by the hand and made him sit on the stool.

Over the next hour, Al took turns trying to eat his meatloaf, green beans, and mashed potatoes and telling Jimmy all about the fishing trip. When Al got to the point in the story about the shore lunch, Jimmy started all over.

Standing up from his stool, he said to Al, "So tell me about the lunch. Did you have Larry's special trout recipe? Did he have the redskins? I've heard of his cookin' and the way he fries the fish and the redskins. Never been with him. Never had his shore lunch. Never had it, but someday I might."

The sincerity and excitement in Jimmy's voice amazed Al. Something as simple as eating fish and potatoes with friends could be so exciting to Jimmy. Al told himself that he would try to make sure Jimmy had the chance to have a shore lunch with Larry.

Al stopped at the office and found it locked. He wanted to check with Ray about the next week's after-hours schedule. He walked to Al and Gracie's house, and as usual knocked on the back door before walking in.

Standing in the kitchen, he hollered, "Hey Ray, it's me. Where are you?"

Before he could move a step, Gracie's voice answered, "We're in the living room, come on in."

Al went into the living room and found Gracie standing next to Ray. He was sitting in his overstuffed chair and looked pale.

"What's up?" Al asked.

Ray piped up, "Nothing much. She's just too worried about me, that's all."

Al asked, "Does she have a reason to be worried? You don't look very good."

Gracie spoke up, "He's not well; the heart doctor told him last year that he needed to take better care of himself. He told Ray to stop smoking and to lose weight. Has he quit smoking? No, he hasn't. Has he lost weight? No, he hasn't."

Al said, "I'll check with you later, Ray. I was just thinking about the rotation for this week."

Back in his cabin, Al got comfortable in his chair and reached for his Bible. He was trying to have a time each day when he would read scripture. He had started reading the gospel of John and always asked God to help him understand what he was reading.

He had sensed in his heart that when he prayed at Agape Station, he was born again. He couldn't give a good explanation of what it meant, but he knew he was. He trusted in Jesus to take his sin away and give him a new purpose. He sensed that the people that came across his path were there for a reason. A few minutes later he was asleep in his chair.

On Sunday morning Al was up early and having coffee at the diner. He had tried to find a church in town when he first came. He wasn't excited about the first two he had visited. The first church was too formal and starchy for him. He didn't really like the parts where everybody repeated specific prayers and readings. He guessed that Reverend Williams and his style made a big impression on the way he thought church should be.

The second church was less formal, and the people were very friendly. Al liked the excitement of the service and the singing, but the preaching was very strict. The sermon on that Sunday was about being separated from the world and how the church should look different from the world, including the way they dressed and wore their hair.

He had noticed when he delivered the papers, that north out of town there was a small church. When he asked Chuck about the little church, he told him that the building used to be a bakery and had closed down a few years back. He said the pastor was a man by the name of Henry, who was a likable fellow and a good handyman too.

Al said to Chuck, "You know that little church you told me about, I'm going there this morning." With that said, he put enough cash on the counter to cover his bill and headed for the door. He had a good feeling that he was going to the right church.

The walk from the diner to the little church took Al almost fifteen minutes. As he neared the church, he realized that he had never really read their sign. It was simple and to the point, "Christian Fellowship—Everyone is Welcome." He pulled the old wooden door open and went in. An aisle ran up the middle of the room and ended near the front where there was an old wooden table. The table was covered in a white crocheted cloth with a vase of flowers in the middle. On each side of the aisle were seven or eight rows of chairs and six chairs per row.

After Al looked around the tiny chapel, an elderly man approached him. Al extended his hand and said, "Hello, I'm Al."

The greeter introduced himself, "Greetings, brother, I'm Tom." Al's instant impression of Tom was of a man as strong as his vice-like grip.

"So Tom, tell me what you do in town."

"I'm a woodcutter for the mill, been cutting for some time now. What you doing in town?"

Al answered, "I work down at the paper. I've been there for a few weeks now."

Tom was dressed in a solid color blue shirt and old grey dress slacks. His white socks were conspicuous, due to his pants being way too short. His black dress shoes must have just been polished as Al watched him buff the top of each shoe by rubbing it on the back of his opposite calf.

Al took a seat about half way up the room. He noticed on the wall behind the pulpit a popular rendition of Jesus. He smiled as he noted that Jesus had long brown hair and a beard.

His facial features caused him to look more Anglo than Jewish, making Al wonder what Jesus really looked like.

As he sat on the folding chair, a few more people came into the chapel. A middle-aged couple sat behind him. They were plainly dressed and didn't move much in their seats. Within ten minutes, the room was about halfway full. Al looked around and observed that the people present represented a good mix of the town. A few people were well dressed, and there was a mix of singles and couples gathered.

At 10:00 a.m. a man sitting in the front row took his place behind the pulpit. "I greet you in the name of the Lord," he said. "I'm Pastor Henry Jones. It is good to see everyone this morning." Just after his announcement, the piano player started playing an old hymn, "We Gather Together to Ask the Lord's Blessing." With no cue, the people started singing.

When they finished singing, Pastor Henry said, "Now it's time to get up and greet your friends and welcome our visitors." The folks started walking around, some shaking hands, some holding the shoulder of the other and smiling. In no time at all a few people had approached Al and welcomed him. He recognized a few of them as customers of the paper, including the owner of the hardware store.

Almost on cue, the congregation began sitting back down. Al was just about in his seat when the couple behind him stirred a bit. Looking beyond them, he noticed Jimmy sheepishly walking up the aisle with his cap in his hand. Al made eye contact with him and pointed to the empty seat next to him.

As soon as the pastor pronounced the benediction, Jimmy was on his feet. The end of the service must have been the switch that turned Jimmy on.

"Well, what do ya know? Al, I didn't know you were coming to my church this morning. I'm so glad you came. Have you met the pastor? Have you met many of the folks here? How come you didn't tell me you were coming here this morning? I would have met ya here if you'd only told me. Man, I'm glad to see you this morning."

Jimmy was still in high gear when the pastor walked towards them. He came up behind Jimmy and put his hand on his shoulder. Jimmy turned with a start and in an instant grabbed the pastor's hand, shaking it as fast as he could.

"Pastor Hank," Jimmy said, "this is my good friend Al. I brought him up to town when he first came here. He's a newspaperman and went fishing with Larry."

Pastor Hank thanked Jimmy for the introduction.

Al said to the pastor, "I'm glad I came this morning. I really got a lot from the service. Your message on 'Acceptance and Movement' really made me think."

"Great," the pastor said, "maybe someday we can get together for coffee."

Al and Jimmy walked about two blocks away from the chapel when Jimmy said, "This is where I turn. I have a little place just down the street, near the end of the block. Someday you're gonna have to come and see my place."

Al answered, "I'd like that Jimmy. Thanks and have a good afternoon."

Before heading back to his cabin, Al stopped by Ray and Gracie's place. Going in the back door, he found Gracie in the kitchen just getting ready to start a pot of coffee.

"How is he today?" Al asked.

"He looks better, but I'm not sure if he feels any better. Not ever sure he's telling me the truth."

Al asked, "Where is he?"

"Pretty sure he's in the living room."

Al went into the living room and found Ray asleep in his

chair. He walked quietly back into the kitchen and informed Gracie that he was sleeping.

She said, "Lot a good another pot of coffee is going to do. I guess I'll let him sleep."

Al spoke up, "Make the pot anyway, I'll drink a cup with you."

Gracie finished getting the pot ready and plugged it in.

The two sat at the dining room table as Ray snoozed in his chair. Gracie told Al how concerned she was about Ray's heart and that he needed to see a doctor and listen to some advice.

As the two drank their coffee, Al asked Gracie a question. "What do you really need me for? The paper can't afford me. The two of you seem to have been doing alright without me."

Gracie responded to his question, "I know we were doing alright. And, yes we could have managed by ourselves. But when Ray told me about you and the relationship you had with him, something inside, call it woman's intuition, call it whatever, kept telling me that you should be here to help. That's why I kept after Ray; I just knew we would need you here."

"Gracie," asked Al, "do you believe in God?"

Surprised by the question, Gracie hesitated before she said, "I used to. As a child, I grew up in Sunday school and attended services with my mom. Later on, I stopped."

Al asked, "Why did you stop going?"

Gracie hesitated again. "My mom died of cancer when I was fourteen. Then my dad started drinking real bad. I guess I buried my faith with my mom."

Al sensed that there was pain in Gracie's heart. He said, "I watched you smile a bit when I asked you if you believe in God. If you don't mind me asking, what was the smile all about?"

This time her smile was not slight. She said to Al, "I smiled because I remember going to Sunday school, singing all of the choruses, and listening to the stories from the Bible. That time with my mom and doing those things at church was important to me."

Al said, "I see this is painful."

Gracie continued, "Even when my mother was dying, and I was mad at God, it was those choruses and stories that brought me peace. Yes, I was mad at God. I thought he took my mother from me. I will always remember the times I was alone and crying. It was the Sunday school songs that helped me. Does it sound strange that I could be mad at God and still find comfort in singing 'Jesus Loves Me'?"

Al and Gracie finished the pot of coffee. On his way out the back door, Al said, "Remind Ray that I'm covering the after hour calls."

Al had a new understanding of Gracie and the road she had traveled. Back in his cabin he took off his shoes and sat down. After a moment he pulled the chair up closer to the bed and put his feet up. As he sat there, he began thinking about the simple message from the pastor a few hours earlier. He had spoken of God's acceptance of us just the way we are and that God didn't demand that we change before we came to him.

The other part of the pastor's message was on "Movement." He had explained that after we come to God and Jesus is a part of our life, he expects us to change. But God doesn't expect us to do it on our own. The Holy Spirit, the pastor said, is the power of God in the life of his children and his church. It is the power of God that changes us. Our movement towards God and godliness should continue until we die.

Al reminded himself that the message was true. God had accepted him, a street drunk filled with pain and bad memories. But God didn't stop there. It was God that had urged him on, bringing him to Salmon Stream Crossing.

That night Al felt a sense of contentment. He knew he was in the right place and felt at peace. And what is not to like about working for a newspaper, living in a beautiful area, and having friends? As he went to bed that night, he felt his life was good. He turned down the table lamp and drifted off to sleep.

The next morning he was up at dawn and heading to the diner for coffee and toast. He was feeling very positive and looking forward to a busy Monday. All the copy would have to be checked and the press ready to run. Chuck brought him his toast and asked if he had seen Ray yet.

Al asked, "Why, what's up?"

Chuck said, "Nothin' much. He was in last night, must have been late, made a small pot of coffee, that's all."

"That seems strange," Al said. "Must have been late and didn't want to bother Gracie about the coffee."

Al finished his toast and coffee and went next door to the office. The front door was unlocked so he went in. He hollered for Ray, but there was no answer. He hollered again, "Hey Ray, you in the back?" Again, no response.

When he walked around the antique counter, his eyes first fell on Ray's black shoes and white socks. Ray was on the floor between his chair and desk. Al ran around the desk and stood over his friend. It was evident that Ray was dead. A sense of confusion started to overtake Al. *What should I do? Who should I call? What about Gracie?* he thought. Clarity began to replace the confusion. He headed out the front door, locking it behind him.

Chuck must have known something was wrong when Al burst in the front door. "It's Ray," Al said, "I just found him; he's dead. Call Larry and get him over here and call Bill and see if he's anywhere near here. Tell them what has happened, and I need them at the office. I'm gonna have to go and tell Gracie. Dear God, how am I gonna do that?"

Chuck was on the phone as Al went out the door and headed back to the office. Standing at the old counter, he put his elbows on the glass top and held his head in his hands and whispered, "Lord, I need your help. Help me support Gracie. Help me to be strong for her. Lord, I have no idea about Ray and you, please be merciful."

Within minutes Larry was standing next to Al inside the office. As they stood there, Chuck came in the door and told them that Bill was on patrol, and it would take him about ten minutes to get to town. Bill also said that nobody should touch the body. The three men walked around the desk and looked down at their friend.

Al said, "He wasn't well a couple of days ago. He looked terrible, and Gracie was trying to get him to the doctor. Yesterday he was doing better and sleeping in his chair when I went over."

Larry spoke up, "Has anybody been to the house? Somebody is gonna have to go and talk with Gracie."

Al said, "I'm going to go over in a few minutes, probably should wait for Bill to get here."

The three men walked back to the front area of the office and stood in silence.

Larry's next statement shocked Al. "Al," he said, "I think you should say a prayer. We ought to pray for Gracie. This is gonna be really hard for her. Would you?"

The three men bowed their heads, and Al prayed for Gracie and then he prayed for the three of them that they might be faithful friends and support Gracie and each other. When Al finished his prayer, Chuck and Larry turned away from Al and each other, their tears evidence of their sincerity.

Bill pulled up in front of the office, and as he came in the front door, he took off his Smokey hat. He asked Al where Ray was, and the four men walked around the desk.

Bill said, "I placed a call to Doc Sam, he should be here in a couple of minutes. Once he pronounces, then we can move the body. Has anybody talked to his wife?"

Al responded, "No, I'm gonna go over in a couple of minutes. I was waiting until you got here."

Bill said, "Well you better go, in this small town folks are already on the phone asking about my car. Even this early in the morning, you'd be surprised to know how many calls are being made. I'll bet my switchboard is lighting up."

16

Gracie Deals with Tragedy

Bill and Chuck stayed in the office while Larry and Al walked the short distance to the house. Al knocked and then went in the back door to the kitchen. Gracie was standing at the sink in her robe and turned when she heard the knock. She was about to ask Al if he wanted coffee when she noticed Larry standing in the doorway.

"Well, good morning, Mr. Mayor, what brings you around so early in the morning? Not another fishing trip is it? Not on a busy Monday morning?"

"Gracie," Al said, "I found Ray this morning in the office."

"Oh I know," she said, "he left early and said he had a piece to work on, normal for Ray. You know how he is."

Al said, "No, Gracie, you don't understand. I found Ray's body this morning. He died."

Gracie collapsed onto the floor, hitting her arms on the kitchen counter.

Al and Larry helped Gracie get up and over to a dining room chair.

"How can that be?" Gracie asked. "He was feeling better. He gave me a kiss going out the door and told me he would see me in a couple of hours." Her voice trailed off into silence.

Larry spoke up, "Bill is next door with Ray. He called Doc Sam, and he'll be here any minute. I know this is gonna be hard.

But after Doc Sam is done, I'll tell Al, and the two of you will have some calls to make."

Larry went out the back door and over to the office. As he rounded the corner, Chuck was coming out the front door and said, "Doc Sam is in with Ray, I'm gonna go make some coffee. Expect we'll be drinking it this morning."

Larry went into the office area and found Doc Sam bent over Ray's body. He had laid his clipboard on the desk and looked up at Bill. He said, "I expect, given his size and the number of cigarette butts in his ashtray, he died of a massive heart attack. I didn't find any signs of foul play. There are no signs of a seizure. I expect, if I did an autopsy, I'd find a destroyed heart."

Bill responded, "I don't see any need for an autopsy. He had a bad ticker for some time. Once you finish your paperwork, I'm gonna let his wife, Gracie, and Al make the arrangements."

Al phoned the Rose Family Funeral Home and talked with Steven Rose. He explained what happened and that he wanted them to come and take Ray back to their funeral parlor and to call back when he and Gracie should come down to make the arrangements. Al sat with Gracie in the living room, and he noticed her looking at Ray's chair. It was like she expected him to come back in the room any moment.

She spoke up, "You know Al, Ray though the world of you. It was much different than a co-worker or boss kind of thing. When he told me about you almost getting killed and then these past months, I saw how he really cared about you. I'm glad you're here. Like I told you before, I think Ray knew this day was coming. He loved what he did. He loved the paper business. He loved his freedom, and he loved eating and drinking and smoking. He loved the things in life that probably killed him. You know I was always after him about the smoking and losing weight. But he was happy, and I guess that I'm glad he was happy."

Late in the afternoon, Gracie's phone rang and Al answered it. A moment later he hung up.

"Gracie," Al said, "that was Steven Rose. He said we could come down anytime and meet with him. I told him it would be a little while."

Gracie was looking at Ray's chair in the living room. Al's words startled her, and she asked, "What was that, Al? I didn't hear you."

Thirty minutes later, Al held Gracie by the arm as they walked into the Rose Funeral Home. Steven met them at the front door. He led them down a hall with deep crimson carpet and cream-colored walls. On the walls, softly illuminated, were the portraits of the Rose patriarchs who started the business. They looked very somber in their black suits, white shirts, and black ties.

Once they were seated, Steven asked, "Gracie, how many death certificates do you think you'll need?"

Her voice shook, "Death certificates, why, I don't really know how many I need."

Al spoke up, "Steven, can I get back to you about the number?"

"Sure," Steven said, "Can we discuss what kind of service you want for Ray? Do you have a pastor that we should contact?"

Gracie said, "No, no, I don't have a church. I don't really know what kind of service I should have."

Steven sensed her discomfort and asked her if she would mind if he asked a pastor friend of his to conduct the service. She looked at Al, and he nodded in agreement that it would be okay.

Steven suggested to Gracie and Al, "Let's go over to the display room. Please take your time. I understand how difficult this can be. In front of each casket is a card that indicates the total cost of the casket and all of our services."

Crossing the threshold into the display room, Gracie hesitated and grabbed Al's arm. Gracie whispered, "Al, I don't know if I can do this."

"Lord, help me," Al whispered. Bending down closer to Gracie, Al said, "Let's just take this one step at a time. Just look around and pick out the one that you think is nice for Ray."

A few steps away Gracie noticed a casket that was bronze in color. "I want Ray to have this one. Al, please take me home." With that said, she simply turned around and walked to the door. On the way out, Al asked Steven to call him later about the times for visitation and the service.

Steven said, "I understand, I'll call you later in the afternoon."

When Steven called, they discussed the details of the printed obituary. Then Steven asked, "Al, how does Gracie want Ray dressed?

Al said, "I'm not gonna ask her about dressing Ray. I can tell you this: Ray never wore a suit, or for that matter, he almost never wore a sport coat. He wore long-sleeved white shirts with the sleeves rolled up. A Bic ink pen was always in his pocket with his cigarettes, and a black or blue tie was always loose at his open collar. That's Ray, and that's what Gracie would want as well."

Two days later the chapel at the funeral home was filled, and the staff had to bring in extra chairs. Al and Gracie sat on large armchairs in front of the chapel and casket. To their left, the organist played soft and somewhat mournful selections. Al wished he would have told Steven not to have such sad and moody music. Ray liked his life, and he lived it the way he wanted. Without a doubt, a popular rendition of "I Did It My Way" would have been more to Ray's liking.

After a few minutes, the organist finished the opening music. It was quiet for a moment, and then Al and Gracie sensed the gathering shift their focus to the back. As Al turned around, he recognized Pastor Henry, who was walking towards the front of the chapel. He paused for a moment in front of the casket and then approached the small pulpit.

At the pulpit Pastor Henry said, "Good afternoon. I'm Pastor Henry Johnson from Salmon Stream Community Church. It's an honor to be with you this afternoon. Al and Gracie, I pray you will find comfort today."

After a brief prayer, he read the official obituary detailing Ray's life. When Pastor Henry began reading the details of Ray and Gracie's wedding, Gracie reached over and took Al's hand. After the reading, the organist played "Amazing Grace." A few people behind Al and Gracie attempted to sing the verses of the great hymn.

After the scripture reading and another short prayer, Pastor Henry gave the congregation an opportunity to make a few remarks in honor of Ray. For a moment the silence was uncomfortable. Al stood in front of his chair, his feet under the front with his shins pressed against the front of the chair. In an unconscious way, he hoped the chair would provide some stability.

Al began, "The most important things I can say is that first, Ray was my friend. Some time ago he gave me an opportunity to write about humanity at its best and worst. Together we witnessed remarkable men and women care for each other, and all too often, die for each other."

Al shifted his feet and continued, "When I was seriously hurt, Ray was by my side. When I got back to the states, it was

Ray who helped me in my new position." Turning his gaze towards Gracie, he continued, "It was Ray and Gracie that thought enough of me to give me the chance to come up here. God had a plan for me, and it included Ray and Gracie. I am really honored to be their friends." When Al finished and sat down, his hands were shaking, and Gracie reached over and took his right hand.

Pastor Henry began his message. He read a Psalm and then a New Testament passage. He talked about life being like a vapor. The vapor appears and then disappears after a few seconds. He reminded everybody that life is short and how so many people want to know how much time on earth they are going to have. "Time on earth," he said, "is never the point. It is what we do with the days, weeks, months, and years we have."

At the end of the service, those attending paid their last respects by passing in front of the casket. Many stopped and gave Gracie a hug. Larry came to her and held both of her hands. As he began to speak to her, he got choked up. Gracie put her hands on his shoulders and hugged him for a moment. He left, and on his way out took Al's hand and just nodded. Bill came up next, dressed in his uniform. He embraced Gracie, shook Al's hand, and quickly left the room. As Al was turning to look at Gracie, he saw Jimmy.

Jimmy walked towards Al and Gracie, clenching his fatigue hat in both hands. He glanced up and made eye contact with Al and continued the rest of the way to the front, looking down at the floor. When he got close to the casket, he paused and knelt down at the altar. After a moment he stood and turned around to face Al and Gracie. A few tears were on his cheeks as he gave Gracie a hug. He turned to Al and said, "I was hoping that one day I would get to go fishin' with him."

After ten minutes or so, Al and Gracie were alone in the

chapel. The two stood quietly for some time. Al had his arm around Gracie, and she leaned her head against his shoulder. She spoke softly to Al, "I never thanked you for helping and talking to Steven about Ray. You know he hated wearing a suit. But he always had to have a clean, long sleeved white shirt. I used to get so mad at him. He'd come home, and the sleeves of his shirts would be so wrinkled! I swear, after a while I couldn't even iron the wrinkles out." Gracie chuckled and reached for Al's hand. Al and Gracie slowly moved to the casket, and Gracie bent down and placed her hands on the edge. Bending over, she placed a gentle kiss on Ray's forehead.

Al drove Gracie to the local veteran's hall on the edge of town. They were providing a luncheon for the family and friends after the funeral. When they came in the door, they were escorted to a table near the front of the hall. Larry, Bill, and Chuck were already there at the table. When Gracie got to the table, Bill pulled out a chair for her and when she was seated, the others followed. Pastor Henry said a prayer asking God to bless the food and the gathering and that the Holy Spirit would bring comfort and peace to Gracie.

The hall appeared to be filled to capacity. Time and time again, Gracie spoke to her friends at the table about being so overwhelmed at the town's outpouring of love.

Larry spoke up, "You know, Gracie, our little town is so much like all little towns. The people here work hard. Whether it is at the mill or out in the fields, they're hard workers. They're also fiercely independent; they love their freedom. The most important quality is that they love and care for each other. When somebody is suffering, the town gathers around them."

Not changing his gaze at Gracie he continued, "I can tell you that there have been many people in this town that reached out to care for their neighbor. Years back when the mill was in trouble, they had to lay off workers. The town's people rallied around their friends. That's what kind of town Salmon Stream Crossing is." When he stopped, he looked at Gracie, and she was smiling.

Bill chuckled and said, "Well, Mr. Mayor, sounds like it's time for re-election."

Al took Gracie back home after the luncheon. She said to Al that she was exhausted and needed rest. Al spent the next four hours getting the paper run completed. The stock was fed into the press, printed, and then cut. The final step was to run the papers through the folding machine. With the paper run complete, Al felt more at ease.

Finished at the paper, he walked through the front door of Chuck's place and found him sitting at the counter. He walked around Chuck and behind the counter found a cup and poured a cup of coffee. Sitting next to Chuck, the two shared a minute of quiet.

Al spoke up, "Gonna be kinda hard around here without him. Sure were a lot of folks at the funeral and the hall. I think Gracie is gonna be alright. It'll take time, but I think she's gonna be alright."

Chuck sat in silence, staring down into his cup. He seemed to be lost in thought and asked Al in a very soft voice, "Do you really believe all that stuff about heaven and seeing God? What about what the preacher said? Is Jesus the only way to go to heaven? Why can't people just be good loving folks and see God?"

"Wow, that's a lot of questions. I'm not a preacher or a scholar in the Bible. I can only tell you about me and what happened to me. I know that I was so messed up. It was in believing that Jesus gave his life for me that brought me peace. I can't speak for anybody else, but it was Jesus Christ that saved my life."

Al headed to the cabin as splintering sunlight fought through the pines. Almost at his door, he remembered he had intended to check in on Gracie. He turned around and in just a few seconds was knocking on her back door. As he walked in, he wondered if he was doing the right thing by walking in on Gracie. He didn't want to barge in on her privacy. He went into the kitchen and called out.

Gracie called out from the living room, "I'm in here, Al, come on in."

Al found her sitting on Ray's recliner, a gentle smile on her face. "I can smell him sitting here, his cigarettes, and his aftershave. It's kind of comforting to me. So tell me, did you get the run finished? I should have been over to help, but I guess I needed the rest. You know, Al, you and I are gonna have to sit down pretty soon and talk about all of this. I mean the paper, you, and me, what we should do."

Al replied, "There will be plenty of time for that. Let's just get through the next little while together."

17

Al, Gracie, and the Paper

Al tried to relax in his chair, his legs resting on his bed. Within minutes of picking up his Bible, he was sleeping. Sometime over the next few hours, his Bible fell from his lap and he slipped into bed. He slept for a solid nine hours and awoke to a rapping on his door. He opened the door to find Larry, pipe in his mouth.

"Come on in," Al said, "what's up?"

Larry responded, "Just checking to see how you're doing. I know these past days have been hard." Larry came in and sat on the chair.

"I'm doing alright," Al said. "I slept well. Have you seen Gracie this morning?"

"Oh yeah," Larry said, "she's at the office."

Al interrupted Larry. "Oh no," he said, "I was supposed to get the papers out to the post office and the stands this morning."

"Well," Larry said, "I think she's already taken care of that."

Al and Larry stopped at the office and found Gracie on the phone. Within a few seconds, she hung up and walked over to the two men. She said, "That was another friend wishing me well and asking if there was anything that I needed. I've been overwhelmed this morning by phone calls and folks stopping by."

Al said, "I'm so sorry for missing this morning. Larry woke me. I guess I must have needed the sleep. What needs to get done now?"

Gracie responded, "Well, nothing much now. This afternoon I have a follow up on an ad. I'll let you handle that."

"Well," Al said, "how about going next door with us for some coffee?"

"Sounds great. Let's go."

The three went into the diner, and Chuck joined them at a table near the window. He brought four cups and a full pot of coffee. As he came near the table, he asked, "Ever wonder why we drink so much coffee?"

In a moment of complete surprise, Gracie said, "If we didn't drink coffee we'd be drunks." Larry, Al, and Chuck just looked at each other.

She continued, "Think about it. We deal with people for a living. Chuck, you run this place. I'll bet you've seen everything. Larry, you deal with people and know the lies and the truth and that some people don't know the difference. Ray and me, we write about the good and the bad." When Gracie realized what she said, she seemed caught and said, "Well, you know what I mean."

After a couple of cups of coffee, Larry left for his office. Getting up from the table, Gracie thanked Chuck for the coffee.

Al said to Chuck, "Thanks for the coffee, and for being here. This place here is a retreat from, well, it's just a nice place to come to."

Chuck got up from the table and took the single step to reach Gracie and gave her a hug and said, "The door is always open."

In the office, Gracie sat at her desk and pulled up a chair. "Al, come and have a seat. We need to talk about the paper."

Cautiously Al questioned, "Don't you think it's too soon to discuss the paper?"

"No, I don't think it's too soon. It's just a question of whether you want to stay and help me. I'm staying here, and I hope you'll stay here with me. I know that with your help we can make a go of the paper. So, what do you say?"

Al sighed and said, "I was afraid you'd want to leave. I'm glad you want to stay and continue. And, yes, I'll stay and help you all that I can."

Gracie smiled and suggested that she and Al each write an opinion piece for the weekly. In their own way, they would thank the people in the community for their support and include the decision to continue the paper.

In her piece, Gracie went to great lengths to thank all the people for their outpouring of love and support. She mentioned the funeral home, the city, and the sheriff. She ended by expressing warm regards to the men and women of the veteran's hall for their work.

Al's article was focused on the welcome he received from the community and how much he enjoyed his work and the people. He ended his piece by writing that the strength of communities is found in the way they love and support each other in times of need.

The day after circulation, Gracie called Al up to the front. Since he had been working in the back, he smelled of cleaner and machine oil.

"Yes, Gracie, what's up," he asked. She was holding a large envelope and motioned Al to sit down.

Tears were running down her cheeks, and the papers in her hand were rustling together. "I have the information from our insurance company. Ray made sure that his insurance would pay off the paper and the house." Wiping her tears she finished,

"Ray made sure that I would be okay. I think we can make it. And I think you should talk to Jimmy about helping out. It would be good for him and give you a hand."

That evening Al was at Chuck's having dinner when Larry came in. "Good evening, Mayor," Al said. "What are you up to tonight?"

"To tell you the truth, I was hoping I'd find you here. I really want to know how Gracie is doing. I know these have been rough days for her and for you."

Al responded, "Well, she's doing better than I thought she would. She just got the news that Ray had taken good care of her and the paper. That relieved a lot of her stress."

Al and Larry talked for a few more minutes until Larry got ready to leave. Al said, "You know, your honor, Jimmy really wants to go fishing with you. He has his heart set on it."

Larry's response was quick, "Well, let's say Friday, good and early, I'll pick you up here. That way I'll make Chuck get his butt out of bed and make us coffee."

"Get my butt out of bed," Chuck growled. "I bet I'm up before you every morning."

Larry laughed as he reached the door, "Just trying to get a response from you, that's all."

Al walked home to the cabin. Getting comfortable in his chair, he reached for his Bible. His bookmark was in the gospel of John the fourth chapter. As he read of the discussion between Jesus and the woman of Samaria, he realized a few things. One of the most striking things was that Jesus didn't care what others thought when he knew he was right. Talking with a foreign woman was against the law. Asking her to bring him water was against the rules of Jewish society. And when he told her that God would pour out His living water to her, a forsaken Samaritan, it was an unspeakable sin. Al concluded that Jesus lived and taught counter to the religious culture of his day.

Early the next morning Gracie knocked on Al's door. After a moment the door opened, and Gracie stepped back horrified. Al looked ghastly standing in the doorway.

He said, "I bet I'm a sight for sore eyes. Come on in."

"Dear God," she said, "What happened to you? Are you alright?"

Al responded, "I guess Ray didn't tell you."

"Tell me what?"

"This is going to take a few minutes," Al said. "Since coming home, I have had recurring nightmares and severe headaches. A while back I had brain surgery, and the doctors removed a growth from the back of my brain. They first suspected the growth was from my injury. After the operation, they discounted the theory about the cause being my injury. They determined it was some kind of tumor."

The look on Gracie's face was one of utter sadness. Al continued, "After the surgery, the doctor told me that the headaches might not come back, or they could come back at any time. He felt the nightmares were not related to the injury and speculated that the stress from the oncoming headaches triggered some type of buried trauma. The doctor said I need to seek help from a therapist. I went a couple of weeks without a headache or the nightmare. I haven't had them as frequently as before, and I don't have any idea when I'm going to be hit by them. The nightmare is always the same; it has never changed, not even one time."

Gracie asked, "Would you like to tell me about them?"

"No, I wouldn't like to tell you about it, but I probably should. Did Ray ever tell you about the attack? When it started, we were all taken by surprise. Oh, we knew something was coming, but we had no idea when it would start. When it started, I got out of our building headed for a bunker. The artillery from the enemy was accurate and heading for the bunker. I was trying to get some good shots of the action, so I was looking around the edge of the bunker."

Al shifted his position and continued. "Right in front of us, a little girl was running and screaming. I saw her in her little buttoned white shirt. Tears were streaming down her face, and as she screamed, she had this look of absolute horror. The young marine next to me tried to get behind me. The marine screamed in my ear that he was going to get her. When he was right behind me, the blast went off, sending me and the marine backward. In the instant between the blast and the concussion, that little girl vanished in a red mist. That's my nightmare—me trying to get a good photograph, and an innocent little girl vanishing right in front of me."

When Al was finished, Gracie was wiping her eyes. "Oh, Al," she said, "What a terrible image you've had to live with. I never really knew what happened. Ray did tell me that you saved the young marine's life, but I never knew the rest."

Al said, "The headaches always come before the nightmare. Lights flash across my eyes, and even with them closed, the lights still flash. The headaches want to crush my skull. Ray knew because I had to tell him the truth. He found me like you did this morning. The only other people that know are the Williams, the doctors, and now you."

Gracie asked, "Is there anything that can be done? Are the headaches and nightmares psychological? Do you feel guilty because you're alive and the little girl isn't? Have you seen a doctor since the headaches and nightmares have come back?"

Al sat right on the edge of the bed and looked into Gracie's eyes and said, "Gracie, I have given the entire episode to God. I have prayed for Him to heal me, and I continue to ask for healing. I have also asked him to help me deal with my guilt. So, yes, at times I do feel guilty about still being alive. But another thing that helps me is that my life today must count for something. I cannot and will not live without making a difference or having an impact. I was spared for a reason."

Gracie left and headed over to the office. After Al showered and dressed, he went to the office as well. When he arrived, Gracie was at her desk, looking perplexed.

She said, "Al come over here and listen to this on the answering machine." Al went over next to the desk, and Gracie pushed the play button. A woman's voice stated that they had been north and stopped at the River's Edge Diner. While still sitting in the parking lot, they noticed somebody walking an elderly man down towards the river. She closed the message with a question, "Do you folks know anything about this?"

Al looked puzzled and said, "What do you think? That diner is near the place where Ray and I went and met Bill. Nothing came from that trip. I don't see anything unusual about a man walking somebody down by a river. What are you thinking?"

Gracie said, "I'm not sure there is much if anything to it. But let's agree that if we get a couple of more calls, we should look into it."

For the next few hours, Gracie was preoccupied with her early morning encounter with Al. She and Ray had never had any children, and her mother's heart was growing towards Al. Gracie heard him in the back room getting ready for their delivery of paper and ink and thought, *Ray taught him well.*

By evening Al had the papers run, folded, and ready for the mailing labels. The stacks for the businesses and stands were tied and ready to be dropped off. As he finished up, he thought that Jimmy would be a great help in this part of the work. He could get the delivery ready and make the drops. Al figured it would only take Jimmy three or four hours, and it'd give him a little extra money. He went into the office and found Gracie in a daze. She was looking at Ray's desk.

When Al came around the desk, he put his hand on her shoulder, and she jumped a bit in her seat. "Gracie, are you alright?" Al asked.

She said, "I was just thinking of Ray. He loved the newspaper business. He didn't talk much about it, but his opinion of a free press and voice was very firm. He told me more than once that a free and uncensored voice would help keep a government honest. It was something that he really believed in."

Al said, "I'm going to find Jimmy, probably next door at Chuck's, and talk to him about helping me out."

"I think it is a good idea," Gracie said. "And I hear you and Larry are taking him fishing. You don't know what that will do for that boy."

Just as he thought, Al found Jimmy sitting on at Chuck's place. He sat on the stool next to him and asked Chuck for coffee. Jimmy seemed agitated so Al asked, "Jimmy, you seem kind of nervous. What's the problem?"

Jimmy fired back, "I don't know, I've been kinda upset these past few days. I know it's been a month or so since Ray left us. But every time I walk by the paper and come here, I think of him. I just hope he's doing okay."

Turning on his stool, Al bent his head towards Jimmy, and whispered, "We're gonna go fishin' this Friday morning. Wanna come?"

Jimmy exploded straight up and off his stool. In a flash he was up and dancing in a little circle and singing, "Gonna go a-fishin', gonna go a-fishin'. Been a-wishin' and a-wishin', now I'm gonna go a-fishin'. Goin' fishing with Larry, goin' fishin' with

Larry. Gonna have me a shore lunch, fried taters and trout. Makes me so happy, think I'm gonna shout."

Al sat on his stool laughing, and Chuck came from the back to see what the commotion was. Jimmy was still dancing his little jig when Al grabbed him by the sleeve and asked him to sit down. Jimmy was like popcorn bouncing in a hot pan. Even when Al finally got him to sit, his legs were bouncing.

Al said, "Now be ready and meet me here at five Friday morning. You don't need to bring anything. Larry will have all the tackle."

18

Larry in Trouble

Chuck opened early Friday morning and came in to find Al drinking his second cup of coffee and eating his double toasted wheat toast.

He said to Al, "See you made yourself right at home. Thanks for saving me some work."

A minute or so later, Jimmy came through the front door. He was dressed in jeans and a flannel shirt and the ever-present fatigue hat. He took a seat at the counter, and Chuck brought him coffee. Chuck came around the counter and said to Jimmy, "So, ya gonna go fishin' with the Mayor and Al. I expect you'll have a great time. I've heard a lot about his Honor's famous shore lunch. It won't be much of a lunch if you don't catch any fish. Now will it?" Chuck smirked and winked at Al.

Just as Chuck finished his little jab, Old Gettem-Up stopped in front of the diner. Larry came in the front door and as only he could, made his grand announcement, "I'm goin' after giant specks. Who's coming with me?"

The grin on Jimmy's face couldn't get any bigger as he swung his legs and propelled himself off the stool, all the while saying, "Don't have to say it twice for me. I've been up since four. Let's get a-goin'."

He was out the door before Al even got off the stool. Al smiled at Larry saying, "I sure hope we catch some fish, and we can keep Jimmy under control." Larry grinned back, his pipe clenched between his teeth.

Old Gettem-Up headed north out of town. Al was in the front seat and Jimmy was on the back bench seat with the equipment stacked around him. As they headed north, the river was on their right side, and the sun was just beginning to transform the hills from the shadowy world, bringing to life the blues, greens, yellows, and the gold of daybreak.

As Larry guided Old Gettem-Up around the first bend and up the rise, Jimmy couldn't contain himself any longer. His rapid-fire questions assaulted Larry and Al, "So what part of the river are we goin' to? How we gonna fish—spinners, live bait? We gonna need waders? What we goin' for beside specks? What size we gonna keep for eatin'?"

Al broke in, "Hold on a minute, Jimmy, slow down before you keel over. I'm sure that when we get to where we're going Larry will fill us in."

Larry took a different two-track off the blacktop than the previous trip. The road was gravel and then turned to dirt and larger stones. The two-track twisted between the pines and second growth poplar. Old Gettem-Up would whine going downhill as the standard transmission kept the speed down. At the bottom of a hill, Larry would shift into first gear and by the time they got to the top, the transmission was whining.

After twenty minutes of going up and down on the two-track, Larry pulled into an opening. The two-track ended on a bit of land with the river in the front and on the right side. The front of the opening had an easy access to the river and a large clearing. In the center of the clearing was a fire pit, and a trail went off to the left. On the right, there were two more openings through the cedars to the river.

As soon as Old Gettem-Up stopped, Jimmy was out the

door and at the water. He ran to the larger clearing in front and then over to the other clearing through the cedars. He was back in a second waiting for Larry to open up the back of Old Gettem-Up and display the arsenal of fishing tackle. Larry pulled out the three plastic tubes and the three old metal boxes.

As careful and loving as before, Larry took each rod out of the tube and the flannel wrap. He put the spinning reel on the rod for Jimmy and another spinning reel on one for Al. When Larry pulled out his fly rod, Jimmy's eyes bulged. He exclaimed, "I'll be a blessed man! You got a split bamboo fly rod. She must be near a hundred years old."

Larry said, "Jimmy, you got an eye for beauty, she's almost a hundred. Ain't she something to behold?"

With the river sweeping to the right, the deeper pools were on the opposite side of the big clearing. The openings on the right led to a straightening of the river and deeper water near the bank. The spots on the right were full of scattered submerged logs. They were perfect places for fish to grow large, and close to impossible ones for a fisherman to get out a monster fish.

Larry suggested to Al that he fish from the large clearing and that he himself would fish the opposite bank in the deeper water. Al agreed and took the rod and metal tackle box to the clearing. Larry told Jimmy that the openings on the right side would be a great place for him to fish, and he was sure he'd catch a few.

He gave Jimmy the rod that was set up with a single hook and small weight a couple of feet above the hook. "Now, Jimmy, the secret here is for the bait to bounce along the bottom. The specks will pick it up real gentle. You got to be ready for just the slightest tap 'cause that big boy isn't going to announce himself to you. Now, in this here cottage cheese container are a couple of dozen worms. Those big guys are gonna eat them right up. Are you ready for this?"

Jimmy's words flew out, "I sure am ready, been ready for this day since I was just a baby, sure am ready."

To say the morning was beautiful was an understatement. The temperature was in the lower fifties; the dew was dancing and sparkling on the ferns. The scent of the pine and cedar mixed as no apothecary could have dreamed. By the time the men had their lines and bait luring the fish, the sun was up and shining between the massive pines. As the sun danced off the moving water, the flashing and shimmering made concentrating on that part of the river nearly impossible.

Al was the first to catch a fish. He had cast a silver spinner into the deep water of the pool and let it sink for a moment. On the third or fourth crank of the reel, the trout took the spinner and headed off down the river.

Al hollered, "Got a fish! He's heading downstream."

The fish tried to turn the bend and head towards Jimmy. Larry hollered, "What ya got on?"

Al, his voice excited, yelled, "I don't know, but it must be pretty big." Al worked his way along the bank, keeping tension on the line. He slowly began making progress with the sleek and strong fighter. A minute later he was kneeling down next to a rainbow over twenty inches long. Very carefully, with wet hands, he worked the hook of the spinner out of the rainbow's mouth and slipped it back into the water.

As he was getting ready to cast again, he heard Larry boasting that his prowess with a fly rod paid off. "Got one for the frying pan," he said. All this time Jimmy was quiet. He never said a word when the two men proclaimed their catch. Larry looked downstream and caught a glimpse of Jimmy's line as the sunlight caught the tiny water droplets falling off it.

"Any luck, Jimmy?" Larry asked. He didn't get an answer, so he asked again. Jimmy's "shh" was louder than Larry's question. Larry was grinning, and he made quite a picture standing in the river, hat on his head, pipe in his mouth, grinning at Jimmy. It wasn't ten seconds after Jimmy's demand for silence that he hollered so loud every creature for miles heard him. "I got one, I got one, I got me one. Oh man, it's a monster! I can't move my pole. It must be as big as a log. Larry, Al, come help me! Oh man, this is a big one."

Larry was the first to reach Jimmy. He could tell it was a really nice fish, the line was moving both upstream and downstream, but the fish never came to the surface.

Larry said, "It's a nice fish, Jimmy. He doesn't want to come to the top. He's gonna stay deep until you tire him out. Keep the line tight and don't let him put any slack in it."

Al got to the clearing, and the two men grinned and chuckled as they watched their frenzied friend do battle with his submerged opponent.

Twenty minutes after his nervous proclamation, Jimmy edged the fish to shore. Larry slid his net under the massive speck. With Jimmy's fish safe in the net, all three men danced the fisherman's jig, slapping Jimmy on the back and giving out a hoop and a holler. The speck was close to twenty-one inches long. As the trout rested safely in the net, the beauty of the fish seemed to overtake the three men. In about six inches of water, the strikingly beautiful blue and gold shimmered in the clear, pure water and mesmerized the men.

Jimmy was looking into the net and said, "I've never seen such a pretty fish before. Look at her spots and the color on her belly. I always thought if I caught such a beauty, I'd want to put her on my wall. I think the best thing is to let her go free." Jimmy stood up, and the other two men agreed. Larry moved the net out into deeper water and pulled it out from under the magnificent trout. As Larry turned back to shore, he was sure he saw a tear in Jimmy's eye.

Larry said, "Alright, the party's over, and if you two boys want lunch, you best be catching some for the pan. I have one, but that won't make much of a lunch, and I'd hate to eat alone." Al headed back to his spot, and Jimmy went over to the clearing where he caught his speck. Al was still smiling as he replayed the scene of Jimmy fighting his trophy.

Al's very first cast upstream was slammed by a fish. Less than a minute later, he had a twelve inch rainbow in the net. "Got one for the pan," he announced.

Larry said, "Not bad for a rookie, but I have two more for my count. That brings our total to four. We best get a couple more because I'm hungry and not feeling very polite when it comes to sharing."

Al heard Larry holler at Jimmy, "Hey, fisherman, you better catch a couple for lunch. If not, you're gonna be really hungry."

Jimmy responded with his usual nervous voice, "I'm trying real hard, honest I am."

A moment later, Larry heard Jimmy talking to himself. Larry asked, "Hey, Jimmy, what's wrong? Don't talk to yourself."

"Aw Larry," Jimmy called out, "pretty sure I got my hook snagged on the bottom or something."

Through the cedars, Larry shouted, "Hold on a minute there, Jimmy, an extra set of hands might help. I'll be right there."

Larry was within ten feet of Jimmy when he saw him leaning out over the water. He was trying to free his line by moving his rod up and down the current and jerking it. Larry hollered for Jimmy to wait at the same instant the small branch Jimmy was holding snapped.

Jimmy fell headlong into the icy water. When he did, his fatigue hat came off, and the swirling current began to carry it downstream. Jimmy bobbed to the surface, spitting out the icy water, and spotted his beloved cap. With a couple of quick strokes, he was able to reach the cap and grab it. He began to swim towards shore, but with his arms flailing, he wasn't making any progress. Larry knew in an instant that Jimmy was snagged on underwater branches.

Larry yelled at the top of his lungs, "Al, get over here quick. Jimmy's in the water, and he's in trouble."

In a panic, Al responded, "I'm coming, I'm coming. Jimmy, hang on."

Larry was on the shore trying to get Jimmy to pay attention. "Jimmy, Jimmy, listen to me. Can you swim to me?"

The fear in Jimmy's voice struck Larry, "No, I can't swim to you, my leg, my leg is stuck on something."

Jimmy's head was just out of the water, and he was struggling. He was trying to tread water with both hands, with one hand clutching his cap.

Larry said, "Now Jimmy, listen to me. I want you to push down real hard with your free leg and when you do, pull with all your might and try to free yourself."

Jimmy said, "Okay, Larry, I'll try, I'll try. I'll try right now." Larry watched Jimmy struggle and go under. In a second Jimmy was on the surface, and he was wildly choking. The look of fear and panic put Larry into action.

"Al," Larry shouted, "I have to go in after him." Without any hesitation, Larry threw his rod and hat on the bank. He waded in upstream of Jimmy, knowing the current would carry him down in a matter of seconds. Within feet of Jimmy, the water had filled Larry's waders, and he started to flounder.

At Jimmy's side, Larry gained footing and was able to hold

on to Jimmy. He knew that if he stood on the same log that Jimmy was on, it would sink deeper. Standing behind Jimmy, with the water chin deep, he knew what he had to do. Assuring Jimmy, Larry said, "It's okay, it's okay. I'm gonna get you to shore."

Jimmy's eyes were filled with fear, and the frigid water was turning his lips blue. Al stood on shore, watching both men struggle in the chilly water. He remembered that Larry kept a length of heavy jute rope in the back of Old Gettem-Up. Running over to get the rope, he was praying for Larry and Jimmy. As he got back down to shore, he yelled out, "Jimmy, I'm going to throw this rope to you, and I'll pull you in."

"Jimmy," Larry said, "listen to me real close. You hold on to that rope really tight. I'm gonna have to let you go. When I do, I want you to pull and jerk on your leg as hard as you can. Do you understand me? Jimmy, do you understand?"

Jimmy answered, fear coloring each word, "Yes sir, I understand, and I promise I'll pull real hard."

"Al," Larry said, "throw him the rope!"

Al threw the rope a few feet upstream of Jimmy; in a second Jimmy had it in his hands. Larry looked at Jimmy and asked, "Are you ready to pull on your leg?"

"Why, what are you—" Jimmy never finished his question. In utter disbelief, Al and Jimmy watched Larry go under the water. Jimmy suddenly felt his leg go free, and Al was pulling him to shore.

In a matter of seconds, both men were looking at the swirling beauty of the trout stream, waiting for Larry to come to the surface. As they watched, Jimmy grabbed a hold on Al's jacket.

Seconds passed and Jimmy yelled out, "Come on out Mr. Larry, Come on out. Please, God, help Mr. Larry."

Close to thirty seconds after going under, Larry burst to the surface. His submerged battle carried him close to thirty feet downstream. Racing down the bank, Al found an opening and threw Larry the rope. Al's throw was right on target. Larry grabbed the rope and quickly was on the bank.

Onshore, Larry fell down next to Jimmy. Trying to catch his breath and help Jimmy, he put his arm around him and said, "I told ya I was going to help."

Jimmy drew close to Larry and said, "Thanks for not leaving me out there. I was getting real scared."

Larry responded again, "I wasn't gonna let the river get another friend."

Al broke in and asked Larry if he had any blankets. Larry told him that in the back of Old Gettem-Up was a box with a couple of old green wool military blankets in it.

Al ran over and brought two back. He tossed one to Larry and put the other one around Jimmy. With the outside temperature below sixty and the water temperature below that, Al knew that his two friends could be in trouble.

Larry must have been thinking the same thing, he said, "We best gather stuff up real quick and get back to town. If the chill sets in, we're in trouble. Jimmy, you grab your pole and crawl into Old Gettem-Up, keep that blanket 'round you. Al, get the other poles and boxes, and I'll grab the fish. You drive so I can keep wrapped up."

The back of Old Gettem-up was quickly loaded, and the three were headed back down the two-track. Al wasn't used to driving a standard, so he spent the first few minutes grinding gears. By the time they reached the pavement, Al was moving right along and pushing Old Gettem-Up hard.

They got into town twenty minutes after hitting the pavement. Pulling up in front of Jimmy's, Larry said, "Now you go in and take a long hot bath, that'll warm up your insides. Be down at the diner by six tonight, we're still gonna have our shore lunch; it's just gonna be at Chuck's and not around a fire."

Al pulled into a spot between the paper and the diner, grabbed the fish and potatoes while Larry changed seats. As Larry was getting in, Al chuckled and said, "Never thought I'd see such a distinguished man in his long underwear. I bet you're glad you had them on. And, by the way, that was an amazing thing you did for Jimmy. Pretty sure he's gonna tell every person from here to the border that you're his hero." Larry chuckled, put Old Gettem-Up in gear, and drove off.

Al took the would-have-been shore lunch provisions into the diner. Chuck asked, "What in the world is going on? Larry never even came in for coffee."

Al said, "I'll fill ya in later, could you put these fish in the cooler, after ya clean them and cut off their heads? I'm not eating fish ever again that stare at me. Larry likes the fish to look at you; I don't. We're gonna come over around five and give Jimmy his shore lunch."

19

Larry's Loss

Larry and Al were back at Chuck's at five. Larry brought all the fixin's for the fish and the redskins. He was not going to impose on Chuck any more than using his grill. As the two men stood in the back room, Larry was preparing the ingredients for the fish.

Al said, "Larry, can I ask you a question?"

"Sure Bub, ask away."

The "Bub" caught Al by surprise, and he asked, "Where did Bub come from?"

"Oh, I don't know," Larry said. "I used to call all of my friends Bub. Does it bother you?"

Al responded back, "Well no, it doesn't bother me, it's just you never used that name before."

Larry said, "What did you want to know before we got off on the Bub issue?"

"Back at the river, you said something to Jimmy. I'm not sure I heard you right or if you remember what you said." Al's subdued tone brought Larry closer.

Larry said, "What do you mean that I said something to Jimmy? I said a lot of things to him."

Al, not wanting to be overheard, said softly again, "You said you were not gonna lose another friend to the river. What did you mean by that?"

The statement and question from Al set Larry back a step. In a flustered attempt to answer Larry said, "We'll have to talk at another time. I've got fish to take care of for Jimmy."

Jimmy came in the door right at six and found a table all decked out. Chuck had decided to play it up a bit and moved a few tables together. He found some firewood from out back and made a pretty good looking fire. The table was set for three, and Jimmy took a seat on the end. Larry and Al came out from the back room, each holding a cast iron pan. They set them on the table, and Larry announced, "Shore Lunch is served."

Before they had the chance to begin eating, Jimmy broke in and said, "I think we should pray and thank God for the food and for keeping all of us safe." Al thanked him for the thought and agreed, asking Jimmy to say the prayer. Jimmy bowed his head and prayed, "Dear Lord, I thank you for this great food we're gonna eat. I really thank you for the new friends that I have. Thank you for Larry and helping him save my life. Thank you for Al who kept thinking about ways to help, like throwing me the rope. Thank you for getting us here safe today. Bless our food and bless Chuck for letting Larry fix it here. Amen."

The shuffling of feet signaled that it was time to eat. Chuck came from behind the counter, holding onto Larry's enamel camp coffee pot. Larry even made sure that the old tin cups were on the table. It was hard to decide if Jimmy was more excited about the trout and redskin potatoes, or eating with Larry and Al.

In a matter of minutes, the fish and redskins disappeared. As Chuck was refilling the cups, he told the three fishermen that he had dessert for them. He brought out four small plates and a cup, saying, "Cup and plate are for me. I'm not gonna miss out on dessert." He went into the back room and came back with a baking dish, smelling of brown sugar, cinnamon, and apples.

The four men devoured Chuck's apple crisp. Larry went on about the brown sugar-oatmeal topping, Al gave his compliments, and Jimmy kept on eating. When they were finally done, Chuck asked, "Okay, now Jimmy, tell me what happened up there this morning. I've never been told the story yet."

"Why, that's as easy as eating all these trout and redskins. Mayor Larry saved my life. I was stuck in the river on a log and couldn't move, not even an inch. The log kept goin' up and down in the deep water. Every time it submerged deeper, I went down with it. Mayor Larry, why he came right over to me, with the water coming into his fishin' boots filling 'em right up. He didn't care 'bout that one bit. He went under the water right next to me and broke off the limb that had my pants all stuck. I came up, and Al was able to haul me in with a rope. They're both my heroes. Mayor Larry, he saved my life."

Al broke in and asked Larry, "How were you able to free Jimmy and then yourself?"

Larry replied, "I knew that I was never going to get out of the river in my waders. Once they filled with water, they were weights on me. So, the best I figured out was to go under and free Jimmy. Once that was done, I had to get the waders off. I keep a knife attached to my vest, so I pulled the knife out, drew my knees up, and reached down to my knees with my knife and cut the waders right up to the top. Did both legs and then pulled my legs out. And here I am."

Al opened the front door of the cabin and plopped on his chair. He was exhausted, and he knew the reason. It was an early morning and an exciting couple of hours fishing. The final minutes at the river were shot full of adrenalin. He hadn't been that filled with the fight-or-flight juice in a long time. He untied his leather boots and kicked them over against the wall by the door. He wanted to relax and let his brain move to the land of nothingness. With his feet on the bed, and his head leaned back in his chair, he was ready to drift off. And then a loud knock on the door abruptly interrupted his desire.

Larry knocked again, and Al reached the door. He invited him in and offered him his chair as he sat on the edge of his bed.

Al began to ask, "What's up," when Larry said, "You asked me about the river. You asked me about the river and something I said."

Al answered, "Yeah, at the river you said something I was not aware of. You said you weren't going to lose another friend to the river."

Larry shifted both his gaze and his position on the chair. He answered, "You're right, I don't talk about it. I never meant to say anything. I guess the reason you never heard is people respect my desire to not talk about it."

"Talk about what?" Al asked.

"Ellie," Larry said, "my wife, Ellie. She's been gone close to seven years. She suffered a stroke almost ten years ago, and it left her in bad shape. I brought her home when she was discharged and helped her with her rehabilitation. I spent as much time with her as I could. When she had to go back into the hospital, I was with her every day. I brought her home again, and things seemed to be going well."

Larry moved in the chair and cleared his throat. He continued, "I came home from the office at noon one day, like I always did, and she was gone. She just vanished, disappeared without a trace. Nothing was missing in the house, nothing broken, no evidence of anything evil or malicious. She vanished; I believe the river took her."

Al was troubled at Larry's story and didn't know how to respond. Larry said, "I know it sounds incredible, ridiculous, far-fetched, and weird, a bunch of different words, but it's the truth."

Al moved on the edge of his bed and cleared his throat. He said to Larry, "Did they ever find any evidence? What did Bill find? Did anybody find anything at all? How did you cope with it? It would send most people over the edge. I never even knew you were married. Nobody ever spoke to me about it." Al's staccato questioning revealed his surprise.

"That's what I said before; people don't talk about it because I don't."

Al sensed that there was more that needed to be said. He asked Larry, "So would you tell me about your wife, I believe you said her name was Ellie."

"Yeah, Ellie was her first name, her full name, not Eleanor, just Ellie. I met her across the border in Canada. I was working for a firm downstate and had to cross into Canada two or three times a month. She was working for the company that I visited, and like any red-blooded American, she was cute, and I was interested. The rest is history and our love story. A year later we got married, and she moved across and became a citizen. You know, the normal stuff happened. We had three children, and they all grew up and went to school. Now the two boys live out west, and my daughter lives down south. I haven't seen them since their mom vanished. They came home for a while, stayed with me while we were searching for her. But after a few weeks, they had their own lives and families to get back to."

Larry moved again on the chair and kept going, "Her disappearance was hard to deal with. Funny thing, for weeks I'd swear that I saw her. I walked up to perfect strangers, thinking it was Ellie. I suppose a few people thought I was nuts."

Al said, "Doesn't sound nuts to me. Seems like you loved her a lot. I'm really sorry for your loss. I don't pretend to understand what that must be like. I've felt deep pain. I know for me, God helped me understand that he is the true source of comfort."

"Ellie was a Christian," Larry said. "She told me that while she was growing up, her mom and dad took her and her sister to Sunday school and Church. She talked about all the choruses she learned in Sunday school and Vacation Bible School. She grew up with church and worship being fun. When she was in high school, the church had a teen club and did all kinds of things together. She said it was the biggest factor in her keeping her head on straight during her teen years. It wasn't that way for me, I mean, for me and church. I went as a kid because I had to. I was forced to study the creeds and confessions so I could recite them and become a member. Later on, after college, I quit going. Today, I go occasionally; I know I need to go, and the folks around here expect it."

Al sat on the edge of his bed and looked right at Larry. He said to him, "Don't go because people want you to go and don't go because you say you need to go. If you go, go because you need God in your life. God was the only power that could help me. He helped me deal with my guilt and pain. You know my story. I wanted to drink myself to death, but God helped me get past that, and quite a few folks have encouraged me to do what God wants."

Al was sensing that he should offer to pray with Larry. Drawing on his sense of purpose, he asked Larry, "Would you mind if I prayed with you about this? I can tell that it's been a burden you've been carrying."

Larry nodded and lowered his head. When Al said "Amen," it took Larry a couple of seconds to compose himself and look Al in the face.

Trying to express friendship and appreciation for the prayer, Larry stood and said, "Thanks, Bub, I needed the prayer."

As the door to his cabin closed, Al went back to his chair. Over the next few hours, thoughts of Larry filled his heart. Trying to imagine the pain and confusion that his friend went through, he prayed on and off for him. The mystery surrounding the area for a couple of hundred years was weighing on his mind. How do people just go missing, how does a person known and loved by their family and friends just vanish? Later that night, he crawled under the handmade quilt and prayed again for Larry.

Sunday found Al and Jimmy back at church. Jimmy continued to amaze Al. His friendly spirit and his excitement over the littlest of things was a reminder to Al about what was important. During a part of the service when Pastor Hank asked for prayer requests, Jimmy was on his feet. He gave a full description of his rescue by Mayor Larry. As he told the story, there were shouts of, "Amen" and "Praise God," from all over the room. Pastor Hank reminded everybody that God has a plan for his children, and the plan will be completed before he takes them to glory.

Jimmy's story fit right in with Pastor Hank's message. Pastor Hank talked about living on this earth. He said that our life is a journey, a time of trials and temptations, of blessings and relationships. But when we come to the end of our days, whenever that is, it's just us and the Lord. He said that when we cross the river, it will be Jesus who will be our guide. Just like Joshua of old led the children of God into the Promised Land, Jesus will guide us across the river to our promised land of heaven.

Al and Jimmy walked back from the church to Gracie's house. As they turned the corner, Al told Jimmy that Gracie had dinner waiting. They went in the back door,. In an instant Jimmy was smiling, and Al was savoring the smell of fresh bread. Gracie had her back to the two men as they came in and she said, "Go on into the dining room, everything's ready; lucky you came in when you did, the bread is just out of the oven."

Al and Jimmy sat down, and Gracie brought the fresh loaf of bread in on a breadboard, with a knife slid underneath it. She put the bread on the table and went back into the kitchen and reappeared with the heavy glass butter dish.

"Now who wants one of the ends?" She chuckled when both Al and Jimmy reached for the bread. "Lucky there's two," she said. "Better get some butter on them while they're warm."

The only sound coming from the dinner table was the tinging sound of silverware against glass bowls and ceramic plates. The two men ravaged the pot roast, complete with potatoes, onions, carrots, and the entire loaf of fresh bread. During dinner, Gracie just picked at her food, watching and smiling as the two men cleaned their plates. A sense of contentment was evident in her smile as two important men in her life enjoyed her labor in the kitchen. When they were finished eating, Al said, "Okay, Jimmy, we get to do the cleanup, not a bad payment for dinner."

With the dishes done, they found Gracie back at the dinner table, a spiral bound pad in front of her.

"Now," she said, "If you want dessert, you have to answer a few questions for me." The two men looked at each other with a puzzled look. "Al," she said, "You can go and make some coffee. I want to talk to Jimmy." For the next twenty minutes or so, she asked Jimmy to retell the story of how the mayor saved his life. Al was smiling as he listened to Jimmy talk.

It seemed to Al that Jimmy didn't miss a detail. Gracie heard how cold the water was; how every time he tried to step on the log, it went further under the water, and he went with it. When he came to the part of the mayor going under the water to pull him free, the excitement and emotion in his voice made it seem as if he were still in the water. Jimmy was a very compelling storyteller.

Blueberry pie, ice cream, and coffee were the perfect dessert. With a bit of pie filling still in the corner of his mouth, Jimmy asked Gracie, "Why did you want to know all about the mayor?"

"Why that's simple," Gracie said. "I'm writing an article on our mayor and how he saved your life. It will be on the front page this week." In an instant, Jimmy was up and out of his chair.

"Oh boy," he said, "Mayor Larry is gonna be a real, honest-to-goodness hero."

Al and Gracie ran the story for Wednesday's edition. Many of the people in town knew ahead of time about the article. It seemed as though every place Jimmy went, he was telling people of his narrow escape and how brave the mayor was. When the townsfolk allowed, not wanting to be disrespectful, he would go over every detail of the rescue. And Jimmy ended the story the same, every time. 'Why," he'd say, "Our mayor is a real live hero." So when the weekly came out, the headline, Mayor Saves Local Man, was no surprise.

After the release, Gracie and Al had a day to breathe. Gracie invited Al over for lunch, and he knocked on the back door as usual. He found her in the dining room with the table already set. She looked preoccupied, and Al wondered what was going on.

She asked him to sit, and she brought out their lunch of chicken soup with dumplings and crackers. She was quiet during lunch, which only added to Al's apprehension. After clearing the table, she sat down and was fidgety.

Al wasn't going to wait any longer, and asked, "What in the world is bothering you? I haven't seen you like this in a long time."

"Al, you know Ray and I cared for you. Since he's been gone, I've come to depend on you more than just at the paper. I feel safe knowing you are around. I know it sounds strange. But you bring a sense of peace to me and to others as well. I know you're a Christian man, and you've helped me think about my own relationship with God. Well, I have a question I'd like to ask. You don't have to give me an answer right away. And, if you say no, I'll understand."

Her fidgeting was getting to him, so he spoke out, "Gracie, what do you want to ask?"

"Al, would you move into the house and live upstairs? There are two bedrooms up there and a nice bath. It's not like you'd be doing something wrong. I understand if you say no because you think people might talk badly about you. Would you please think about it?"

Al looked at Gracie and smiled. He said, "Well, you pretty much take care of me already. Does it mean pot roast and meatloaf, baked chicken and noodles?"

Gracie's laugh was his answer as his smile was hers. He chuckled when he said, "If people want to talk, I guess they will. Just means there's no other gossip in this town. And it would mean you have good taste."

They both laughed, and Al got up to leave. At the door he said, "I'll tell the folks at the cabin office that I'll be out by the end of the week."

The following day, Bill, the deputy from the sheriff's department, stopped at the paper's office. Al and Gracie were talking about ads that they were running and trying to decide on their column size and place. When Bill came in the front door, both Al and Gracie turned to see who it was. Al greeted Bill. Looking at Gracie, Bill tipped his hat.

Bill said, "I was in town, and I thought I'd just stop by and see how you folks are doing. I haven't seen the both of you since, err, ahh, the funeral. Sorry for stumbling so, Gracie."

Gracie smiled, and said, "Oh that's alright, I understand. The weeks have gone by fast. Al's keeping me busy here, and we're running more copies than we have in a long time. I guess it helps when we have a famous mayor. I hear folks downstate have heard about Larry and Jimmy."

Bill said, "Well, yes, I guess they have. Another river story for the books, 'cept this is a good one."

Al asked Bill, "That reminds me. Whatever happened to that old man, you know the one who left his car by the river? Did you ever figure that out?"

"No, nothing ever came of it. Never found a body. We had the car towed, and his kids never came to get it, or for that matter see if there was anything inside the car they wanted. It's a strange case and pretty strange people if you ask me. Got to be going now. See you two later." Bill turned and headed out the door.

Al said to Gracie, "Nice guy, I'm not sure I would want his job. The strange things that happen around the river, they ever get you to thinking?"

"I don't know. I've never really thought too much about it. That was Ray's thing, you know what I mean. He liked to look into stuff like that. I will tell you this, the river and the name of this paper, that's what drew Ray to this area."

It only took Al a couple of hours to get his belongings upstairs at Gracie's. The hardest part was moving his chair, the only real piece of furniture he had. Jimmy showed up just in time to give Al a hand. With the chair up the stairs, Al realized he had more room for himself than he could remember. Gracie had the room decorated with a few things. A couple of pictures hung on the walls. Against another wall a small built-in bookshelf hung over an old desk with an old banker's lamp on it.

After they finished the move, Al and Jimmy went to the office. Gracie was at her desk writing on a notepad. When Al and Jimmy headed past her to go to the back, she stopped Al. "I want to talk to you about something, maybe in an hour or so."

Al responded, "Sure, what's up?"

"Oh, probably nothing," she said.

Al and Jimmy set about cleaning the back room. Jimmy was singing as he swept the floor and helped Al move supplies.

Al remarked, "Jimmy, you're always such a happy guy. You're always smiling or laughing; you're a fun person to be around. What's up with you?"

"Why," Jimmy replied, "you should know what makes me happy. Jesus makes me happy on the inside. Knowing God loves me, that's what makes me happy."

Al sat down on the edge of a pallet of paper and asked Jimmy a question that had been on his mind for a long time. "Jimmy," he said, "Please tell me about your cap and your brother." The statement stopped Jimmy in the midst of his sweeping.

"Why do you want to know?" he asked. Al sensed discomfort in his reply.

Al said, "I didn't mean to upset you. You're my friend. I just wanted to know a little more about you. I know how important the cap is to you."

"Sorry," Jimmy said, "I know you didn't mean anything bad."

For the next half an hour, Jimmy talked about his brother and how they used to go fishing together. They would stay up all night catching worms and then be at the river when the sun came up. They would fish for hours and then go back to their apartment. Jimmy said, "My brother was almost ten years older than me. My mom and dad were killed in a bad car crash. My

217

brother took care of me until I graduated. Later he joined the Marines and got killed in the war. His cap is the only thing I got of his."

Gracie walked into the back room and said, "Sorry to interrupt."

Al said, "That's fine, Jimmy and I were just getting done back here, been talking a while. What's up?"

Gracie said, "I was writing down some information when you came in. We had another message on the answering machine, kind of like the one back a while ago. Remember, somebody saw a person escorted down by the water. It seems like it happened again. This one is different in a way."

Al looked puzzled, and Gracie continued, "The message was from a man, said he was a fisherman. Seems like he was on one side of the river, and he watched an outdoorsy type guy escort an old lady down to the water. He swears they got into a western style float boat and headed across the river. He said they were floating past him, about a hundred yards out. Said his view was blocked by some cedars, and he swears it was only for a moment, and the boat disappeared. He thought he might have lost them in the trees, but he's pretty sure he didn't."

Jimmy sat quietly listening to Gracie. When she was finished, he seemed nervous. Al picked up on it, and asked Jimmy, "What's the matter, Jimmy?"

In a nervous voice, Jimmy responded, "Been strange things goin' on around that river for as long as I can remember. You know the talk, goes way back, even to the times of the native folks. There's something strange 'bout that river."

Gracie went over to Jimmy and put her hand on his shoulder, saying, "You don't believe all that do you? You know, this is the kind of stuff Ray lived for."

Al told her that the story seemed more mysterious than the

previous one, but he wasn't sure that there was anything worth looking into. She agreed and told him that she'd keep the information. If something else came up, they should look into it. Gracie went back to the office area and put the note up on her board.

That evening Al was sitting in his chair reading from the works of Saint Augustine. On the stand was a book of Poe's writings that he had started and put down. Al thought, *Poe must have been a very troubled soul. Everything was dark for him, no joy, or hope, such a sad man.* Al's head dropped as did the book by Augustine. Al slid into sleep with Augustine on the floor.

Sometime in the night, when the stillness is only interrupted by nocturnal creatures, flashes of light, a child vanishing in a red mist, and infant cries, sent Al falling off his chair. As he tumbled to the floor, he hit his head on the stand, sending his reading lamp crashing down. As he fought away the voices and the vanishing child, he placed his hand on his forehead, the warm blood covered his cupped hand.

Startled by the noise, Gracie quickly ran up the stairs and knelt over him. "Dear God," she said, "What happened? Did you have one of your nightmares?"

With his hand on his forehead, Gracie went to the bathroom and got a wet cloth. She pulled his hand away, placing the cool damp cloth to his head. After a minute she said, "Better let me take a look; you might need a couple of stitches." Gently moving Al's hand away, Gracie said, "I think I should call Doc Sam. You ought to have some stitches."

"No Gracie," Al said, "after it stops bleeding, just put a couple of butterfly bandages on it. I'm not going to the doctor."

By daylight they had finished a pot of coffee. Gracie was trying to convince Al to go downstate and see a doctor. She had told him that the general practice doctor wouldn't be able to help him. Near dawn he agreed that if things didn't get better, he'd travel downstate and see a specialist. She tried to pin him down to a specific date when he would call and make an appointment. She'd have to be content with his word that if things didn't get better, he'd make an appointment.

Sunday found Al and Jimmy sitting together in church. Just before the service began, Jimmy heard the door open and turned to see who was coming in. He elbowed Al in the side, and Al turned to see Mayor Larry coming towards him and Jimmy. Jimmy stood up and let the mayor get past him and Al. He took the chair next to Al.

Al whispered, "Good morning, Larry, and glad to see you here."

Larry said, "Glad I came and really glad the place didn't fall in on me."

After the service, the three men walked back through town. About a block from the paper, Jimmy turned and went down the street to his place. Larry and Al walked to the diner and found Chuck sitting on a stool. With his back to them, he was hunched over, his paper hat almost touching the counter. At the sound of the door, he sat up and turned to see the two men come in.

He said, "Well, what brings you two in? What's up, Al, Gracie not cooking for you today?"

Al quipped back, "Oh, shut up, you're just jealous because you don't get the treatment like I do." They chuckled, but Al could tell something was bothering Chuck.

20

Chuck Opens His Heart

After enjoying a cup of coffee, Larry left and headed for home. Al and Chuck sat in silence for a moment. Chuck cleared his throat as he moved on the stool. He looked down and said, "I got a question for you. Do you believe that God heals people?"

The question took Al by surprise. He answered, "I believe God heals people. I believe He healed me. When I left the bottle, I didn't suffer withdrawals or anything. Why are you asking?"

Chuck struggled for words, saying, "I got a call from my daughter. She lives downstate; she says she has cancer." With that, Chuck struggled and cleared his throat and continued. "I told her I have a friend who's a Christian and will ask him to pray for her. Her name is Caroline."

Al said, "I'll begin to pray for her, and you, every day." Moving a bit on his stool, Al said, "I think we should say a prayer for her right now."

Chuck's hat was nearly touching the countertop as his head was bowed. Al prayed, "Dear God, I thank you for my friend, Chuck. He has been such a welcome friend to me. I ask you, dear Lord, be close to him and to his daughter, Caroline. Please touch her body as she has cancer. I know you can heal her. And God, be real close to my friend. The burden is heavy on his shoulders. Help his love to be strong and bring assurance to his Caroline. Amen."

When Al said "Amen," Chuck turned his head away and reached for the chrome napkin holder on the counter. He fumbled for a napkin, and three or four came out. He moved quickly to wipe his eyes and then his nose.

"Thanks,Al," he said. "I'm glad you're here. I'll keep you posted when I hear more from Caroline."

Al went in the back door of the house and up the stairs. He thought about what just happened with Chuck. Taking out a piece of paper from his Bible, he added Chuck's and Caroline's name to his list. He spoke a brief prayer and sat back in his chair, thinking about all the things that seemed to be taking place. First was Ray's death, and then Jimmy in the river, his move to the house, and today. *Wow, today, what a day. Larry comes to church, and Chuck tells me about his daughter having cancer.*

Monday night was council meeting time, and Al took his usual place in the gallery area of the chambers. The beginning of the meeting went as it usually did. The pledge was recited, and this meeting it was Pastor Henry, Hank to most people, who gave the invocation. Al had heard the pastor pray quite a few times, but something about this prayer was different. There was more passion in his prayer, and he seemed to be pleading with God for the leaders of the town to be given wisdom.

At the end of the meeting, Al noticed the pastor and Larry over by the wall engaged in conversation. Al wondered what the two were talking about. As he got to the door, Pastor Hank approached him.

"Al," he said, "Can I see you a minute?"

"Sure, Pastor. What's up?"

Pastor Hank said, "There's something I need to talk to you

about. Can we meet for coffee at the diner, say eight tomorrow morning?"

Al responded, "Sure, sounds good to me. See you in the morning."

On his walk home, he wondered what was on the pastor's mind. Coming in the back door, he found Gracie sitting at the dining room table with a concerned look on her face. Al took a seat and asked her what was wrong.

She replied, "I've been doing a lot of thinking these past couple of days. Actually, since you had that dream. I've been praying too—something I haven't done in a long time. I'm concerned about you. Have you given much more thought to going downstate to see a specialist?"

Al said, "Yes, I've been thinking about making that call. I have a meeting with the pastor in the morning, and then I plan on calling."

Gracie seemed relieved as Al told her goodnight. He went upstairs to write out his notes from the council meeting and do some reading. He was enjoying the space there. It was a lot more comfortable than the cabin and had twice the room.

Before eight in the morning, Al was talking with Chuck at the diner. Chuck brought him up to date on his daughter, Caroline. "She is supposed to undergo a new kind of test at the end of the week. At the University Hospital, they have some type of new machine that can take pictures of the inside of your body. I asked her if it was an x-ray, and she told me that it was something new."

Al said, "Remind her that people are praying for her. And remember that I'm praying for you too every day. Being a dad must be tough some days."

Right at eight, Pastor Hank came through the front door. Al got up and greeted him, and the two sat at a table in the corner.

Chuck brought the pastor a cup and filled them both. He asked the pastor if he wanted anything to eat. Pastor Hank responded, "Yes, I'll take an order of wheat toast and double toast it, please. I don't like wimpy toast." Al chuckled at the pastor's order and said, "You don't like wimpy toast. I was sure that I was the only person on the face of the planet that used that term, wimpy toast."

The pastor smiled and answered back, "Well, then, you know what I mean—when you hold a piece of toast by the corner and it's still soft and kinda flops over. I can't stand that kind of toast. That's wimpy toast. I don't want it burnt, and I don't want it limp like noodles either."

Al said, "I'm glad there's another person in the world that doesn't like wimpy toast."

At that, both men chuckled, and Chuck just shook his head and went behind the counter.

The small talk between the two men didn't last very long. Pastor Hank said, "I'm going to be blunt. I hear that you're having some serious medical problems. Don't ask me how I know; this is a small town. So, I know about you from others. I would like to hear from you what's going on. If you tell me it's none of my business, that's okay."

Al moved in the bent chrome chair and looked at his pastor. "I don't mind telling you about myself," Al said. "I came close to getting killed, and the results left me with pretty bad headaches and nightmares. Close to a year ago I collapsed, and the doctors found a growth in the back of my brain. They did surgery and told me that my future was uncertain; the growth might never grow again, or it could come back."

Al paused a few seconds and then continued, "I went a few weeks without symptoms. And I really thought that the headaches and dreams were over, but they're not. I can live with what is going on. It might sound strange to some people, probably not you, but, I'm okay with whatever happens. The Lord is in control of my life, and I know that."

He took a deep breath, gathering his courage, and went on, "I haven't told anybody what I'm about to tell you. On my way here, I think I met an angel. Her name was Edith, and she was one of the sweetest old ladies I ever met. We traveled together for a while and she told me some pretty incredible things. She told me that God wanted to use me in a very wonderful way, and she really encouraged me. We had coffee at one of the stops and then she said she had to meet her family and walked away. The funny thing was, she said she was walking around the corner and down the street. When we first had gotten out of the bus, I remember looking around the coffee shop, and there were no houses down the street. Just the coffee shop, gas station, and a couple of old, abandoned clapboard buildings."

Pastor Hank said, "That's an incredible story. God must have his hand of guidance on you. I don't understand what this little town has to do with any of it. But what I know isn't that important. It's what God has planned that is vital. Now, as far as an angel is concerned, that's fascinating. I've heard of people who believe they witnessed or talked with an angel. What made you think Edith was an angel?"

Al said, "That's simple. She knew things about me that nobody knew. She spoke with an authority that I've never heard before. And I knew in my soul that there was something strangely wonderful about her."

Pastor Hank asked, "So what's going to happen about your headaches? Are you just going to live with them? Is there any help available for you?"

Al chuckled and said, "You've been talking to Gracie, haven't you?"

Now it was Pastor Hank who chuckled and said, "Some things a minister has to keep confidential."

Al was at the office by nine and found Gracie on the phone. When she hung up, Al sat across from her smiling.

"What's with the smile?" she asked.

"Oh, I just had coffee with Pastor Hank. Seems a little bird has been talking to him about me."

Now Gracie was smiling as she quipped, "So now this town has talking birds. Strange place this town is."

"I planned on calling the hospital this morning. I'll go back to my desk and keep my promise. And you can tell Pastor Hank."

With that, Al walked back to his desk. Close to ten minutes later, Al was back in Gracie's office.

"Okay, the hospital says they'll be sending me a packet of forms to fill out. Once I send them back, they'll get the records from my surgery. Once they have those, they'll call me with an appointment."

Gracie was relieved with the information. She never told Al, but the headaches and the nightmares were a constant worry to her. She feared that they might increase in their frequency. She thought that if they ever started hitting him in the middle of the day, his life could be in danger. The thought of him driving to cover a story and being hit with the blinding lights and headache was more than she wanted to think about.

Al and Gracie spent the rest of the day getting the paper run ready. Jimmy showed up in the afternoon to help. He was always fun to have around. Al cared about the young man who chauffeured him to Salmon Stream Crossing. Jimmy was an open book. You knew when he was happy, which was almost all the time. And you always knew when something was bothering him. It was long after dark when the two men finished in the back room, and the papers were ready to take to the post office and the stands the next day.

On Wednesday, Al and Jimmy got the papers distributed. It was much easier for Al having Jimmy around. Before, he would have to stop at each business or corner stand, get out and stack the papers, get back in and go. Jimmy was a great sidekick. Because he loved jumping out of the vehicle, grabbing an armload of newspapers, and stacking them in the right place, Al's job was made much easier. By the end of Wednesday, the two men were tired, and Jimmy's arm muscles were pretty worn out.

Al said, "Jimmy, now that we're done, Gracie wants us to come over for dinner. We better get moving. She might not want to wait for two dirty newspapermen."

As the two were coming in the back door, Gracie yelled, "You two, go into the laundry room and wash your grubby hands before you come in here. Lucky you came in when you did. I was just gonna sit and eat it all by myself."

The slight smirk on her face told Al what was going on. Jimmy began to apologize with torrents of, "I'm sorry Gracie, really, really, I am. I'll work faster next week, promise I will."

Gracie couldn't hold back any longer and laughed. She said, "I was joking with you, Jimmy. You'd better get used to me joking, especially if you're gonna be coming around here. I'll have dinner ready in a minute. You two just stay in your seats."

Dinner was one of Al's favorites—baked pork chops with scalloped potatoes, extra cheddar cheese, and green beans on the side. The two men were speechless for ten minutes until the clear glass baking dish was empty. There wasn't even a spoonful to put in the fridge.

Al and Jimmy cleared the table and washed the dishes. Afterward, Gracie brought out dessert. She set the pie on the table with three small plates and dessert forks. The crust had the

227

look of perfection, golden brown center with the edge being a bit darker than the center.

Looking at the pie, Jimmy said, "I bet it's blueberry."

To which Al challenged, "Nope, it's dark raspberry."

Gracie said, "Both of you boys are wrong. You'll never guess. It's an elderberry pie." It really didn't matter to the two men. All that mattered was it was pie and Gracie made it. As Al enjoyed his second piece, his mind went back to an old boarding house and Bee's pie.

On Friday the information from the hospital arrived. Al read through the papers and signed the release form for his medical records. He walked the two blocks down to the post office and dropped the envelope into the outgoing box. Back at the office, he found Gracie on the phone, as usual. As he walked past her, she waved for him to stop. Motioning to the phone, he turned and came back to her desk. He heard her say, "All right, Bill. I'll tell Al, and I'll talk with you soon."

From the snippet that Al heard, Gracie had his attention. When she hung up, he asked, "What was that all about with Bill? Something I need to know?"

Gracie said, "Bill called to say they found the remains of an elderly man in the river about two miles downstream from where you and Ray were. The coroner said the man died of a severe blow to the back of his head, and it would be consistent with a victim falling backward and hitting his head against a large rock."

Al said emotionlessly, "I guess that pretty well answers that mystery at the river."

That evening, while Al and Gracie were in the dining room, Gracie gave Al a brown paper bag.

"Open it up," she said. "I ordered this more than a month ago. Folks from the mail order company never heard of us.

Seems like some people don't even know we exist up here. I wanted to get it for you a while ago. Well, anyway, here you go." Al looked with surprise at Gracie.

Al sat with the paper bag on his lap, curious as to its contents. He opened it and then pulled out a plastic bag. Al looked into the clear plastic bag and pulled out a natural brown leather portfolio. His broad smile brought an instant smile to Gracie.

Gracie said, "I can't have you going to council meetings and other important appointments carrying around just a tablet of paper, can I?" Al was motionless for a moment and then pushed back his chair, bending over he gave Gracie a hug. He said, "Thanks, I've never had a leather case, and this one is beautiful and my favorite color."

Saturday morning was blessed with a cool breeze. The sounds of birds coming in Al's window added a sense of peace. It was a morning to read. He opened Poe again and came to the conclusion that Poe needed the divine purpose for life. He had an emptiness in his soul. After the darkness of Poe, he continued his study of Augustine.

After putting down the writings of Augustine, he picked up his Bible. He was reading from Ephesians. The words he found were hard to understand. "God," he read, "wants to fill His children with His divine nature." That, he thought was past his understanding. After reading he spent time praying for the needs on his prayer list.

Lunch with Gracie was homemade chicken and noodles. Her cooking so reminded him of Bee; his heart ached a bit when he dwelled on the circumstances that led him to leave her. After cleaning up, he went back to his room and continued reading.

21

Gracie Joins Them

Al found his usual seat in church Sunday morning. Larry and Jimmy joined him a few minutes later. As he sat waiting for the service to begin, he thought that Pastor Hank must be doing something right. Over the last few weeks, about half a dozen new people started attending. The preliminary music was just beginning when Jimmy turned his attention to the door. Both Larry and Al caught Jimmy's movement and looked towards the door. Spotting Gracie, all three men stood up.

Gracie saw them right away. She made her way to where they were standing and slid past Larry and Jimmy, taking a seat between Al and Jimmy. Al leaned over and whispered in her ear, "I'm glad you came this morning. I think you kind of surprised a few people." During the service, all three men were dumbfounded as Gracie sang with a beautifully clear soprano voice. More than once the three men stopped singing so they could enjoy the pure voice of the most important lady in their life.

Pastor Hank spoke on "The Unexpectedness of God." He used a couple of biblical stories to enforce the truth that what we see as unexpected is not that at all. God uses events and circumstances for whatever his purpose is. He said that when Jesus turned the water into wine, it was totally unexpected. He challenged everybody to be ready and expect the unexpected. "And don't be surprised when God brings it to you."

At the end of the service, Larry excused himself and headed out the door. Gracie tried to talk to him before he left, but Pastor Hank was quick to get to the back and welcome her. The pastor talked with her for a minute, and then she joined Al and Jimmy waiting outside. There was a chill in the air as they walked the few blocks down the street.

Before Jimmy turned off, Gracie invited him over for dinner. She told him to come around six and not a minute later. As they continued on, she said to Al, "I was intending on asking Larry over as well. I didn't want to seem to be forward, but I missed talking to him."

Al said, "I'll see Larry in a couple of hours. I'll tell him we expect him for dinner at six."

By six o'clock, all three men were already sitting at the table. Al was getting up to help Gracie when she said, "You three just stay where you are, I'll bring out the food and then we'll eat." She went in and out of the kitchen bringing in the roast, mashed potatoes, carrots, and then the biscuits. When she sat down, she said, "I'm going to ask the blessing this evening."

Al's smile across the table connected with her for a brief second. Gracie prayed, "Dear God, I thank you for the food you have provided to us. I thank you for my friends. They have blessed me in so many ways. Thank you, dear God, for your love, and for Jesus who came into the world to save us. Amen."

For the next twenty minutes, the only sound was silverware against china, and the tinging of glass serving bowls. If ever a cook outdid herself, it was Gracie. She had put an extra-large beef roast in the oven before she left for church. She let it cook low and slow, all day. When she came home, she prepared her baked carrots, putting them in a large baking dish and covering them in a layer of brown sugar. She started the pan with the potatoes in it and put the carrots in the oven. When the potatoes were done, she mashed them, adding fresh butter and garlic.

With the last forkful from each plate was consumed, Gracie spoke up, "I just want to say something before we have dessert. Dessert comes after you three do the dishes." She chuckled and said, "No, I'm kidding. What I want to say is, on Friday I realized how God has been taking care of me. Since Ray left me, the three of you have been helping me continue on. You have become my friends and, and, my family. This is the way I wanted to say thanks. You know, they say a way to a man's heart is through his stomach. So, how did I do?"

She wasn't ready for the onslaught from the three men at her table. The comments and laughter were a powerful message.

Al told Larry and Jimmy that they wouldn't get dessert until the table was cleared and the dinner dishes done. Larry announced that he was gonna wash, Jimmy said he would dry, and that left Al to put the dishes away. It didn't take the men ten minutes to get everything washed, dried, put away, and settle back at the table.

Gracie brought out the apple pie and put it on the table. The top crust glistened with a mixture of sugar, butter, and a sprinkle of cinnamon. Al stood to cut the pie and asked, "Gracie, is it all right just to cut the pie into four pieces?"

She said, "If you do, there won't be any left for later. Anyway, wait a minute, I have to get the ice cream."

After dessert, Larry and Jimmy left, and Al and Gracie sat in the living room talking. Al was interested in Gracie's new attitude.

He asked her, "What happened on Friday? You said you realized something. What happened?"

Gracie said, "I was thinking about Ray. And I realized how blessed I am to have you helping me. I know that God wanted you to come here. I thought of Jimmy as well. He's such a blessing to have around. He's so full of excitement and joy; he's almost infectious. And Larry has been concerned about me and is willing to do anything for me."

Gracie continued, "Since we talked about church and I told you about being a child and going to church and Sunday school, I sense the Lord has been talking to me. I've been praying, and I'm going to try to get closer to the Lord. I know Jesus loves me, and, and I want to live for him. I know that I need to keep praying, get back to reading my Bible, and keep going to church."

Al said, "Gracie, you're a blessing to me and other folks around here. Now I'm going upstairs and sticking my nose in a book."

On his way up the stairs, Al leaned over rail and kissed Gracie on the cheek. "Good night," he said, "Thanks for a wonderful evening, and I don't mean just the food. You're a blessing to me." Gracie smiled as he went past. When she heard him go up the stairs, she sat back in Ray's chair. With her eyes closed, it would be difficult to see the tiny tear form.

Al sat on his chair reading for an hour or so and then got ready for bed. He knew the week would be busy, and he was going to be dragging by Wednesday night. As he got into bed and pulled up the fresh smelling sheet and comforter, he thanked God for Gracie. Before giving in to his tiredness, he thought about the sermon of the morning and prayed that he might be ready for the unexpected from God.

The flashes of light were blinding. Al tried to make out the hands on the big wind-up alarm clock. It was just past midnight. The flashes increased to a steady strobe. The pillow over his head did nothing to mitigate neither the pain nor the nausea. After an hour of wrestling with the light and the pain, exhaustion won, and the battered man fell asleep.

The morning light found him on the floor, halfway to the bathroom. He didn't want Gracie to know, so he pulled himself together and made it into the shower. He let the hot water run over his aching and tired body. After getting shaved and dressed, he headed down the stairs and made it past Gracie. Once out the door, he walked over to Chuck's place.

He found Chuck sitting at the counter and greeted him. Chuck said, "You know where the cups and the pot are, help yourself."

Al got his coffee and sat next to Chuck. "Any news about Caroline?" Al asked.

Chuck responded back, "Nay, nothing yet. I talked with her last night, and she said it might be a few more days. I hate this waiting stuff, enough to drive a man over the edge."

Al said, "Remember I'm praying, and so are a lot of other people."

"Thanks, I never really thought a lot about praying, before this, I mean."

Al nodded and shared, "I guess I never thought much about praying either. As a kid I never went to church, and praying wasn't a part of my life. I don't remember any friends who even talked about praying or going to church. When I was at Agape Station, the pastor and his wife took me under their wings and taught me the first things I learned about faith and being a Christian. They told me that praying is never supposed to be difficult. If we believe that God loves us, then we should talk to God that way."

Al got up to get more coffee and continued, "While I was with them, I found a small book that helped me. It was written hundreds of years ago by a monk. He worked in the kitchen of the monastery and did the same job over and over, every day.

Well, he says in the book that he learned to pray even while he was working and that God was with him. That God didn't care if he was peeling potatoes or scrubbing the floor. He called it, practicing the presence of God. I know praying works because I'm still alive."

22

Mystery of the River Deepens

Coming in the front door at the office, Al found Gracie at her desk. He walked past her into the back room to make sure the supplies were ready for the next day. He spent an hour moving a few things and cleaning around the outside of the receiving door. With the weather change coming in a few weeks, he didn't want to be caught off guard. Folks around town talked about the first frost and how snows can happen suddenly. After finishing the cleaning, he went back to his desk. The phone rang, and Al told Gracie that he would answer it.

Al introduced himself, and asked, "What can I help you with?" As Al was listening, he stretched out the phone cord as far as possible and waved for Gracie to come over. "Sir," Al said, "I'm going to put you on speaker phone. Is that okay?"

The voice on the other end said, "That's fine with me."

"Okay," Al said, "let's start over. I introduced myself. What is your name? What's going on?"

Through the speakerphone came, "My name is Charles. I am a dentist in a small town north of Eagle Ridge. I fish the river at least once a week. For the past few weeks, I've been fishing just downstream from a small restaurant, River's Edge Diner, I think that's the name. Last week I thought I saw something strange. Today I was at the same spot, and I swear that what I'm going to tell you is the truth."

Al interrupted, "Excuse me, Charles. Is it okay for me to take notes while we talk?"

"Sure that's alright," Charles said. "You're going to think I'm nuts, so what's the difference?"

Gracie spoke up, "Sir, we're not judging you; we want to hear your story."

"Well okay," Charles continued, "I was at the same spot this morning. And again, I saw this fellow walk down to the river with a man who looked about middle age. They got into the same guide boat I saw last week. They headed across the river and caught the current heading my way. About a hundred yards away...you're not gonna believe me. The darn boat started to sparkle as if stars were exploding from it, and then they were gone, vanished, and the boat with them."

Gracie had been staring at Al during the phone conversation. Al asked Charles, "Can you come down to the office and talk? I really want to hear what you have to say face to face. I'll be here all day." Charles told Al that he was using a pay phone just down from the river, and it would take him an hour or so to get to the paper. Al told him that he would stay at the office until he arrived.

A little more than an hour later, an older pickup truck pulled in front of the office. Al and Gracie were both looking out the front window as the man got out and walked around the front of his truck. Al and Gracie were trying to size him up. Al had made the remark to Gracie that they might be dealing with a nut case and that's why he wanted the man to come to the office.

The man was wearing jeans, a long sleeved heavy cotton shirt, and high-quality leather boots that laced up over the ankles. He was clean shaven and presented himself very well. When he came through the door, Al met him with an extended hand.

His grip was firm as he introduced himself. Charles said, "Let me begin by saying a few things. First, I've been fishing the river for quite a few years, so I know the river pretty well. Second, I used to fish upstream, but a friend told me about the spot by the diner. It turned out to be a good spot. The first time I watched the guide boat I didn't pay much attention, except for the fact that I loved the boat. When it vanished, I just thought that I had lost it behind some of the overhanging trees. Not this time. I watched the boat from the time it left the bank on the other side of the river."

Al asked, "Where did the boat leave from?"

Charles' answer was without a moment's hesitation, "Right where the footpath comes down from the diner. The footpath is across the river and about a hundred yards upstream from where I fish. The river must be close to two or three hundred feet across right there. It was almost directly across from me when the boat and the two people in it started to sparkle. You know, like the river sparkles when the sun bounces off. There was nothing else on the water, nothing."

As Charles was talking, both Al and Gracie were jotting down notes. When he finished his story, both Al and Gracie thanked him for stopping by. Al said, "I'll follow up on this. You have given us some good information about some things we have only heard of."

As Charles went out the door, he turned and said, "I hope you follow up because I know what I saw, and I'm not nuts."

With the front door closed, Al turned to Gracie and said, "This is very strange. For years people have been talking about crazy things happening along the river. And, now we have this guy come in, who swears he saw two people and a boat sparkle and vanish."

Gracie looked at Al and spoke up, "You have to admit that

the guy seemed credible. He didn't seem like a nutcase. I'm gonna suggest something to you. When your deliveries are done on Wednesday, get your stuff together and bright and early Thursday morning head north. Now, this is just a suggestion. I will leave the final decision up to you. But I am the acting editor, am I not?"

Al smiled at her and said, "You know what, great minds must think alike because that is exactly what I was going to suggest to my editor and boss."

On Tuesday morning Al made sure that his copy was in order and ready to be set. Gracie finalized the ads and the story she was working on. She had decided to put a teaser on the second page about the supposed strange occurrences on the river. She didn't give any details and ended it by telling the readers the information was being investigated. By Tuesday evening everything was set, and Al and Jimmy would be ready for their deliveries on Wednesday.

Jimmy was at Chuck's bright and early Wednesday morning, sitting at the counter when Al came in. Chuck said to Al, "Grab your cup. I'll have your toast in a minute, and yeah, I remember; now you don't like wimpy toast. Wimpy toast, you never even said that before the preacher said it."

Al got his cup and sat next to Jimmy who was antsy as usual. Turning on the chrome stool, he asked Al, "Are you ready for the day? Got the papers done? Did you have to finish last night? Did you need my help last night?"

Al was shaking his head and smiling saying, "Jimmy, I don't know what I would do without you, but at times I don't know what to do with you!" Putting his arm around his friend, he said, "We still have work to do. We have to do the sorting, get the labels on them, and then get them delivered. We will have a full day."

Done with his toast and coffee, Al asked Chuck if he had heard any news about Caroline. He told Al that he was expecting her to call tomorrow. Al left with Jimmy and reminded Chuck that he was still praying for her, and Chuck surprised him when he said, "I've been prayin' too." Al and Jimmy took the few steps back to the paper. They went into the back room and started on the sorting and labels. By early afternoon they were on their way to the post office and the stands.

Back at the office, Gracie was waiting for the two men. She knew that by this evening, Al would be exhausted. Around four, Al and Jimmy pulled in front of the office. The two came in the front, and Gracie asked Al, "Are you ready for tomorrow?"

Al answered, "Yeah, I plan on leaving early in the morning. I want to get up there and poke around for a while. See if I can find a local to talk to. I'd really like to be back by noon. It'd be nice if I could get back even sooner."

Jimmy's curiosity got the best of him. He asked, "Where ya goin'? Need me to come along?"

Al answered, "No, Jimmy, I'm just going north for a few hours. Got some information I need to follow up on."

Jimmy's nose for adventure was picking up on something, and he asked again, "Aw c'mon. Let me go. I won't get in the way."

Al answered him, "No, Jimmy, not this time. If I have to go again, I'll think about it."

Al told Gracie, "I'm tired. I think I'll go over to Chuck's for something to eat, and I'll turn in early."

Gracie protested, "Why, you don't have to go to Chuck's. I can make you something for dinner; it's no trouble."

Al said, "I know it's no trouble to you, but the way you take care of me bothers me some."

Al walked next door, leaving Jimmy and Gracie standing in

the office. Jimmy thought that she looked upset, and he tried to help. "I'm sure," he said, "He didn't mean anything of it. He's probably tired."

"I know," Gracie said, "I'll talk to him tonight when he gets back."

With that, Jimmy walked out the front door and headed over to Chuck's place. Jimmy took a seat next to Al, and Chuck brought him a cup of coffee and asked him if he was gonna eat. Jimmy told Chuck no. For over a minute, he sat silently next to his friend.

With his foot bouncing a hundred miles an hour on the lower rung of the stool, Jimmy asked Al, "You alright? Please don't mind me for asking. You seemed a little upset with Gracie."

"Oh, I'm alright I guess," Al said. "I just think Gracie does too much for me. I'll talk with her tonight."

Jimmy laughed and said, "That's exactly what she said, that the two of you would talk tonight."

Walking into the living room, Al found Gracie sitting in Ray's chair. A sense of sadness welled up in his heart. He thought, *She'll always be drawn to that chair. The smell of Ray's aftershave and tobacco will linger for a long time.* He sat on the edge of the sofa just a few feet from her.

"Gracie," he said, "I want to apologize for what I said at the office. What I really wanted to express to you was, I think you do too much for me. You cook most of my meals, and you've been doing my laundry."

Gracie started to tear up; a moment later she looked at Al and said, "It's been hard these weeks and months, you know, losing Ray. He was such a large part of my life. We loved our work here. For years it was Ray that worked hard. He didn't want me to work. But when we came here, it was different for both of us. Ray wanted me to work, and we were a great team. I think when I lost Ray, I still needed to take care of somebody. I guess that was you."

Getting up from the sofa, Al went over to Gracie. He looked intensely at her and said, "I miss Ray. He'll always be a very important person in my life. He allowed me to come here, and I'll be forever grateful. By coming here, I got to know you. You're such an important person to me right now. Please forgive me for being sharp with my words. You're the last person I would want to hurt." By this time both friends were wiping away tears. Before getting up, Al took both of Gracie's hands in his and kissed the back of them, "I love you," he said.

Coming down the stairs Al's senses of smell were delighting in the fusion of coffee and bacon. Gracie was over at the counter getting out two plates and cups. She asked Al, "Do you still like your eggs over medium? While I get the eggs going, would you make some toast?"

Al responded, "Sure, I'll make the toast, it's the least I can do for such a great breakfast."

He pulled the bread out of the bread box and put two slices in for Gracie. When hers were done, he spread butter on them and put his in the toaster. He turned the dial up so the toast would darken. Gracie was basting the eggs in the bacon grease and finished just about the time the toast was done.

At the table, Gracie said, "I'll say the blessing. Lord, bless this food to our nourishment. And please guide Al today as he travels. Keep him safe on the roads. We thank you for your love and grace, amen."

After breakfast Al gathered his jacket and portfolio, making sure that he had a couple of ink pens and spiral tablets. Giving Gracie a kiss on the cheek, he said, "I should only be a few hours unless something spooky happens."

They both chuckled as he headed for the door.

"Wait a minute," Gracie said. "I almost forgot your thermos of coffee." In a second she was back holding a green steel thermos. "Ray has had this for years, still keeps the coffee hot," she said.

Saying his goodbye, Al went out the door and got into the old four-wheel drive and headed north.

23

Al Meets Rose

Al pulled away from the house not long after sunup. The drive north was pleasant and relaxing. He had fallen in love with the countryside, with the massive pines and rolling hills. The farther north he got, the more rugged the terrain appeared. The beauty of the land was intoxicating.

After an hour on the road, he pulled off on to a two-track that went to the river. He was on the opposite side of the diner and figured he was at the spot Charles talked about. Al had told Gracie that he was going to poke around, first where the fisherman was and then to the footpath at the river. He parked and got out, walked to the edge of the river, and looked across. He could hardly make out the footpath on the opposite side of the river, so he began thinking he must be a little farther downstream than Charles had been.

Driving out of the clearing, he noticed tracks through tall grass going to the river. Making a sharp right turn, he followed the grass that had been bent over and found another clearing. Now, even looking through the window, Al could make out the footpath in plain sight as it snaked up the hillside towards the diner. Not seeing any boat near the path, he took a break and poured a cup of coffee from the steel green thermos.

Ten minutes later Al pulled onto the asphalt heading down the grade to cross the river. It was close to a four hundred foot drop to the river, and the old four-wheel drive's transmission complained all the way. He crossed the old timber and steel framed bridge and climbed the grade, pulling into the gravel lot of the River's Edge Diner. Al remembered the first time at the diner. That night along the river had been cold and long, and he was glad Bill and Ray had wanted coffee.

Al got out with his jacket over his arm and portfolio in his other hand. In the full light of day, the diner looked older and more worn than the first time he saw it. The white clapboard siding was in need of paint and repair, and the old worn concrete steps coming up to the front door looked to be in as bad a shape. The old screen door dragged and twisted as Al pulled on it. When he pushed on the storm door, it gave way, and the bell on the top of the door clanged.

One step inside and a voice from the back welcomed him and told him that he would be taken care of in a minute. As he stood there, he was positive of two things: the first was the voice was not that of the petite old lady that was there the first time. The second being the voice was strangely familiar, and it was not that of a white northeasterner.

As Al stood there, the voice from the back said, "Go ahead take a seat; I'll bring you coffee in a minute." Al sat by the front window from where he could just make out the edge of the river on the opposite bank. *It's a pretty steep hill* he thought as he looked out. He heard the swinging of the back room door and turned in his seat. "Good morning, I'm Rose," she said.

Walking towards him, Rose was carrying a cup and saucer. She set them down and said, "I told you who I am, who might you be?"

Al introduced himself and told her he was a reporter from Salmon Stream Crossing.

"A reporter? What in this world brings you up here?"

Al said, "I'm just following up on a couple of things. Seems people say they see strange things along the river."

Rose answered, "Near as I can tell they say strange things been happenin' on this river for a couple of hundred years."

"Well, what do you make of it?"

Rose answered, "Nothin' happened around here that wasn't supposed to be happenin'."

Rose turned and went back behind the counter. Looking over at Rose, he thought she looked familiar. His mind went back to Sarah, and their time on the coast. "No, it couldn't be," he said to himself. "Wasn't the woman at the old roadside diner named Rose?"

"Rose," he said, "could I talk with you for a couple of minutes?"

"Well sure," she said. Coming over to the table she sat right across from him.

Al asked, "Have we met before? You look familiar to me."

She answered, "We sure could have. I've been all over and there and back a few times."

Her answer didn't do anything for his confusion. So, he decided to ask her a direct question, "Have you ever been in southeast Virginia?"

"I suppose I have," she said. "This is all pretty confusing to you. You come in here, and I haven't given you a simple answer to any of your questions. You really don't know why you're here, do you?"

Al's response to Rose was quick. "Well, yes, I do know exactly why I'm here. I'm here because strange things have happened along this river for a long time. And just a few days ago a guy walked into my office, telling me an incredible story about a man, a boat, and the two times he thought he saw the boat vanish. That's why I'm here."

Rose smiled and said, "That's what brought you here. But that's not the reason you are here. I wanted you to come here for a story that will help lots of folks."

Al's chair ground on the old wooden planks as he tried to pull it back.

She said, "Leaving won't answer the questions still in your soul. You asked me about the south. I know more about you than you realize. I know about the diner and Bee. I know Sarah and how she broke your heart. I know about your little baby girl. I know about Agape Station."

Al sat still as concrete, stunned, as she continued, "I know Stan, the hotel manager. And. I know Edith."

Al stammered, "How did you find out about me? Did Ray talk to you or something?"

"No," she said, "Ray never said a word to me. I have something to tell you that I must help you believe and understand. I know that the image of that precious little girl has been burned into your soul. Do you remember what happened in the instant before the blast?"

"Well," he said, "if you know all about me, you tell me."

"Whoa, wait a minute," Rose said. "I'm just trying to help clear up some fog. If you'll just try to remember, I'll help you, and it will bring peace to your heart."

Rose asked, "Would you please close your eyes and recall what happened right up to the explosion."

Al resisted saying, "What good is it going to do, nothing will change."

"Please," Rose said.

Al reluctantly said, "Alright. The first explosions knocked me out of bed. I made it down the street to a bunker. The enemy started zeroing in and moving the artillery down the street. I wanted to get some action shots of the explosions, so I moved to the edge of the bunker. Both the marine next to me and I saw the little girl running towards us. Both of us started yelling at her to run faster. I was looking around the bunker and waving at her with my right hand. At that point, the marine hollered at me that he was going out to get her."

Rose said, "Now this next part is important. What do you see just before the explosion?"

Al said, "I saw the marine moving behind me, and I turned to him. He was yelling at me, but I couldn't hear because an artillery round went off. In an instant, I was back looking around the bunker and yelling at the girl. And, then the explosion occurred and sent me flying backward. In that split second, the little girl vanished in front of me."

Rose asked, "Where was your camera just an instant before the explosion?"

"Why, what difference does that make?"

"Please," said Rose, "Just tell me where your camera was."

"Well," Al said, "when the marine started to go around me, my camera was on my left." When Al realized what he had just said, he stared at Rose. It took a moment for Al to regain his awareness. He asked Rose, "How did my camera save my life? If it was on the ground, how in the world did it take the blast?"

She answered, "I needed you here. You're going to work on the most important story of your life. I'm going to help you record an incredible series of events. Believe me when I tell you, people will have their lives changed with your writing. Over the past months, how many people have told you that God wanted to use you? Your pastor just preached about expecting the unexpected. This is it—the unexpected."

Al stammered, "What do want me to do?" Close to being speechless, he continued, "I do want to be faithful to what God wants from me. There is just so much I don't understand."

Rose responded back, "There's a lot you'll never understand, at least not here. In a few minutes, precious folks will begin coming in. I'm going to take care of them. They're going to have the most fantastic meal in their memory. As they come in, I'm going to tell you about their lives. I want you to write it all down. And don't just write what you see and hear, I want you to write what you sense too."

Al asked, "Can you explain a little more to me? I'm supposed to try to find out what's been going on around here. Gracie is expecting me to come back with a story or a dead end."

Rose said, "I know this is confusing. Your story will come together but in a different way. As time goes by, you'll understand the purpose of your writing. And I am going to help you see things that have been hidden, kind of like your camera on the ground."

Rose got up from the table and said to Al, "I'll get you a cup of coffee and be right back. And, by the way, in two minutes an elderly man by the name of Gene is gonna be coming in. When he does, I'll be paying attention to him and what he wants. I'll come by and tell you about him. Make sure you're ready to write down his story. You do have your nice leather portfolio from Gracie, don't you?" Al looked at her nervously as if he didn't know if he should smile or look worried.

Two minutes later an elderly man pushed the front door open. He hesitated a moment, looking around, and his feet shuffled on the old linoleum as he made his way towards the tables. Al noticed a few things right away. He looked like the world had been hard on him for a long time. He wore a waist length, brown corduroy coat. The stubble on his face and the hair on his head were the same length. As he walked past, Al noticed a skin condition on his chin and around his mouth. The way he puckered and moved his lips told Al that the elderly guy was missing most, if not all, of his teeth.

"Good morning, Gene," Rose said, "I'm so glad to see you this morning. I'm here to bring you the best meal you've had in a long time. I know you like your coffee with cream and sugar. I'll bring it right over."

Gene said, "How did you know about my coffee? I've never seen you before."

By the time he finished his statement, Rose was at the table. She put her hand on his shoulder and said, "Gene, I know all about you. I'm gonna make your breakfast as you remember it. I know you like thick cut, maple smoked bacon. I know you want your eggs and potatoes cooked in the bacon grease, and white toast, just slightly toasted. Relax and have a good breakfast. I'll be bringing your food right out."

Al watched Gene, and he didn't seem as nervous as he was just moments before. Al sensed that Rose's voice had put Gene at ease. Al noticed Gene reach down in the pocket of his coat and pull out a paperback. The wrangler depicted on the cover told Al the theme of Gene's book. Rose went back behind the counter to the grill and started transforming bacon, eggs, bread, and potatoes into a meal Gene would remember.

Even though he had eaten two hours earlier, the smell coming from the grill was putting a spell on Al. Visions of Bee cooking some of the best food he had ever eaten filled his mind. He was thinking that even though thick cut peppered bacon was his favorite, the smoked maple sure smelled wonderful too.

It took Rose about ten minutes to have the food ready. Before taking it to Gene's table, she refilled his coffee cup. She brought Gene his breakfast and said, "Now I expect you to enjoy it, and if you need anything, like more bacon or another egg, you just speak up. I know what you were just gonna ask. I'll bring the hot sauce right back." She winked at Al as she went behind the counter and brought back the hot sauce.

Walking over to Al's table, Rose took a seat and said, "Gene will be done in a few minutes, and then I'll have to leave you. During a Sunday school class when Gene was six, he asked Jesus to come into his heart. That moment he began a wonderful relationship of believing and loving. Gene was just twelve when his dad was killed in an accident on the farm. He was the oldest son, so the majority of the work and responsibility fell on his shoulders. His mother wanted to sell the farm and move away, but Gene persuaded her to stay and that together they could make a go of it."

Al shifted in his chair, and Rose said, "I'll answer your question in a minute. Working six days a week, from sun-up to sundown they made the farm work. Gene never went back to school, but he made sure his brothers and sister finished school. Life was hard on Gene, but he never stopped believing in his Father's love, nor did he ever blame him for a hard life. Gene loved his Father in heaven. He'd pray with his mom at night, and they would pray for their family and the work that had to be done. They were so thankful for the blessings they had."

Al asked Rose, "Are you sure I shouldn't be writing this down?"

She said, "Don't worry, it'll all come back later. When Gene's brothers and sisters were out of school and his mother had passed on, he had to leave the farm. It was a life that he loved. He wandered around for a while. It was hard on Gene. He didn't finish school, and the skills he had were for farm work. One day he drifted into a town and walked through the door of a storefront ministry."

"Excuse me a moment," Rose said. Getting up from her chair, she walked over to Gene and asked, "Well now, is everything okay? Let me get you more coffee." Gene raised his cup and nodded as Rose walked to the counter. Bringing the pot, she refilled his cup.

Back at Al's table, she said to him, "Now back to Gene. It didn't take long for Gene to make friends. The two women that worked in the office found comfort with Gene sitting in the other room, kinda protecting them, that is what he told them. Strange people had been known to come into the office, and Gene was there to watch over things."

Rose got up from her chair and said to Al, "I have to be with Gene for a few minutes now." She walked over to Gene's table and sat across from him. Moving his plates and cup out of the way, she reached out and took his hands. Al couldn't hear what was being said, and the conversation lasted a couple of minutes.

Then Rose got up from her seat and went over to Gene's side of the table. Gene got up and Al noticed tears on his face as Rose put her arm around him. He bent over and gave her a hug. Gene was a massive man, and her head was well below his chin. He looked over at Al and through his tears, he was smiling. After letting her go, she walked with him towards the back door.

Just before Rose and Gene got to the door, it opened and in stepped a man. He was dressed in dark green brush pants, a dark rust colored heavy cotton shirt, and an oiled dark olive hat. As he stood in the door, his presence was powerful and striking. The stubble on his face, hair to his shoulders, and his countenance gave the impression of a very rugged woodsman.

Stepping forward, he took Gene's hand and pulling him forward, the two men embraced. As they turned to the door, the newcomer looked across the diner and caught Al's eye. He gave Al a slight smile and nod of his head.

Gene and the rugged looking man walked out the back door. Rose turned towards Al; her face was glowing as she walked to the table. She said, "I'm filled with joy every time I see Etche, the River Guide. And, when I get to introduce a traveler to him, well I'm so filled with joy, I just, I just want to shout."

Al was silent as Rose sat on the seat across from him. Finally he said, "What's really going on here? And, who is this Etche, the River Guide?"

"All in good time. All in good time. I have another traveler coming in just a couple of minutes. I have a couple of things I need to get ready."

Rose walked over behind the counter and brought out a starched white table cloth and a centerpiece filled with freshly cut carnations and baby's breath. She set the table with shining table service and what looked like a soft pink rose pattern antique cup, saucer, soup bowl, and plate. In the midst of her busyness, she said to Al, "You're going to love Hazel; she should be here any minute. She reminds me of a lovely flower."

Al was feeling a little more at ease and asked Rose, "Is it alright if I just keep my cup full?"

She answered back, "Sure it's okay, and it'll help me out."

As he was walking over to the counter, cup in hand, the front door opened. Standing in the doorway was an elderly woman. Al's first impression was that she was a person of means and substance.

Her white hair was meticulously in place. She stood in the doorway wearing a sandy brown skirt and sweater. Around her neck was a strand of pearls with matching pearl earrings. As she came in, she placed her hand on the top of a chair, and Al saw perfectly manicured fingernails painted an opaque white that nearly matched her pearls.

Standing next to Hazel's table, Rose said, "Good morning, Hazel, it is so good to see you. Come right over, I have your table ready."

As the visually impressive and elegant woman walked to her table, Rose pulled out her chair and helped her to her seat. Rose said, "I'll have your English Breakfast Tea ready for you in just a moment. I'm bringing the water to a boil."

Hazel responded, "Why, thank you so much."

Hazel's voice was an enticing blend of Southern charm and Midwest plain speak, soft, gentle, and friendly.

Rose brought over the teapot and the tea ball for Hazel. Hazel put the ball into the pot and closed the lid. As she did, Rose said, "Hazel, my dear one, I would like to suggest that you have my eggs benedict with Canadian bacon. I have a wonderful cinnamon and raisin toast, and I would never forget your favorite, grits and honey."

Hazel's eyes seemed to be sparkling as she spoke to Rose. She said, "I've been looking forward to this day for many, many years. You know exactly what I enjoy, and I'm so thrilled to be here with you."

As Al was listening, the peace and composure of Hazel surprised him. She spoke like a woman of tremendous grace and poise, seasoned with experience and wisdom. It took Rose only minutes to have Hazel's meal prepared and on her table. When Rose turned from the table, she was smiling and whispering a song, "A wonderful woman, a wonderful woman, a wonderful woman of God."

As Al watched Hazel, he was moved at how at peace she was in her surroundings. The diner was not a perfect example of class and ambiance; it was quite the opposite. The stark difference between this woman of grace and the old diner was staggering.

Watching her pour another cup of tea, she caught his eye. As Hazel smiled, Al sensed tremendous warmth coming from her.

Still whispering her song, Rose sat down next to Al. She said, "I only have a minute, and then I have to get busy again. Isn't she a remarkable woman! I'll tell you about her in a couple of minutes; you're gonna be really surprised."

Al thought, *How can I be any more surprised?*

Rose got up from the chair and said, "I've got to go to Hazel."

Rose sat across from Hazel, placing her hands on the crisp linen tablecloth. Al could tell Rose was talking to Hazel, but this time he couldn't understand what was being said. A moment later, Rose put her hands on both of Hazel's. Then she walked around to Hazel's seat. Hazel stood and the smile on her face was absolute glowing. As she turned to walk to the back door, the front door opened again.

Hazel turned around to see a man dressed in khaki slacks and navy sports coat standing in the doorway. Without a moment's hesitation, she said to him, "Frank, it's real; this is such a lovely place. I've been waiting for this day for a long time."

Rose walked over and introduced herself and said, "I'll be right with you, Frank. I'm just getting ready to introduce your wife to Etche, the River Guide. Please allow me to walk with Hazel to the back door."

Frank spoke up, "It's okay Hazel, my dear. I'll be with you in just a short time." Al watched stunned and emotionally moved as Frank walked to his wife and took both of her hands in his. He bent forward and kissed her on the cheek. Al heard him whisper, "I'll see you in just a few minutes."

Just as Hazel turned back to Rose, the back door opened and in stepped the River Guide. He took Hazel's hands in his, bent forward and whispered something in her ear. As they moved towards the back door, Hazel turned and gave Frank a wink and a smile. Rose said to Frank, "Welcome, Frank, I'm honored to know you. Please come and have a seat." Rose guided Frank to the table his wife had just occupied.

Rose said, "Frank, I'll go get your coffee." She came to the table with a cup and the pot, just getting ready to pour when Frank interrupted. "Excuse me, Rose, I would really like to use Hazel's teacup, if you don't mind." Rose smiled as she poured the coffee into the antique rose cup. She said to Frank, "I'll have your oatmeal and cream ready momentarily, and your toast, it is whole wheat and dry, isn't it?" Rose didn't wait for Frank to answer and headed behind the counter.

Al watched as Frank held up the teacup. Cradling it in his hands, every so often he took a sip, but he kept holding onto the cup. Rose got Frank's oatmeal and toast ready in a few minutes. She brought the items to his table on a tray with cream. When she set the items down, she said to Frank, "There's a little extra cream; I know how you like to dip your toast into your oatmeal." Frank's smile was almost like a child's cookie jar confession. Rose put her hand on Frank's shoulder and said, "Don't worry; I won't tell a soul."

Rose came to Al's table and sat. She said, "I'll tell you about Hazel and Frank and their special life together. Frank will be finished in just a few minutes. I'm gonna check on his coffee and have a chat. After Frank goes with the River Guide, we'll have time. I know you have questions, and I'll try to answer as many as I can."

Al was amazed as he watched Rose. She seemed to love every moment in the diner. He thought, *It's like she was made for this place, as if she's always been here.* Her smile and joy permeated everything from the coffee makers to the worn out bent chrome chairs. As Al sat, he realized that only the people Rose was expecting had come into the diner. An old pickup truck never stopped; a fisherman never came in for coffee. Another question was now trying to work its way into his confused mind.

Rose went to Frank's table and sat with him. Al figured she was talking with him like she did with Gene and Hazel. To Al's surprise, Rose began laughing. From his perspective he could tell, even looking at her back, that she was fully engulfed in laughter. He watched a good twenty seconds or more until she stopped.

As she moved her chair back, Frank was already standing and waiting for her. He was grinning and reached out and took Rose's hand. Al heard him say to Rose, "It's been a delight to have spent this time with you, but I'm on my way to be with the two biggest loves of my life."

Rose walked with Frank to the back door, and he bent down and kissed her on the forehead. As he did, the back door opened and the River Guide stretched out his hand to shake Frank's. When both men shook, they pulled themselves together and embraced. As they did, the River Guide looked over at Al and smiled. Without any effort, he pivoted and walked with his arm around Frank's shoulder.

Even before the back door was closed, Rose was heading to Al. Her smile and the sparkles coming from her eyes were magical. The moment she sat, she said to Al, "I love doing this; it makes me so happy to be with people before they meet the River Guide and cross over."

"Cross over," Al said. "What do you mean by that?"

Rose said, "Look at your watch, what time is it?"

Al looked at his watch and said, "It's eight forty-five, why?"

"What time did you get here?"

Al answered, "I looked at my watch when I pulled in. I have

to keep track of the time I spend on a story. My watch said it was eight thirty when I parked."

The bewildered look on Al's face was evidence of the truth that just hit him. He sputtered and said, "I know I've been here more than two hours. What in the world is going on?"

Rose said, "You've used that term more than a couple of times."

"What term have I used?" Al asked with a frown.

"Why," Rose said, "you've said, 'What in the world is going on?' What is going on here is not of this world. Al, I've brought you here for a reason. I'm sure it's obvious to you that this is no regular diner. The River Guide is not a local fisherman or outdoorsman just taking people on a floating trip down the river. You're going to write about people, people who believe in the Lord and in the power of his love. Folks of every economic and social standing are gonna come into the diner and meet Etche, the River Guide. They're folks who've been on a journey with God. Their journey has its greatest fulfillment here at the diner and crossing the river with Etche."

Al looked confused and amazed. He asked, "Will you tell me about Etche? He looks like a pretty rugged man."

Rose answered, "Sure, I'll tell you about him. I've referred to him as Etche and the River Guide. His name is Etche, which goes back generations to the early people of the land. In the tongue of the early people, it means, Canoe Man. That's why we call him the River Guide. Every traveler will meet him as their guide."

After pouring Al some more coffee, Rose continued, "Etche knows every traveler intimately. He knows all about their life. He has watched over every minute, every event; every joy and tear has been etched upon his heart. He knows when their heart was moved towards God."

Rose stopped for a moment and looked at Al; the twinkle in her eyes was gone. She said, "That's why what you're doing is important. Many people think that the way to cross over is to be good or have certain teachings memorized."

At this point Rose was getting back to her joyous form. Continuing, she said, "Since the beginning, it's never been about memorizing, or quoting, or reading certain things. It's always been about love. It's always been about my Father's love for mankind, his plan to rescue travelers by providing his guide, Jesus. God desires us to have belief and love, which are so simple. I don't understand why everybody wants to make it so complicated."

Al was sitting quietly, trying to understand what Rose was saying. He sensed an intensity building within his heart. He knew he must ask the question. "Rose," he said, "Is Etche—?"

"Yes, Al, he is. The day is coming when teachers and scholars will make the crossing complicated and confusing. Teachers will entice people with stories and mysteries. Some of them will get rich in their enticing. Their false words will be their curse. Men will turn the simple into the impossible to understand. They will transform the importance of relationship into religious confusion."

Al stammered, "How could he… How did you know what my question was? I'm having a hard time understanding this."

Rose smiled and said, "I understand. It's okay that you do not understand all of this. That will come later. What's important, though, is that you're here and writing these stories."

Al settled back, knowing he was going to hear another interesting story from Rose.

"Now, let me tell you about Hazel and then Frank," Rose began. "Hazel comes from a very influential family from the South. Her father was very successful in business, and her great,

great-grandfather made a fortune in the textile business. It's shameful that he did it using the toil of chained-children, slaves, as you know them to be. I prefer, chained-children. The world has been full of slavery for thousands of years. Hazel had the best of everything. She went to the finest schools, wore the finest clothes, and ate the finest foods. Just after college, she met Frank; he was in business and called on her dad's firm. It's funny, after his first visit and dinner party, he made his business calls there much more often."

Getting up, Rose brought the coffee pot to the table and re-filled Al's cup. After putting it back on the warmer, she returned. "Al," she said, "Hazel was a young woman brought up in the graces and charms of the South. Frank was from the Midwest. He was raised in a small town where he learned to work hard. He had a solid work ethic. As a youngster, he delivered newspapers every morning before school.

"Frank's mom died when he was just a teenager. Her death brought him into contact with godly people who helped him and his dad deal with their grief. It wasn't long after that, Frank and his dad met Jesus. When Frank met Hazel, it was very natural for him to talk with her about loving God. Within weeks Hazel had made the same decision, and the Lord began leading the two of them into a wonder-filled life.

"Hazel fell head over heels in love with Frank. With her dad's blessing, she and Frank were married. It was hard for her to move north because she had to leave behind her family, friends, and culture. She loved Frank and made his life her life.

"It didn't take long for her to become good friends with many people. They fell in love with her spirit and charm. She was involved in all kinds of activities that helped people in need. Hazel wasn't able to have children. So, instead of complaining, every child became her child."

Al said, "She sounds like she was, or should I say, is, one lovely person."

Rose responded, "She was and always will be a lovely person."

"Now," Rose said, "Let me tell you about Frank and Hazel's life together. Believing and loving would be the two words that every person who ever met them would use to describe them. Their loving hearts drew people in. Once you met Frank and Hazel, they were friends for life. It was impossible to be an inconvenience to them."

Al asked, "Did God bring them together?"

Rose laughed, and said, "Frank and Hazel were convinced God brought them together. They were strong in their beliefs, yet they never used them to send people away. It was their love of Jesus that opened their hearts to those around them. Frank was very successful in his career, yet they chose to live a very modest life. Their heart found its greatest satisfaction in helping the less fortunate and innocent children around the world. Your world would be so much better if there were more Frank and Hazels."

Rose got up from the table and put her hand on Al's shoulder. She said, "You'll have peace over all of this. Remember, I'll be helping you. In a few minutes, well, four to be exact, a remarkable lady is going to come in. Now she may frighten you or make you laugh; her name is Lilly, and she has quite a story. Some of her story will break your heart, and other parts will open your eyes to a new understanding of people and our Father."

Al was looking at Rose as if some revelation was beginning to dawn on him. He had to have an answer to a question. He asked Rose, "How do you know so much about these people when so many are older than you are?"

Rose said to him, "So you think these people are older than I am? I guess I should thank you for the compliment. I'll let you in on a secret and answer your question. Before everything you can see began, I was here."

Looking at Rose, Al's hands fidgeted on the table. Rose could feel the floor and table vibrate from his bouncing feet. His mouth fumbled, "Do I understand this…"

Rose interrupted, "Yes, you do understand. Etche and I have always been and always will be. The Father, your heavenly Father, has time in his control and we're part of his kingdom and plan." Reaching across the table, she took Al's hands. The warmth of her hands brought tears to his eyes, and a very gentle sensation moved throughout his body.

With his voice quiet and at times trembling, he asked, "Why would you choose me? I'm not the best person to do this. Are you sure that I'm the right person?"

Rose looked at Al and said, "Because you feel inadequate, you're the right person. I'll make your inadequacies a thing of the past. I wouldn't have brought you to this place if you weren't the right person." With a laugh, to help Al, she said, "You should know by now that I don't make mistakes."

24

Rose Continues

Al sat and watched the front door. In precisely four minutes, the door opened. Standing in the doorway was an elderly woman dressed in mismatched skirt and blouse. Her black shoes looked to be at least four or five sizes too large, and her white socks had slidden down around her ankles. She was wearing eye make-up that was the color of black and blue bruising.

Rose walked up to her and took her by the hand. "Well, I'll be, it's Lilly. I'm so glad to see you." Rose smiled over at Al and continued, "Come on in, I've been waiting for you. I have something very special planned for you."

"You do?" Lilly asked and continued, "I love special things, and you're doing it just for me."

Rose responded, "Oh yes, Lilly, this is just for you." She escorted the woman over to a table that had a bright red and yellow striped tablecloth. In the center of the table was a vase with a single white rose. Attached to the vase were three strings, holding in place three helium balloons, red, blue, and yellow.

Rose pulled out the chair for her, saying, "It's so wonderful to have you here. I've been waiting a long time to see you again. I'll have your hot chocolate with marshmallows in just a minute. It will take me a couple of extra minutes to make your special pancakes. You know how special they are, and I'm gonna make them just the way you've always liked them."

Lilly said, "You know, Miss Rose, it's been such a long time since I had my pancakes. I hope you remember how I like them."

Rose said, "Sure, I remember. But most people don't know the recipe like I know it. It's the extra special ingredients that most people leave out—the lemon juice, vanilla, and confectioners' sugar. That's what makes your pancakes so delicious."

Al watched Rose turn and walk to the grill. Coming back she had Lilly's hot chocolate and set it on the table in front of her. As he watched Lilly, he noticed she seemed to be talking to herself. It wasn't loud enough for him to distinguish her words, just a word here and there. He did understand, hot chocolate and pancakes, not much else. Lilly took a sip of her hot chocolate with marshmallows. When she lowered her cup, the foam highlighted her mouth. With her foamy mustache, she smiled at Al and said, "I sure hope you have some of Rose's wonderful hot chocolate. It's so delicious, just like I used to have back home."

Al watched Lilly smiling and clapping her hands quietly. As she clapped, she rocked a bit in her chair. Al thought, *How could she be so happy and excited over hot chocolate and pancakes?* He was trying to determine what might be wrong with her. She seemed simple but not what people would call retarded. Rose appeared from behind the counter with a tray and on it were Lilly's pancakes, butter, and maple syrup.

Rose said to her, "Here we are. Now you tell me if everything isn't perfect. I mean everything. I can make more pancakes, and I have plenty of butter and syrup."

Lilly answered, "Oh Rose, I'm so happy. I'm sure they're gonna be perfect. Thanks so much, you're such a wonderful friend."

A moment later, Al was surprised to hear Lilly clapping her hands and laughing.

"O Rose," she said, "You made a chocolate chip smiley face on my pancakes. I just love them."

At that she began to butter and cut her pancakes. She poured the maple syrup over them, and the smell reached Al. As she ate the pancakes, a smile crossed her face, giving Rose the signal that her treat went beyond her expectations.

Rose came over to the table and sat next to Al. She said, "Don't you just love her? She's just the sweetest thing, not a mean bone in her body. I'll tell you about her in a few minutes. After she goes with Etche, we'll have time to talk and for you to write."

Rose glanced over at Lilly's table and told Al, "She's almost done; Etche should be coming in the back door in a minute." Rose got up from her seat and walked over to Lilly.

"So, Lilly my dear," Rose said, "how were the pancakes? Did I do okay?"

Lilly smiled back and said, "They were wonderful, just like I remember. This is so much fun. The tablecloth and the balloons—this is wonderful" She was smiling and rocking a bit on her chair, and as she did, she silently clapped her hands. With her hand on Lilly's back, Rose bent over to talk to her. After a moment Rose pulled Lilly's chair out for her, and the two headed towards the back door.

Etche opened the back door and stepped in. Without hesitation, Lilly took his hand. She turned and looked at Rose and said, "Thank you, Rose, you're such a sweetie. I'll see you later." As Lilly headed out the back door, she looped her arm through the big arm of Etche and skipped once or twice towards the door. Al and Rose heard Etche laugh as the back door closed.

When Rose turned away from the back door, Al saw a tear on her round cheek. "Folks like Lilly are such a blessing to me," she said to Al. "The Father has very special people in the world;

you might call them different. Their belief and love have not been complicated by the cares and worries most people carry around. Etche has such a deep love for them. He calls them his heart-children. Love motivates them. He wishes that everybody would look at God the way both young and old heart-children do."

Rose sat and looked at Al. She said to him, "Please begin to write your impressions of Gene, Hazel, Frank, and Lilly. Once you start writing, everything will flow. Take care with your words. Protect each piece of paper like a priceless treasure. After you're finished, we'll talk." With that said, she put her hand on his shoulder, and the pressure from it was ever so slight. As she did, Al felt a sensation move from her hand across his shoulders and down to his fingertips.

Al began writing. At the top of one page he wrote, General Impressions, and then he put the names of Gene, Hazel, Frank, and Lilly on the top of individual sheets. He wrote for what must have seemed close to an hour, though it was hardly minutes. When he moved to the pages with the names, his writing was quick and deliberate. He never crossed out a word, idea, or thought. In a matter of minutes, he had two or three sheets filled for each person.

After a few minutes, Rose came over to the table and sat down. "Well," she said, "How's it going?"

Al smiled at her and said, "In all of my life, I've never written this fast and self-assured."

Rose smiled and asked, "Any special insight so far? Is there anything that they had in common?"

"That's easy," Al said. "They didn't talk about churches or denominations, they talked about Jesus. It was easy to see on their faces and even within their words that believing and loving Jesus was what their life was centered on."

Rose smiled and said, "I think you're on the right track."

When Al was finished writing, he slid the papers into his leather portfolio. "Rose," he said, "I have a question."

"I know you do," she said. "It's about Lilly. There are special people in this world. You folks put labels on them; we don't. Lilly was not always as she appeared. I guess you would say she had a normal, whatever that is, childhood and upbringing. Her father was a professor at a university, and her mother was a professional musician."

Al noticed Rose's expression change as she continued. "When Lilly was six, she was hit by a drunk driver and suffered severe head trauma. When that happened, her mind moved into another world. The world she lived in, up to her meeting with Etche, was centered on love and acceptance. She loved people without any barriers and just wanted people to return that kind of love. Some heart-children are born into a world of love and acceptance. Some, like Lilly, move into that world later."

Al said, "That just doesn't seem fair. She had wonderful parents and endless possibilities in her future and then, what, a wasted life."

Rose stood up from her seat and got close to Al. She said, "Now you wait a minute. Who said she had a wasted life? That's what's wrong with so many of you folks. You judge and compare by a wrong set of standards. Many of you would say of Lilly that she could never live a fulfilled life. Just let me tell you, she had more love in her heart and kindness on her lips than hundreds of sad, rich, and educated people that I've known. And, believe me, I've known more in my time that you can imagine."

Al knew that he had touched a nerve with Rose. He said, "I'm sorry for offending you. That's just the way so many people think. I wasn't trying to be judgmental."

Rose smiled and replied, "I know you weren't. I just get a

little testy when the innocents get hurt or misunderstood. You folks have got so much of living screwed up. Now in a few minutes, Elizabeth is going to be coming in. Let me tell you just a bit about her. She's a woman of great beauty and character. Her inner beauty has helped to create a distinguished person of great grace and talent. She's a musician, a pianist to be exact, of the highest caliber. She began her lessons when she was four. And, like most children, she hated them for a while. That was until she was seven, and she played a number for her Sunday school. Jesus touched her that day, and she's been in love with him ever since. She told me once that she would close her eyes and see Jesus smiling at her."

Al looked at his coffee cup. It was still full, but it was cold. He couldn't remember the last time that ever happened. Rose was smiling at him when she said, "Cold coffee, how long has it been since that happened?"

Al responded, "Well, I bet you know how long it's been." He chuckled at the end of his statement, and Rose's smile just got bigger. Still grinning, she said, "Elizabeth will be here in just a moment. I have a few things to get ready for her."

A moment later the front door opened again, and Elizabeth stepped into the diner. Al was taken aback for a moment at her beauty. The contrast between the diner and her beauty was extreme. She was dressed in dark gray slacks and matching jacket. Her white turtleneck offset her jet black hair, tied in a bun on the back of her head. She stood still just for a second, looking around, and smiled at Al.

Rose came from behind the counter and said, "Hello, Elizabeth, it's so wonderful to have you. Come on in, and I'll show you to your table."

As Rose walked her to the table, it was easy to be impressed with the woman's physical stature and the gracefulness of her movements. She seemed to move on air. Rose led her to the table that Hazel had used. The table was now covered in a light pink rose table cloth. The centerpiece was a single white rose in a lead crystal vase. The plate, cup, and saucer were patterned royal blue, gilded in gold. The service was the same silver that she used when Hazel was her guest.

Rose stood next to the table for a moment and said, "Elizabeth, I'll right back with your black coffee."

Al moved in his chair at the "black coffee" comment. He figured she'd be a tea drinker. Rose came back with coffee and commented, "I hope you like the setting. I knew your favorite colors, although some may think that the pink doesn't go well with the royal blue. But this is for you and not anybody else."

Elizabeth answered, "The setting is strikingly beautiful, the patterns are pleasant and yet magnetic to the eye."

As Rose headed to the grill, she paused at Al's table. She said, "I'll take care of Elizabeth and be back. Her story is amazing and very powerful." She headed behind the counter, and Al could hear the grill starting to sizzle and pop. It didn't take Rose long to have her guest's food prepared. Elizabeth loved French toast with creamery butter and strawberry preserves. When Rose brought the food to her, a bright yet controlled smile crossed Elizabeth's face.

Placing the food on the table, Rose said, "I know that this has been a favorite of yours. The strawberries are fresh, and the butter is unsalted. I'll bring you more coffee, and then we can have a wonderful conversation."

Elizabeth said, "This is far more than I expected. Thank you so much for the thoughtfulness and consideration. I must tell you that the aroma is absolutely wonderful."

Rose excused herself and came over to the table and sat, not across from Al, but next to him. She said, "I told you that she has an amazing story. Just wait a few minutes and what I have to tell you will be astonishing."

Al said, "Now that's not fair. Why can't you tell me now?"

Rose replied, "Because I don't want to shock Elizabeth." With that comment, Rose turned on her chair. She could feel Al's stare right through the back of her head. With a big grin that Al couldn't see, she got up and headed back to her guest.

Rose took a seat next to Elizabeth and held one of her hands. Even though Al couldn't understand the conversation, he realized that Elizabeth seemed upset. Rose kept her hand on her, and the conversation continued for some time. At one point Elizabeth removed a hand-stitched handkerchief from her pocket and dabbed her eyes. A few seconds later, Rose stood and pulled her chair out. When Elizabeth stood, she embraced Rose. Their embrace lingered until Rose stepped back. As the two walked towards the back door, Elizabeth was still holding her kerchief.

Within two steps of the backdoor, it opened and in stepped Etche. His smile radiated warmth and love. He stepped forward and embraced Elizabeth. With his hands on her shoulders, she seemed to want to continue the embrace. When he whispered to her, Al could plainly distinguish every word.

Etche said, "You don't need to worry; I'm right by your side, just like always. We're going to the place you have dreamed of for many years." With that said, Etche and his traveler, endowed with striking beauty and grace, went out the back door.

Rose came and sat next to Al. She said, "You'll have to give me a minute to catch up. I've loved Elizabeth for a long time."

She and Al sat quietly until he said, "I've got to get a cup of hot coffee; you just sit here, and I'll get it myself."

Rose laughed and said, "Feeling kind of comfortable around here, are ya?" as he went and filled his cup.

Al returned and brought up something troubling him. "Elizabeth seemed upset. Even when Etche was holding her, she was pretty emotional. She settled as they walked to the door. What was wrong?"

Rose said, "Nothing was wrong. Elizabeth thought a lot about heaven. Some people react differently when faced with their own crossing. That's why I place my hands on every traveler. You see I use my touch to bring back the travelers memories of their greatest delights and joys. With my touch, their spirit understands what glory awaits them."

"The Father," Rose said, "has a wonderful way of working things out. People throw around words like fate, circumstances, coincidence, in the cards. Now, how stupid is it to say that it's just in the cards. Life is not a poker game. There are reasons for things to happen. The tragedy is people want an instant answer, but there are few instant answers in life."

Al asked, "Why can I understand some of the conversations? Like just now with Etche and Elizabeth. Other conversations, I don't understand a word of what is going on."

Rose grinned. "That's easy. You understand what is important to understand."

"You were going to tell me more about Elizabeth, remember."

Rose said, "Now don't get cheeky with me, young man. I plan on telling you. Elizabeth came from what you would say was an average working family. Her dad was a police officer in Washington D.C., and her mother worked in the local bank.

"When Elizabeth was three, she loved to listen to music. Now that is not so unusual, but she especially loved to listen to piano music. Her mother took her to the local college to listen to a pianist. The pianist was a young lady who began practicing when she was four. Elizabeth was enthralled with the music and told her mother that she wanted to be just like the pianist. Later her mother called her aunt, an elderly lady who knew how to play. Her aunt agreed, on a trial basis, to teach her the basics.

"So, she went to her auntie's for her lessons. Her auntie had a beautiful piano in the front parlor of her boarding house. Now, you might remember who I'm talking about. Her auntie is a wonderful follower of Jesus. I believe you called her Aunt Bee."

Al almost fell off of his chair. "Aunt Bee," he said, "How in the world did that ever happen? I knew she played, but I had no idea she... I guess it was something she just didn't think was relevant." Still somewhat in shock, he continued, "Aunt Bee gave her lessons, and she shows up here." With that said, Al looked at Rose and began to ask, "Does that mean that..." Rose stopped him and said, "No, that doesn't mean that Aunt Bee has finished her journey."

Al scratched his head and said, "I've been trying to take in all of this. I have to admit I'm still in the fog on some of it. Let me see if I have this straight. I've been writing about men and women who believe in God and love him. They come in here, and you treat them like they're part of your family, and then they walk out the back door with Etche."

Moving around on his chair he continued, "Once out the back door, they take a ride in a boat and then vanish. Is that pretty much what's going on here?"

Rose smiled and said, "Yes, pretty much that's what has been going on. But not just here, we've been doing this for a long time. We'll talk later. Gramps is ready to come in the door. I mean to tell ya, this guy will bring a tear to your eye."

As Al was looking at his watch and shaking his head, Rose was grinning. What had just taken more than two hours in the diner had only taken five minutes on his watch. He was beginning to understand that time was meaningless at the Rivers

Edge Diner. He turned in his chair when the front door opened once more. In stepped a man with a small build and a huge smile. His close cut hair was white, and his eyes twinkled. His smile made the crow's feet by his eyes curve up, enhancing the twinkle in his eyes.

Gramps was dressed in blue jeans and a heavy cotton work shirt. His clothes were worn, yet clean, and seemed to match him perfectly.

From the back room Rose called out, "Hey Gramps, have a seat, and I'll be with you in a minute."

Seeming to be at perfect ease the elderly man sat next to Al's table. When he stepped past Al, he said, "Good morning, young man. How's everything with you? Isn't today just a perfect day!" Al didn't take his statement as a question but more of an exclamation.

Rose came out from the back and stopped at the counter. Picking up a coffee mug, she carried it and the pot to Gramps' table. Al noticed how absolutely joyous Rose was, her smile filled her face. As she set down the filled mug, she put her hand on Gramps' shoulder and said, "I'm so happy to see you, I could just sing and celebrate. We're gonna have a party the likes of which, well, you'll just have to wait and see. I'll have your breakfast out in a few minutes. I haven't cooked this much for one man in a very long time."

Al glanced over at Gramps sitting on the old chrome chair. Gramps caught his eye and smiled. His smile was as mesmerizing as the twinkle in his eyes. The aroma from the grill was wafting out to Al and Gramps.

Al spoke up, "Man that sure smells good. Smells like black peppered bacon."

To which Gramps answered, "That's what it is, thick cut peppered bacon, nothing better. And knowing Rose, my eggs and potatoes will be fried and splattered with the hot bacon grease. Just before my eggs are done, the clouds will open, and she'll rain down the pepper on them."

Gramps had just finished when Rose appeared from behind the counter. With a platter in one hand and the coffee pot in the other, she got to the table and announced, "Just the way you have always liked it. Peppered bacon, thin sliced fried potatoes, eggs splattered with the bacon grease, and thick cut homemade wheat bread."

As she sat the platter down, she chuckled and said, "I don't know how you can eat all of that and keep your shape. Look at me—I just cook the food, and ole Rose looks like this."

Rose grinned turning towards Al. Gramps bowed his head and Al heard him say, "Father in heaven, I thank you for this day and your care for me. May my life be used according to your will. Amen."

Rose came to the table and spoke quietly to Al, saying, "That man sitting there has touched people all over the world for Jesus. I'll tell you about it when he's done." She got up from her chair and went to the counter, picking up the coffee pot she topped off Gramps' mug. She said, "I've got a few more potatoes and two more slices of bacon, would hate to see them go to waste." Gramps' smile and nod sent Rose back to the grill, and she returned in a second, reloading his platter. "Lord," she said, "it does my soul good when folks enjoy my cookin'."

Rose walked over to Al and said, "Etche will be here in a couple of minutes. I'm gonna sit with Gramps until he gets here." She turned and sat next to the older gentleman. Even though they were only a couple of feet away, again Al couldn't hear a word of their conversation.

Al watched as Rose put her hand on Gramps. He was smiling as she held his hand. Al heard Rose's chair squeak, as she tried to get up from the table. Before Rose could even get up, Gramps was over to her chair and pulled it out for her. Al noticed that they were both close to the same height as they walked with their arms around each other to the back door. Within two steps, the back door came open and Etche stepped in. Etche towered over Gramps. As Etche put his arm around Gramps, Al caught a glimpse of a mark on the back of his hand. Etche and Gramps moved as one out the back door.

Rose came over to the table and sat down. She said to Al, "This time I think you should write as I tell Gramps' story. It won't be long, and all the men like him will end their journey." Al pulled out a fresh sheet of paper and wrote "Gramps" on the top.

Rose said, "Gramps grew up in a rough house. His father didn't know how to deal with the problems of life, and so he tried to drown his troubles. The problems were only made worse. You can't hide from life trying to drown yourself. Gramps grew up hard and fast. When his dad was at his worst, Gramps was the one who faced his wrath. The physical pain caused by his dad faded., but the emotional and mental scars were always just under the surface."

Rose seemed bothered as she continued, "When he was old enough he left the house. He joined the military at the time the entire world was engulfed in the madness of war. That war, started by the hatred of men, came close to the destruction of freedom and free thinking."

Al was writing as fast as he could, and as Rose paused, he looked up at her. "You can keep going," he said.

"Fine," she said, and continued, "The war was changing, and there was a plan to bring the death to an end. Gramps was part of the group of men that would attack and stop the madness. He was one of the first men to place his feet on the sandy beach.

Within seconds Gramps was changed forever. That stretch of beach sand turned red, and hundreds of young men ended their journey. The images that filled his eyes left scars on his soul."

Rose hesitated a moment. Al noticed that she was agitated and on edge. He said, "You seem bothered by this. I don't want to be disrespectful, but if you know everything that happened, why do you get upset?"

Rose answered him back, "I do know what's going to happen, but that doesn't stop me from feeling pain and anger. So many times I wished that man would learn lessons from history. They don't learn; they just rewrite the same failures. You need to understand that our Father gave mankind the ability to choose their own actions, freewill you call it."

She paused for a moment and then continued, "After that season of killing, Gramps returned to his hometown. He was a different man; he may have looked the same, but that is all that remained of the man who left. Gramps took up where his dad left off, drowning the past and damaging the future. Within a short time, he married a wonderful young lady, and they began to raise a family. A wife, family, and destructive drinking never lead to wholeness and happiness. He had neither; his soul was as lifeless as the bodies strewn across the beach that awful day. He was facing a crisis. His life hung in the balance, not just his, but his wife and children's as well."

Al said, "So many things happen in life that can destroy the soul of people. Why doesn't God just stop all of it?"

Rose said, "Let me go on, and you'll have a better understanding. Gramps had to make a decision. He had to decide to die with the bottle or live without it. He made the right decision but was powerless to keep his promise until the day he met Jesus. His relationship with Jesus was profound. It changed his life, and it changed history for countless people."

Al looked puzzled at her statement. "Let me explain," she said. "When Gramps fell in love with God, he knew that his entire life was saved. He decided that he would spend his extra time and energy making a difference. He was pretty handy and loved working with wood so he came up with the idea of making tiny crosses out of wood. He passed them out to every person he met."

She continued, "When he came in here today, he had passed out thousands of little wooden crosses. Today, they are all over the world. The love Gramps has for Jesus reached around the world. Just think what would happen in your world if there were more men and women like him. Well, I'll tell you what'd happen. The kingdom would be here, and this world would be washed over in love."

Rose got up and walked over to the counter. She returned with the coffee pot and an extra cup. She refilled Al's cup and then poured one of her own.

"I need to repeat something," Rose said. "It's so easy to misunderstand God. So many people think that they have to say the right words or believe certain phrases or prayers. That's religion. God's not reached by any set of rules or regulations. He's touched by faith and love. People come to have faith in what God provided through Jesus, and then they fall in love. They love God with their whole heart and soul and mind, and they love their neighbor. That neighbor part is so important. It's part of the whole. When you love Jesus, you'll love everyone around you."

25

Understanding His Purpose

Rose stopped talking and looked at Al. She said, "I've been talking a lot, and you've been here a while. Are you hungry? Won't take me long to make something for you."

"Well," he said, "that bacon sure smelled good. But I've got to tell you that my all-time favorite meal is—"

Rose didn't let him finish. "It's pot roast, baked carrots, potatoes, and fresh bread. And you'll finish off the meal with peach pie, and the pie crust must be made with lard."

Al smiled. "Of course, you knew what I was gonna say."

Rose said, "Give me a few minutes. I put the roast, potatoes, and carrots in the oven some time ago. I think the bread is ready. Do you want me to bring you a couple of slices to get started with? And sure, I'll bring you the heels, nice and warm with creamery butter." She turned and headed to the oven.

As Al sat there, he looked over his notes from the day. He put them into a file folder and slid the file into his portfolio. He placed the portfolio on the chair next to him and took a sip of his coffee.

Rose brought over a small plate with the ends of the bread loaf still warm. Two pads of butter were next to the bread. Al noticed that the warmth from the bread began to soften the bottom of the butter pads. Al was quiet and content as he enjoyed the fresh bread.

As soon as Al finished his bread, it took Rose only a moment to bring a platter over to the table. The pot roast was perfect. The top of the roast had a very slight crust, yet he cut it with his fork. The carrots were not hard, nor were they mushy like mashed potatoes. The potatoes were slightly browned, yet Al mashed them with little effort. After putting butter on the potatoes, he added the usual heavy dose of pepper. Slowly, with intense concentration, Al separated bite-sized portions of the roast with his fork. For the first minutes, he continued with his treatment of each item—contemplation, concentration, and consumption.

When the platter was clean, wiped spotless by the last of his bread, Al sat back. Rose came over, took the platter, and refilled his cup. She said, "I'll be right back with your pie. The peaches came from Georgia just a couple of days ago." Returning, Rose had cut him a quarter of the pie, and instead of putting it on a dessert plate, she used a dinner plate.

The smell of the peaches hung like a cloud, lingering, wafting their sweet warmth around Al's head. The perfectly browned crust gave way with a quick crunch. For a lingering moment, the only sound to be heard in the River's Edge Diner was fork against crust.

With the last bit of crust and peach on his fork, an unsettling thought entered Al's mind, a thought that turned into a question that demanded an answer.

"Rose," he asked, "is Etche coming for me?"

Rose's voice was tender as she answered, "Yes Al, he is. He'll be here in just a few minutes."

He tried to clear his throat, saying, "I sure didn't see this coming."

Rose spoke up, "You're wondering why today, now, this place, this way. Let me explain. Every traveler will come to the end of their journey. Some travel for what you think is a long time. Others folks travel for a few winks. In the Father's Kingdom, all of time is but a wink. Your travels have brought you through many experiences that have made you who you are. Some of your travels we helped with, you know that now. Stan, at the hotel, Aunt Bee, Edith, Reverend and Mrs. Williams were willing to be used for your coming to this place. Some of your travels broke our heart. MiSong, her death broke my heart. The death of your child broke my heart. Those events were the results of choice."

Al questioned, "Why now? I thought that I had so much more to do. What about the friends I have back in town, what becomes of them?"

Rose said, "The work you started here is going to continue but in the hands of someone else. You'll be able to watch it unfold and be amazed at how things come together. Your friends back in town are a vital part of this story. A few of them will take what you have started and carry it down the road until others pick it up."

Choking back tears, he whispered, "You said 'MiSong.' Is she the child in my dreams?"

Rose said, "Yes she is, and not just in your dreams. That was her name. She was raised in the village next to the orphanage where her mother worked. Do you remember the woman running behind MiSong? She was her mother. There are other things that you need to talk about. Etche will be here soon. Ask him the questions that linger in your soul. I want you to understand the importance of your life."

When she finished talking, she walked over to his chair and pulled it out. "Etche is coming for you. He'll be right here," she said.

With Al standing, Rose came over and wrapped her arms

around him. He was overcome with a sense of warmth and peace. It was like standing in front of a warm fire of dancing flames and glowing coals. The warmth of Rose's presence penetrated deep into every cell, tissue, and bone.

Rose was holding on to Al as they heard the back door open. When Etche stepped in, Al was met with a sense of energy, almost electric. Etche reached forward and took Al's hand, pulling him close. Grasping hands, Al could plainly distinguish a scar at the base of Etche's hand.

At Etch's touch, Al's senses exploded. The sun coming through the back door was more brilliant than any he had ever seen. He could distinguish the song of every bird. His eyes were able to focus on every object with absolute clarity. Even the rustling of his clothes was magnified and clear.

Held in Etche's grasp, Al's senses were filled with the sweet aroma of fresh pine, the grip of Etche's powerful hands, the look of his discerning eyes, and his own breath. As they moved apart from each other, Al sensed Etche's eyes penetrating deep into his soul.

Etche said, "We have many things to talk about, my friend. And we will have plenty of time." The sound of Etche's voice was deep, filled with absolute confidence, yet gentle and easy to listen to. He spoke again to Al, "It's time for us to walk down to the river." Glancing at Rose, Etche said, "After we leave, please remember what I asked you to do."

Al stepped out the back door into the forest of majestic pines. A brilliance came out from among the branches that gave him the essence of exploding stars. In front of Al was a trail that led right from the back door. Etche came to Al's side and simply put his hand on Al's shoulder, saying, "Let's walk down to the river."

As Al stepped off the single cement step onto the trail, the very sound of his first footfall on the soft pine needles echoed in his ears. The needles lay thick on the trail, and when they yielded themselves to Al's footsteps, they graced the air with their fragrance.

When Etche finally spoke, he said, "People are waiting for you on the other side of the river—some you know and others you do not. Your crossing will be peaceful and illuminating. There will be a time in your crossing when you will see things with perfect clarity. The clouds and fog of misunderstanding will vanish." He stopped for a moment and looked directly at Al. "There will be no secrets to protect on the other side of the river." Al became startled and confused at the comment.

The walk down the trail was a mixture of fragrances and bright splashes of light. Al smiled as he listened to the birds that lived among the pines. No longer did he hear chirping; now he listened to their music. He listened to the pine squirrels play and scamper far into the forest. Now, instead of running, their tiny feet were dancing on the carpet of needles.

Just before the trail ended, it dropped steeply down to a small clearing at the river's edge. Etche's arm across Al's shoulder grew more powerful as he led Al down the steep incline to the bank. There on the bank, pulled up on the sand, was Etche's guide boat. The absolute beauty and simplicity of it took Al completely by surprise.

Etche said, "Let me tell you about my craft. I built her in your western guide boat style so she would glide across the currents. With her shallow draft, I can slip upstream or down with little effort. Her ribs and framing are ash, her strength and beauty were revealed as she yielded to my hand and tool. The rest of her is white cedar held in place with seasoned and boiled pine pitch. She is light and powerful. And finally, I used red cedar to make the oars; they'll last a hundred years or more."

The breeze was cool and refreshing as Al stood on the patch of sand. Embracing the wind, the limbs and branches of the pines danced in perfect rhythm. The water, just inches from Al's feet, was as clear as glass. The small sand spot where the boat rested gave way to marble-sized gravel of every color and hue.

Etche held on to Al's arm as he guided him into the boat. Sitting in the front, Al was amazed at its craftsmanship. Looking around the inside of the boat, Al couldn't find a knot or blemish anywhere. He watched as the hair on his arms stood up, and a tingle ran down his spine, causing him to shiver.

Without effort, Etche pushed his craft into the current. Al looked over the side and was amazed that even in the deeper water, he could easily make out every pebble and stone. The water was mesmerizing as the colors and ripples danced in his eyes.

Etche and his craft were just yards from shore when he spoke up. "Al," he said, "When we get to the other side, you'll find the answers that you've been seeking. They're the answers that all people really seek. But, along our way, there are a few things we need to clear up."

Etche continued, "Aunt Bee loved you very much. I know why you didn't get in touch with her, but that is no excuse for not trying. You don't know how she worried about you. You were there one day, and the next you're gone. She leaned on me as she struggled with your disappearance. A letter or phone call would have eased her troubled heart."

The only noises on the river were the droplets of water falling off the oars and Al's movement on the seat. Al, trying to clear his throat and wipe tears from his eyes, was gazing into the water.

"Al," Etche said, "it's alright. I know your heart. What is in the past is gone."

Etche masterfully kept his craft still in the flowing current. Unknown to his traveler, they had drifted but a few feet during the conversation. Progress across the river would begin the moment Etche released the pressure on the oars. And that wouldn't happen until Al had come to grips with the present issues.

Al asked, "Why wouldn't you let me stay until my work was done? There was so much more to write and tell people. I was learning so much about believing and loving. I just think I could have done more."

Etche replied, "There will always be more to do, more to accomplish, more to write, more to say. What I needed from you, you completed. Others are coming right behind you to take up where you left off. They too will accomplish what I need."

As the craft floated across the current, a visible transformation was taking place within Al. Facial lines of stress and pain disappeared. A sense of repose and contentment filled him. As Al watched, the trees waved their praise. The clear river headed to paradise. Etche, his River Guide, smiled at him. A strange energizing sensation swept over the traveler. In that same instant, Etche smiled. A brilliant flash of light blinded Al for the slightest bit of time. As his eyes regained their focus, Etche had been transformed into the likeness of a man, shining with the brilliance of the sun.

The craft drifted in sunlight more brilliant than any mortal had seen. As Etche's craft drew close to shore, Al could see people standing on the golden colored sand. Etche said, "There are people waiting for you. But, my friend, there will be thousands more who will come after you, and they will thank you for your faithfulness and influence."

Within yards of the shore, Al recognized the Marine standing in his dress blue uniform. His brother in the faith, Pfc. Williams, was standing next to a woman and child. Drawing closer, Al gasped. MiSong was standing next to a woman he recognized as her mother. MiSong was grinning and waving. Standing next to them Al's immortal eye's recognized his wonderful Sarah. In her arms she was cradling a baby. With a very slight sound, the sand surrendered to Etche's craft. Coming to rest, Al stood up. As his foot came to rest secure on the shore, his soul was smiling.

ABOUT THE AUTHOR

T.A. Galloway has been married to his wife Donna for forty-five years. He is the father of three daughters and is Bumpa to three grands—Allie, Ayden, and Avery—and a fourth grand is on the way. He was ordained in 1979 and in ministry full time until he suffered a debilitating spinal cord injury.

His first book, *A Mother's Heart Moved the Hand of God*, reached number two on Amazon and chronicled the birth and struggles of his third child who was born in the Zambian bush.

Since retiring he has given himself to writing novels. His inspirational blog is at http://aservantsheartministry.blogspot.com. He can be reached by email: tedd@teddgalloway.com